STICKS IN A BUNDLE: TRANSITIONS

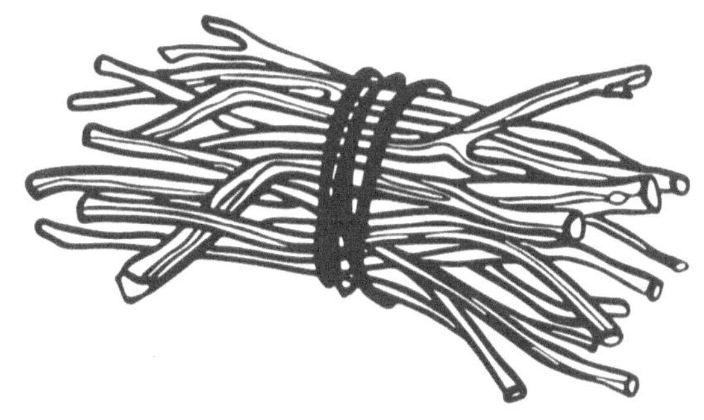

PAT SPENCER

Book II of the Sticks in a Bundle Trilogy

Seaside Writer Imprint

Contents

Praise for Sticks in a Bundle

"The life of Eshile Mthembu as recounted to the author while aboard a bus from Zimbabwe to Johannesburg" is "a richly told story. The characters are vivid and unique and offer a window into 1960s South Africa." —*The Booklife Prize.*

"The writing is absolutely stunning, conveying a strong sense of place as well as vivid characters." —*The Bookouture Team.*

"All Eshile knows is her own small circle of the world. It becomes something like Holden Caulfield trying to figure out himself in relation to society–only in reverse–Eshile is trying to figure out society in relation to herself." —*Cherri Randall, author, The Memory of Orchids, and developmental editor for Writer's Digest.*

"Sticks in a Bundle is a riveting foray into the challenges of a mixed-race family struggling to hold tight under the rule of apartheid — designed to tear families apart. It's beautifully rendered through intimate, gritty details of the towns and daily lives of the people who lived in those places during those times, so much so that elements of the story continue to draw this reader back into it." —*Marlis Manley, author, Trophy Girl and Is that Your Mother Calling?*

"We experience empathy for a hard-working multiracial family as they cope under the Apartheid rule of South Africa. For me, I found a story of family togetherness, love, and survival in the throes of a world that considers prejudice the norm. Of course, I feel this family's poverty, but also their pride. You might say apartheid Africa has been written about enough, but never like this." —*Jacqui Murray, author of The Crossroads and the Dawn of Humanity trilogies.*

"The combination of living poor, striving for an education, enduring and fighting apartheid, surviving the death of loved ones, and experiencing loving relationships and more is well done. Told in a natural, easy manner that's both educational and satisfying storytelling." —*Nada Chatwell, moderator, California Writers Circle.*

"Through the introduction of this mixed-race family, author Pat Spencer brings forth a culture not known to many people. The characters come alive through hardship, happiness, death, fear of the ruling government, and prizing family." — *Arlene E. Bernholtz, author of nonfiction and poetry.*

"Dr. Pat Spencer is a superior author with the talent to generate feelings on the page that can, as Thomas Paine wrote, '*Try the Souls of Men*' (and *Women*). The emotions of helplessness, fear, and care bubble off every page and let one feel the despair of fellow humans. This story is about one woman in one family, yet it is really the story of women in society, acting as the glue to keep the family together. Well done is all I can say." — *Jim Takos, author, Southern California Writers Association.*

"Compassionate, gripping, absorbing. Eshile's story will linger in your mind for a very long time." —*Steve Iman, author, California Writers Circle.*

"We feel the anger against apartheid. Excellent writing and a plot that keeps offering surprises. I couldn't stop reading." —*Sandra Homicz, author, California Writers Circle.*

The story, set against the backdrop of 1960s South Africa, is richly woven with clear prose. Pat Spencer's writing immerses readers in the historical and cultural landscape of the time. She skillfully conveys a strong sense of place, bringing the era to life with evocative descriptions and nuanced details. Characters are rendered with depth and authenticity. A compelling and memorable read. —*Clive Aaron Gill, author, My Short Stories, Literature that Matters; The Diary of Natan Borenstein: A World War II Prisoner and Partisan Fighter.*

Other Works of Fiction and Nonfiction by Pat Spencer

Novels

Sticks in a Bundle: The Early Years
(Historical & Literary Fiction)
Story of a Stolen Girl
(International Thriller)
Golden Boxty in the Frypan
(Historical Fiction)

Nonfiction

A Baker's Dozen For Writers: 13 Tips for Great Storytelling
Hair Coloring: A Hands-On Approach

Upcoming Novels

Sticks in a Bundle: The Decision
(Literary & Historical Fiction)
The Unfortunate Conversation
(Historical Fiction)

Short Stories & Articles

Oceanside: A Healing Place
Winner Write On! Oceanside Library Literary Festival
(Available on Amazon)
Ouija (Available on Amazon)
Why Aren't We Marching in the Streets? (Vine Leaves Press)
Isibambiso (Literary Yard)
Passing On (Potato Soup Journal)
Bittersweet (Scarlet Leaf Review)
Action Beats v. Dialogue Tags: A War that Must Be Won!
The World is Not Black and White
(Almost and Author)
When an Apple is More than an Apple (Word Dreams Authors Writing)
Writer's Block (Academy of Heart and Mind)

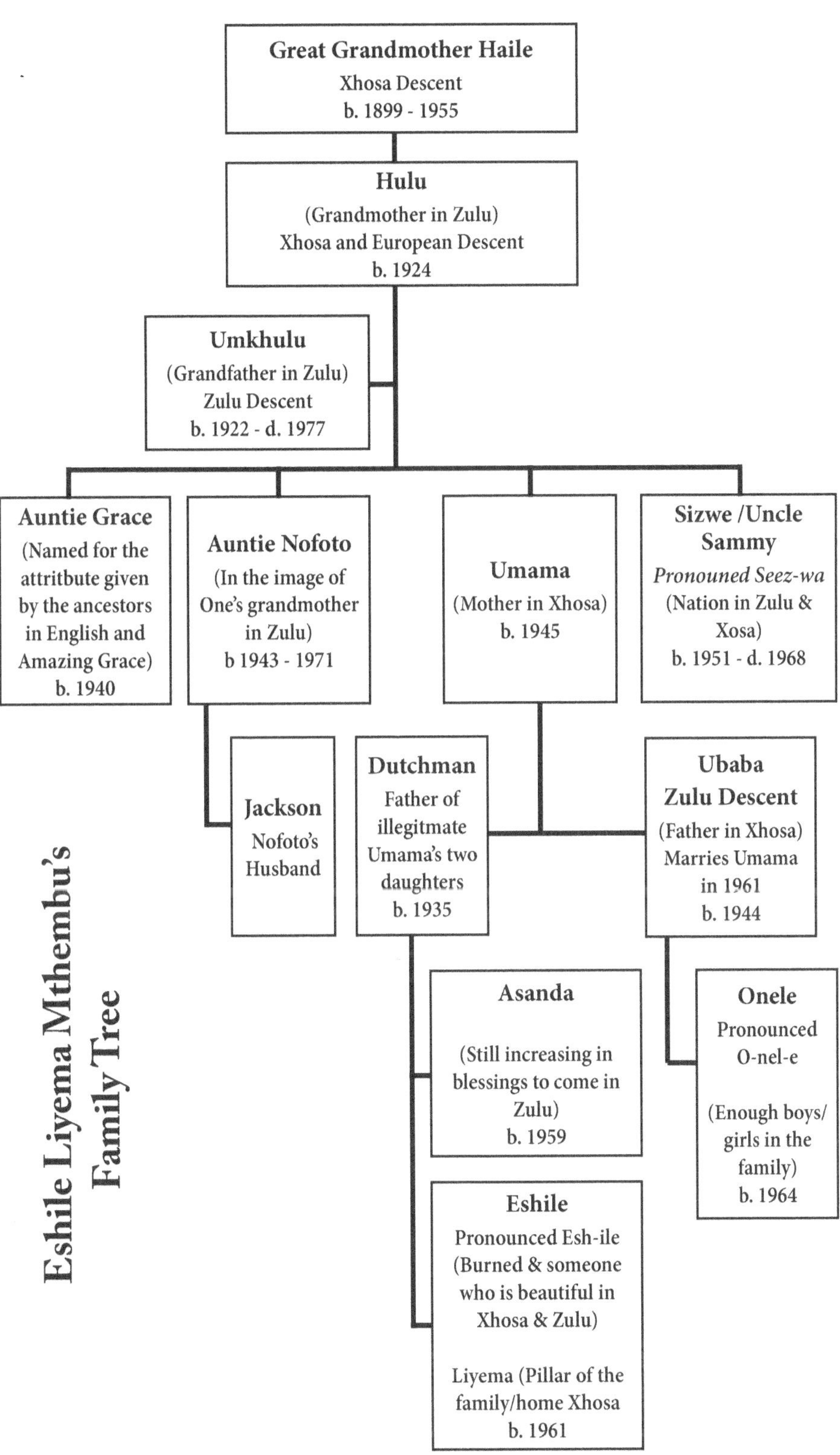
Eshile Liyema Mthembu's Family Tree

Great Grandmother Haile
Xhosa Descent
b. 1899 - 1955

Hulu
(Grandmother in Zulu)
Xhosa and European Descent
b. 1924

Umkhulu
(Grandfather in Zulu)
Zulu Descent
b. 1922 - d. 1977

Auntie Grace
(Named for the attritbute given by the ancestors in English and Amazing Grace)
b. 1940

Auntie Nofoto
(In the image of One's grandmother in Zulu)
b 1943 - 1971

Umama
(Mother in Xhosa)
b. 1945

Sizwe /Uncle Sammy
Pronouned Seez-wa
(Nation in Zulu & Xosa)
b. 1951 - d. 1968

Jackson
Nofoto's Husband

Dutchman
Father of illegitmate Umama's two daughters
b. 1935

Ubaba
Zulu Descent
(Father in Xhosa)
Marries Umama in 1961
b. 1944

Asanda
(Still increasing in blessings to come in Zulu)
b. 1959

Onele
Pronounced O-nel-e
(Enough boys/ girls in the family)
b. 1964

Eshile
Pronounced Esh-ile
(Burned & someone who is beautiful in Xhosa & Zulu)

Liyema (Pillar of the family/home Xhosa
b. 1961

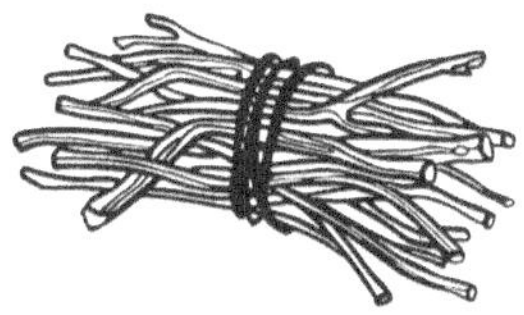

Whether the ancestors were wise to choose me, or whether they made a tragic mistake, it is too early to know.

Eshile Liyema Mthembu

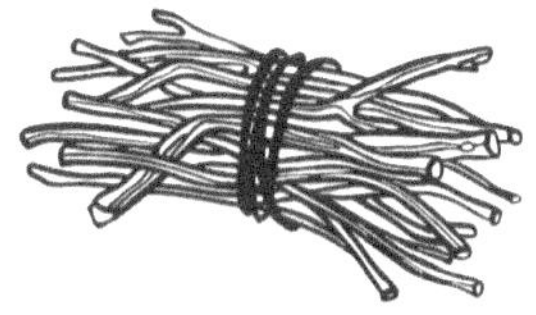

Author's Comments

We had completed a third of the bone-jarring ride from Johannesburg to Zimbabwe when Eshile's head bobbed against her chest. I fought to keep my eyes open, but the dry, hot air did nothing to keep us alert. It seemed an act of kindness to let her sleep, no matter how much I wanted to hear more.

My eyes closed even though my mind whirled with so much to think about.

When I awakened out of my restless nap, my arm tingled from the awkward position I'd pinned it in and the weight of my head. Sticky sweat pooled in the folds beneath my chin.

The washcloth I'd dampened earlier now rested atop my backpack on the floor. Finding it stiff and dry and my water bottle empty, I sighed with despair.

"It was a time of uncertainty. Overwhelming for me, a young girl of only eleven." Eshile's brows pinched questioningly. "Are you sure you want to hear more?"

I brightened and wiped sweat beads from my forehead with the back of my hand. "Oh, yes. Please, if you don't mind. There's nothing I'd like better than to hear more of your story."

Eshile patted my knee and resumed where she left off before the heat and rhythm of the old bus had rocked her to sleep.

CHAPTER ONE

An Important Walkabout

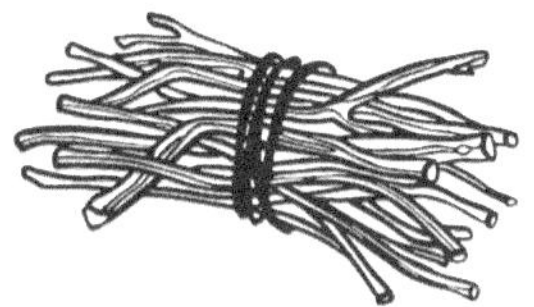

EyeSilimela (Month of the Pleiades) June 1972

I lay in my new bed, afraid to move. What would I do if Baas John returned to say it was all a mistake, and he had given the job to another man? Could I invent a compelling story of why he should fire the other fella and keep my father?

Or had last night been a dream? Had I imagined the enormous upside-down baobab tree and the lush path we followed to end up at the Ilanga Safari Lodge? This place that would be our home, was it real? What might happen if I reached out and touched the wall? Perhaps there was no lodge, no rondavel. Had I wanted so badly to live in such a place that I created it in my mind—invented it to wipe out the memories of our arduous journey? But that made no sense. If we made the journey, we must be here. Still, I pinched my eyelids shut for fear if I took the smallest peek, I might find myself returned to Soweto.

Umama's whispers perked my ears. "Husband, it is only half past four. Eat a piece of fruit."

"But what if I lose my way? Baas John said I should meet him where we first turned off the path. What if I take a wrong turn? I must not be late for my work assignment. What would my new boss think of me?"

The scuffling of feet tempted me to open my eyes. But not until I heard my mother chuckle, then the sounds of her shoving my father out the rondavel door, did I dare.

Still, I felt torn. A gentle light cast an inviting glow into the bedroom where my sisters and I slept in bunk beds. My stomach growled its desire for the fruit Ubaba didn't have time to eat, yet I dreaded lifting my head from the pillow. It was even softer than the one I slept on in my grandmother Hulu's pink bedroom.

Big sister Asanda had not stirred. I hung over my bunk rail and watched my little sister Onele flip onto her stomach, expel a wet snort, then return to her soft kitten snore. I wanted to extend this time of peace and quiet. It was rare not to hear Onele whining or Asanda issuing commands. I inhaled the clean, soapy fragrance of the bedcovers and welcomed the heavy haze taking over my brain.

That's the last thing I remembered until Onele's stale morning breath curled my nose as she repeatedly rammed her index finger into my collarbone. "Wake up, Eshile. We're really here, and Umama's cooking eggs."

"Smells good!" Asanda threw one long leg over her bunk railing, twisted to place a bare foot on the ladder, then thudded to the floor. "I'm hungry."

I grabbed my throbbing arm as I rose. The dense, woody boxthorn bush I had run into during the excitement of last night's dark arrival left more damage than I realized. The swollen red wound, made by the stab of a four-inch gray spine, burned as hot as if punctured by the fork our mother Umama used to poke coals in the *braai*. Yet the pain didn't stop me from racing my sisters to the kitchen.

Asanda was first to the table, but Onele and I weren't far behind. We dove into wooden chairs and snatched up the knife and fork Umama placed at each seat.

"You look like street beggars eager for a handout." Our mother's smile wrinkled her cheeks up to her twinkling eyes. "Guess I don't need to tell you to eat it all."

These eggs were more delicious than any I had ever eaten. My sisters must have thought so too because we fell silent and shoveled in our food.

When we finished, Umama said, "After you change your clothes and unpack, we will explore this wondrous place where we now live."

I swallowed my final giant bite of fluffy yellow egg and ran to our bedroom. How could we be so fortunate? What had we done to deserve to live in paradise? I wanted to cheer, laugh, and shout a million thank-yous to the ancestors, but I collapsed, couldn't even draw a breath until Umama sat beside me and massaged the back of my neck. My sisters gawked as if I'd lost my mind. Maybe I had. I'd never felt so overwhelmed in my entire eleven years of life.

I waited for my sisters' teasing. Instead, they smiled encouragingly. I experienced one of those rare moments when an epiphany hits a person as hard as a bag of boulders. My personal insight was that I take my family's love for granted instead of thanking God for it every day.

Onele bounded to her woven bag and dumped her belongings on Umama's jute rug. I hadn't spotted the closet the night before. Shelves lined the far corner of the structure and a silver bar, holding a supply of wire clothes hangers, extended across the length at Asanda's eye level. We hung our clothes, each an inch apart, so it appeared we had more than we did. Then I closed the white cloth that served as a door.

My younger sister frowned and slid the curtain back. "We want Umama to see our good work."

Onele and I slipped on our drawstring shorts, then yanked tee-shirts over our heads. Asanda took her red, ankle-length *pagne* from a hanger, spread it on the bed, and smoothed out the wrinkles. She also put on a, but it was her nicest, one she wore to Sunday services, not an after-school play shirt such as mine. The problem was that she was taking forever to get ready.

Onele asked, "Can't you hurry just a little?"

Asanda rolled her eyes and slowly ran a comb through her wavy hair. Onele and I buckled our sandals and fidgeted impatiently until our mother and eldest sister Asanda joined us at the door.

Asanda had tied the cloth of her *pagne* in a knot that resembled a rose. The skirt brushed the tops of her ankles and her apricot-colored hair flowed softly to her shoulders. Umama had braided her hair, then twisted until it resembled a small, finely woven basket. She had secured the braid at her nape with the ivory hair comb from the International Imports Emporium that was our grandmother's gift to our mother two years ago for her twenty-fifth birthday. Both she and Asanda had dressed as if headed to Sunday services or dinner at Hulu's.

No one needed to tell Onele and me that we had made a mistake. This was an important walkabout. Our play clothes were not appropriate. Avoiding eye contact with our mother, we scurried to our room. Onele changed into her pink ruffled worship services/birthday/Christmas dress. I could have put on the yellow dress Hulu ordered from a mail-order catalog, the dress Ruthie claimed made me look like a chicken. However, I didn't wish to risk that happening again, so I wrapped my ankle-length multi-colored *pagne* around my waist and tied it in a neat knot. The tee-shirt I wore was my favorite, so I tucked it neatly into my skirt, and out we went.

I turned to run back when I realized I had forgotten to rub mafura oil into my skin. But my panic lasted only a moment. Instead of looking ashy, my skin was supple and moist from Ilanga's humidity. Confident that I looked worldly and sophisticated, I followed Asanda and our mother along the path. Onele flounced behind, her ruffles bouncing with each step.

We passed a num num hedge like the one I helped Hulu plant at her lemon meringue house. After the glossy green foliage grew thick and healthy and white flowers bloomed, we had picked the small red berries, then cooked up an amazing jam. I told myself to remember to return to this num num bush and bring a bowl.

Onele poked her fingers through the openings of a chicken wire enclosure that surrounded deep pink flowers with white star-shaped centers perched atop long green stems. Before she could pluck a delicate bloom, Umama smacked her hand away, shot me the squinty-eye, raised-eyebrow glare, and pointed to a wooden sign.

"Eshile, why aren't you watching out for your sister? Can neither of you read?"

Impala Lily

Used as arrow poison for hunting.

Do not touch.

Wide-eyed Onele locked her hands behind her back, appearing to wait for a full-fledged lecture. When Umama walked on silently, I breathed, long and slow, holding in the damp earthy scent of rich, dark soil as if it would wipe out my memories of Soweto's stink.

When we reached a fork in the path, Umama stopped and extended her arms so we couldn't pass. "I wish I'd asked your father where we are allowed to walk and where we may not."

I asked, "How would he know? It's his first day too."

"Ah, yes. Perhaps we should not walk on any paths."

"Umama, the growth is too thick," said Asanda. "We'll rip our clothes. Look at what happened to Eshile last night when she crashed into that thorn bush."

Umama patted where she had slipped her pass book into her brassiere. "Police worry me more than thorns."

I squinted in the opposite direction from which we had traveled. "The sign says employees only. It's best we go that way."

Umama put her finger to her lips, scrunched her body, and tiptoed. My sisters and I followed suit, like shoplifters sneaking away, until four people in swimwear stepped out onto the pathway, sipping tall icy drinks, the color of fresh cream with swirls of pink. Then we scurried to the 'Employees Only' sign and stepped off the gravel that sparkled like gold in the morning sun and onto a thin dirt trail.

We walked until the trail opened into a large clearing. Though it had been only a few moments, I felt as if I had wandered into the past.

The Bantu Education Act of 1953 required Blacks to attend schools designed to prepare us for the lowly jobs the South African government expected us to hold. I was insulted by the requirement to spend school hours learning needlework despite the fact that it trained me to earn my first rand from Umama's former employer, Mrs. Cromwell.

Since history was not part of our curriculum, Miss Odili, who taught Life Skills for Girls, took it on herself to provide lessons from the past. As we stitched, she talked of events gone by that weren't in our school-books. We learned of our country's contribution of troops and materials for the Desert War in Egypt and Libya. Miss Odili shared a photograph her father took when he was in the war. And now, in this strange and wondrous new place, stood long, narrow barracks that replicated those that housed the South African Army and Air Force soldiers during World War II. If it hadn't been for the signs reading *Men's Dormitory* and *Women's Dormitory*, the *potjie* pots hanging over burned-out firepits, and the large *braai* with meat traces burnt on the grill, I would have thought I'd been whisked back in time

Two men wearing khaki-colored trousers and matching long-sleeve, button-up shirts brought me back to the present by walking out of the dormitory closest to where we stood. *Ilanga Safari Lodge* was embroidered in red over each shirt's right pocket. The men paused their conversation, glanced our way, then continued toward another trail.

Umama nudged Onele. "Suppose we might as well follow them. They seem to know where they're going."

A woman called from behind the paisley dress she was clipping to the clothesline. "Good morning, ladies." She left the straw laundry basket at her feet and bustled toward us. Bits of silver hair glinted at her temples, and her welcoming smile crinkled the skin around her eyes. Since her cheeks were full and rounded like two deliciously ripe apples, I found her name befitting.

"I am Rosie. You must be the Mthembu family. I've been eager to meet you."

Umama extended her hand. The woman, short albeit substantial, shifted to evade Umama's intent, grasped her shoulders, gave them a little shake, then drew my mother close as if they were old friends who hadn't seen each other for years. Given how thin my mother was, she almost disappeared. I expected this woman's hugs to be like Auntie Grace's, and I hoped she'd hug me too. Instead, she hefted Onele into her arms. "My, my, aren't you the cutest child?"

Asanda took two steps backward. Not me. As soon as the woman set Onele down, I walked into her embrace and inhaled her fragrance, the rich nutty scent of *yangu* oil made from seeds of the Cape Chestnut tree. I'd been right. This woman was as soft and welcoming as my Auntie Grace—a bit of home.

"Two aprons to hang, then I'll walk with you."

Onele scampered after Rosie and removed the aprons from the basket. I wished I had thought of that. I wanted this woman to like me best.

"Some paths we may walk on our day off, others only on our way to our jobs." As we circled the compound's perimeter, Rosie warned us not to be seen wandering around the pool, restaurant, lodge entrance, or gift shop.

"Our parents have pass books." I asked, "Rosie, do we girls need them too?"

"Will you apply to work for the government?"

I shook my head.

"Perhaps you seek a policeman's job?" Rosie's eyes twinkled mischievously.

"We're too young," giggled Onele.

"Ah, I see…" Rosie rubbed her chin as if deep in thought. "Then you have no need of a pass book." Then she looked at Umama. "I wish I could say apartheid does not reach this far. Regrettably, that is not quite true. But no police lurk around the corners or behind the shrubs. You won't get arrested for making honest mistakes, but we are still Blacks living in South Africa. Just remember, we're the help, and our responsibility is to make our guests' vacation dreams come true."

Rosie bent to Onele's eye level and cupped her chin. "For beautiful girls like you, your job is to go to school, enjoy your new life in Ilanga, and learn the ways of the magnificent animals that surround the lodge every day. Now, come. Let us walk."

We stopped at a short trail that broke off to the left. Rosie pointed to three steps leading up to a wooden porch and a wide-open door. "This is the employee entrance to the big kitchen, and where I slip special treats to my favorite children."

I was devising a scheme to become Rosie's favorite when she interrupted my thoughts. "A few paces farther, then turn right. We'll visit the employee supply shed. Did Baas John explain the system?"

Umama shook her head.

The shed reminded me of ole George's grocery, only an eighth the size. Rosie pulled a large key from her pocket, then inserted it into the lock. Shelves made of wooden planks held toilet tissue, bath soap, dish and laundry detergent, and rows of canned goods—more than I'd ever seen in one place, except for the SuperMart.

Rosie lifted a clipboard that had a pencil tied to it with a string. "Baas John marks the amount of your allocation and you sign out for what you need. Like your living quarters, these supplies are part of your pay. You may have whatever you want. If you go over the allocation, the bookkeeper deducts the amount from your wages. Providing him with these records is one of my duties." When she thumped her heart proudly, just above her breast, the sound reminded me of Umama testing a watermelon for its ripeness. "You need something, you come see Rosie."

I don't think any of us knew what to say. I certainly didn't. A shed from which we could take whatever we need? What kind of miracle was that?

Umama broke our silence. "Oh, my. So much more than expected—how shall we repay you?"

"Me? *Hayi, hayi*. Not me. Thank Baas John." Rosie's chuckle rumbled and bobbed her chest. "The owner provides, but it was Baas John who made it happen. He has no children, so he takes care of us."

Rosie let us stand in awe for a moment longer, then pulled four brown paper grocery sacks from a shelf. "Let's get you started with the necessities."

We held our sacks open. My mouth was also wide open. Besides the canned goods, toilet paper, and different soaps, Rosie loaded boxes of oatmeal, flour, maize, and best of all, a Betty Crocker apple cinnamon upside-down cake mix. When we could carry no more, she grabbed a cardboard box and loaded it with bags of rice and dried beans, balanced it against her hip, then motioned toward the door. "It's a jaunt to the family rondavels. Come, I'll help you carry all this. Then we'll walk the route to church and down to the watering hole." Rosie wiggled her eyebrows. "You might never find it without me. The path is so overgrown guests rarely notice it. Baas John keeps it that way so the animals will feel safe."

My mind filled with the photos printed on two frayed and yellowed pages of my school book—lions, elephants, hippos, and giraffes. My imagination ran wild when Rosie put my hopes into words.

"At the watering hole, you will see the most amazing animals as they behave naturally—things city folk, even our own tourists, will never see."

Hours later, after stuffing ourselves with the dinner Umama cooked in our very own kitchen, Asanda and I washed dishes, then wiped the counters. Our mother hung her apron on a hook beside the refrigerator and heaved a heavy sigh as she lowered herself into the rocking chair. Since I hadn't sat in it because its dark wood was buffed slick and smooth, I watched in case she slid out and needed my help.

Ubaba sat on the sofa. Seemingly afraid he'd soil the cloth, my father took particular care to not let his bare arms touch the white flowers in the print. Asanda tossed the dishtowel on the counter, then joined our father. Rather than assuming his awkward position, she spread her skirt and leaned into the soft cushions as comfortably as if she were back at our grandparents' lemon meringue house.

Onele dropped onto the blue braided rug, rolled onto her back, and stared like Anathi, the blind fortuneteller from Soweto, had cast a spell on her. I followed my sister's gaze, not understanding why I hadn't noticed the light. Darkly stained wooden poles radiated from the ceiling's center to the top edge of the rondavel's walls, and from this raised center hung the most amazing lamp.

A single lightbulb that glared down from the end of a thick black cord had lit our Soweto shanty. This light, now hanging over our heads, encased in a two-foot-square wire frame wrapped in powdery white gauze, looked like a gigantic marshmallow. Instead of the harsh shadows cast by our former naked bulb, I felt this lamp's soft, warm glow, almost as if it were the sun.

I joined little sister Onele on the blue braided rug. When she snuggled against me, I slid my arm beneath her neck and gave her a squeeze. The night was silent, except for insects and the songs they make rubbing their wings together. I assumed we were consumed by our individual thoughts, with Umama offering prayers of thanks and Ubaba worrying about how fragile our new life might be.

My father was a man of few words, and those words were always carefully considered and most likely came from his heart. Understanding this left me haunted by the African proverb he had recited to our mother the previous evening. A chill ran along my spine.

Even the most beautiful fig may contain a worm.

CHAPTER TWO

Adjusting

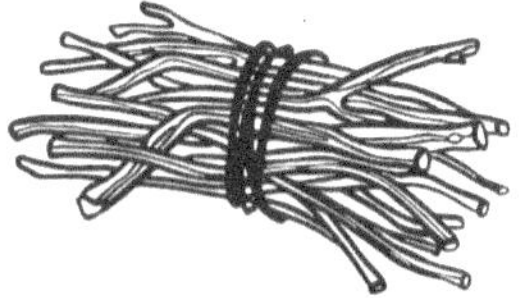

EyeThupha (Month of the Buds) August 1972

After my father began working at the Ilanga Safari Lodge, Baas John assigned my mother a job. I learned it had always been the plan that they both work, and what entitled my family to the glorious rondavel in which we now lived.

By early in the month, we settled into a routine. Both our parents worked six days a week in ten-hour shifts anywhere from 5 a.m. to midnight, depending on whether the lodge was in high or low season, and what events the staff had planned for the guests. Our mother divided the household chores and assigned them to us girls. This was a lot more responsibility, but I didn't complain. Each evening, I either wrote in my journal or penned a letter to Bini, describing what a gift it was to live in such a beautiful place.

My sisters and I excitedly prepared for our first day at our new school. For the first time, our parents were able to buy us new uniforms instead of secondhand, even new shoes and socks. And on this shopping trip, Umama made sure we each had a three-ring binder like the one Asanda had been given at her former Catholic School.

But as exciting as I found all this, our daily trips to the watering hole were my most beloved part of settling into our new home. Each morning, we perched on the edge of the rough-cut deck. Our skinny legs, shades of dark to light, dangled at three different lengths.

One particular morning would live forever in my mind. Two months had passed since the day we recognized the belly swell in *Kuhle*. The rainy season, the time during which most elephant mothers birthed their calves, was over. For the previous twenty-eight days, well before dawn, we had taken up our post, hoping to witness this arrival. We were not about to miss it by sleeping in.

Mist rising from the watering hole softened our view. The only sound was our breath as we filled our lungs with sweet, earthy smells. My sisters leaned against me. The warmth of their arms touching mine warded off the chill.

We gasped when a single ray of sun cut through the branches of the marula tree and illuminated *Kuhle's* newborn as he stretched his trunk, trying to grasp her spindly tail. She led him to the water's edge and showed him how to drink. We later learned it can take a baby up to a year to learn to control the many muscles in his trunk. But at that moment, we stifled our laughter when he shot the water between his legs.

After that, rarely did we miss our morning viewing at the watering hole. Sundays were the only exception. Umama's meticulous attention to what we wore and how our hair was arranged often delayed us.

Baas John's method of scheduling work allowed employees to request Sunday off at least every other week. On our first day of rest, we attended church services. I slipped out of our bedroom while Asanda scolded Onele for not putting on the dress she told her to wear.

Onele screamed, "I'll wear what I want!"

Ah, the irony… After my parents received their first pay, we hitched a ride with the employee who cared for the lodge's swimming pool and serviced the vans. This was our first shopping trip to Phalaborwa, and the first time we girls each owned two store-bought Sunday dresses. I considered scolding my sisters for their pettiness by reminding them how in Soweto we owned so little, we had no opportunity to argue about which dress to wear. But I'd lost patience with them both, so I walked out.

My sisters and I normally visited the watering hole together. That morning, I was ready for a bit of alone time. Moving briskly, I eagerly greeted the morning and hoped *Kuhle* would be there when I arrived. She often left her herd, and I assumed her reason was the same as mine, a solitary break from family. Baas John predicted Kuhle might give birth soon, but one can never know for sure with wild elephants. With an animal of that size, some say it's impossible to recognize the signs of pregnancy. Baas John said he could tell because he'd known her all her life. Excitement tingled through my body just thinking how I could brag if I saw the newborn elephant first.

The fragrant purple flowers on elongated stems like those Umama cut several days ago and arranged in the water pitcher she repurposed as a vase, now peeked out from behind a dense shrub. While I had little time to gather them, a bouquet could put me in a good light, especially in view of my sisters' cranky behavior. I was deep in the shrubs, selecting the fullest blooms, when two uniformed cleaning women, both older than Umama, though not grandmotherly like Rosie, passed by me.

"You know why we have to walk so far, don't you, Lily?"

"Course I do. Baas hides the Blacks' living quarters because they're old and rundown."

Lily clicked her tongue. "Girl, you got that right. He thinks we should be the ones to keep them up and do the repairs, before and after we finish our work assignments."

The older woman harrumphed. "It's not fair. That's supposed to be our free time."

These women—mean as honey badgers—had no right to talk badly about Baas John. The long thin buildings, one each for the unmarried men and women, had showers with running water and toilets that flushed. They slept on beds, not grass mats on the floor. These ungrateful women angered me. The dormitories had luxuries I knew better than to even hope for in Soweto.

After the women turned onto a side path, I peered out between the purple blossoms of Umama's favorite flowers, then stepped over a dry rocky area where Pyjamas grew tight against the soil. Rosie, who worked in the big kitchen alongside Umama, had explained everybody called them Little Men in a Boat because of the six tiny buds centered among the soft green and white striped leaves.

I didn't realize I had taken the wrong path until the guest entrance to the lodge came into view. Just as I turned to go back, a police car sped up the path and stopped in front of the beautiful hand-carved wooden doors. Two White policemen got out. One patted the holster attached to his belt. I'd witnessed this scene many times in Soweto. It never turned out good for the residents of the house. I ducked behind a thick bush and listened and waited. Who would they bring out? Which employee had broken the law? Someone who should have had their pass book in their pocket? Or someone accused of talking back, or maybe theft? My emotions whiplashed from curiosity to fear to dread. Confident this was a warning sent by my ancestors to not become complacent about apartheid laws, I sunk a bit deeper into the bush.

My mind whirled with possibilities, all of them bad until Baas John walked out with the two officers. "I'll alert the staff to keep an eye out for the boy. I doubt he's here. Ten years old, you say. You know that's the age when traffickers kidnap them and sell them as slaves to work in the mines. Hopefully, he's just wandered away. Otherwise, he'll probably never be seen again."

Kidnap! Horrible memories of the men who tried to kidnap Onele roared into my brain. I renewed my commitment to watch over my little sister. This place was not as safe as I'd first thought.

The policemen shut their car doors. Baas John raised one hand in a farewell motion as they drove away. I would learn no more from my hiding place in the bush, so I headed back to the main path.

When I reached the big kitchen, cheery sounds of chortling and singing were coming from the staff. Even though I had eaten the plateful of the mealie bread and fried eggs Umama fixed for breakfast, the sweet scent of corn and butter wafting out the open window caused me to crave a taste. I pushed my worries about the boy to the back of my mind and thought about tapping on the back door. If I did, Rosie might slip me a small bowl of *krummelpap*, a traditional African porridge prepared for the tourists, but time was getting short. So, I scurried past the dining room, descended the terraces made of flat, earth-toned stones, skirted the reclining chairs shaded by grass-canopied umbrellas, pushed aside the brush leaning across the path, then hurried down to the waterhole.

I hefted myself up on the rough-cut viewing platform and squinted into the misty air. On the left bank, the upper tips of the tallest reeds swirled silently. Baas John said that meant some critter was digging up the roots. I listened for the crushing of thick grass being trampled by enormous feet and perhaps the breaking of tree branches. The stillness surrounding me should have amplified any sound, yet I heard nothing except my own sigh of disappointment at not seeing Kuhle approach.

The rising sun framed the Marula tree in brilliant gold. The warmth seemed to pull the mist from the ground, enabling me to see the far side of the watering hole. I searched quickly, eagerly, but dared wait no longer. The day would not go well for me if I made Umama late for church.

My mother claimed the location of the church was another blessing from the gods. It rose from the rich brown soil and surrounded by lush greenery. Three trails and two roads converged on the church and its idyllic setting—such a beautiful place that worshipers from local villages and smaller clusters of homes looked forward to the stroll. Other parishioners drove battered pickup trucks or Volkswagen *kombis*. Tourists, men wearing cargo shorts and women in gaily colored sundresses, walked barefooted or arrived in vans with the names of other safari lodges painted on their doors.

Rosie's schedule gave her the same Sundays off as my parents. While walking alongside us, she slapped her thigh. "Had a good chuckle two weeks ago. Baas John said a young couple felt disappointed because they expected tribal rituals. They had hoped to see a Black man wearing a headdress, shaking a spear over his head, rather than a Catholic priest reading Psalms 23."

At first, I was leery of Father Richard Chipo. But his huge smile and welcoming open arms brought me around. I'd never met anyone more enthusiastic about his role in saving our souls. He believed in the gospel and the power of gospel music. He handpicked his choir to ensure dominant vocals with strong harmonies delivered the Christian lyrics. And he conducted the singers by thrusting his hands and raising his arms to convey sufficient emotion to bring the heavens, or at least an angel or two, inside his church.

Father Chipo also believed it was our Christian duty to employ the call-and-response technique of repeating each phrase in case God was so busy with important tasks that He didn't hear the congregation the first time. Ubaba complained we made so much racket, it was a wonder the birds didn't head north to Zimbabwe.

I was enthusiastic about attending church. It seemed my best chance of making friends. I hoped folks might be different here. But I guess some things are universal. The same as the Catholic Church in Johannesburg, people checked out my mixed-race family when they thought we wouldn't notice. I never seemed to know how to fit in.

Still, Rosie swore color was of no importance to anybody at this church. All shades were welcome. After our initial worship service, the composition of my family, Black, Coloured, and White, may have still baffled the employees, but only the tourists whispered among themselves. Still, I preferred to sit in the back, but Rosie wouldn't hear of it. So, my family followed her down the center aisle and sat in the front row pew, for everyone to see, just as we had at our Xhosa service in Soweto.

We grew accustomed to tourists' curious stares. Rosie, who had a theory on every aspect of human behavior, explained it was a natural reaction—like opening a package of biscuits and finding double chocolates and chocolate chippers in the company of vanilla and lemon wafers. "Honey, you got to love all the biscuits. Still, you're surprised to find the different kinds mixed in together."

Except for the local veterinarian who cared for the animals—from the lions roaming Kruger National Park to the feral cats keeping down the rat population at Ilanga—and his wife and son, Asanda was by far the palest of all the locals. This didn't escape her notice and caused her great discomfort, sufficient that during the socializing after services, she slipped away from us and inched closer to Dr. Vorster's son. On the third Sunday of our attendance, she spoke to him.

Neither Onele nor I had made a single friend yet, and according to Rosie, we didn't have many opportunities because few children lived in Ilanga. Not that we had sought the ones who did. My sisters and I clung to each other as if afraid to venture out. And I guess we were. Every time I took a step away from Onele, she grabbed my hand and whispered, "Please don't leave me here alone."

With my sister's words, all of Soweto came rushing back. For the first time, I realized we had lived in a state of fear—so pervasive we barely recognized it—constantly aware of which street we walked or bus we boarded; finding a Blacks' restroom; being out later than the government-mandated 9 p.m. curfew. But as part of our daily lives, we hadn't called it fear. The only thing that brought terror deep into our souls was the threat of our parents' arrest because of Asanda's whiteness.

So, in this new place, among unknown people, apprehensive of whom to trust, I kept a close watch on the veterinarian. Rosie claimed he was the most respected man in the region. I had two reasons to be unsure.

My grandfather Umkhulu had respected the White men with whom he had conducted joint business adventures. He had trusted that their friendships were real, until renewed support and enthusiasm for the laws of apartheid cleansed native Africans from certain areas of Johannesburg, Cape Town, and other desirable townships. This renewed implementation of these laws cost him his International Imports Emporium, his beautiful family home, as well as the position he thought he held in the community. But what I hated most was to see his spirit break, bit by bit, when all those who could have helped pretended not to know him.

My second reason to harbor mistrust of the veterinarian was more remote and less emotional, yet still big in my mind. Vorster was the last name of South Africa's president, a man who enthusiastically adhered to apartheid policies. In President Vorster's earlier role as Prime Minister of Justice, he oversaw the Rivonia Trial that resulted in Nelson Mandela's sentence of life imprisonment for conspiring to overthrow the state. A chill ran down my neck as my grandmother Hulu's words returned to me—*You had to be there, watching Mandela burn his pass book.* The scene flashed into my mind, as alive as if I were there to watch it happen. I saw the terror on Hulu's face, her fear authorities would also imprison my grandfather for his daring act of support of this man brave enough to cause Blacks to unite and rise up against the ruling Whites.

I vividly remembered the hatred my friend Shaka held for Vorster and the articles everyone said were so radical when he published them in a 1962 edition of his underground newspaper, *Staan Op!* That was one year after I was born. But Mr. Wallace, knowing the importance of documenting this piece of African history, had packed away many copies, so I was able to read them.

Was this doctor President Vorster's brother? Cousin? Or another relative? If so, could his philosophy be different from this president's? Was the doctor hiding out in Ilanga? Disassociating? Hoping no one made the connection?

My mind raced to what I should do once my questions were answered. At this point, my only source of information was an underground newspaper Rosie tried to hide. Yesterday, when she noticed me and shoved it deep into the rubbish, I realized the paper was worth digging out.

I strolled alongside Rosie until we reached the big kitchen. As soon as she shut the door behind her, I returned to the rubbish bin and retrieved the paper. *Inyaniso Yethu*, translated from Xhosa to *Our Truth*, was printed in large bold letters across the top of the first page. Now weeks old, the paper's four leaflet-size pages were damp with meat drippings and tomato sauce. That didn't sway me from reading the articles, all of which were the type that authors end up in prison for writing. This was an older issue with a front-page story similar to one I'd read prior to leaving Soweto. Student Onkgopotse Tiro had been chosen to deliver a graduation speech at the University of the North. The paper said Tiro made the university officials uncomfortable by pointing out that the families of the Black graduates stood outside while White people took up most of the seats inside the hall.

After pausing to wish I'd been there to see the officials' faces, I read more. Officials expected Tiro to thank those who implemented the Bantu Education Act for the opportunities it offered to native citizens. Instead, he said, "The Bantu system is very poisonous, and we are not really impressed with it, and the day of liberation is going to come. And when that day comes, not even the military might of this country is going to stop it." Neither school nor government officials took kindly to his words. They swiftly expelled him and denied him his degree.

I admired Tiro's determination. He had worked at a manganese mine as a dishwasher and general hand for seventy-five cents a week to be able to attend college. Now he risked his education and job, perhaps his life, by urging Blacks to come out of the fog of fear that enveloped them. I was in awe of his strength and bravery. While I couldn't see myself delivering speeches to crowds of hundreds, his bravery fueled my intentions to make my thoughts public through the written word. Eager to read more, I wiped away a red smear that looked like spicy peri-peri chili sauce.

And I read every word. This paper might publish my firsthand accountings of educational inequalities between Whites and Blacks, as *Staan Op!* had. But nowhere was an address, not a city or township name. Still, if I gained Rosie's trust, she might reveal the source.

CHAPTER THREE

Settling In

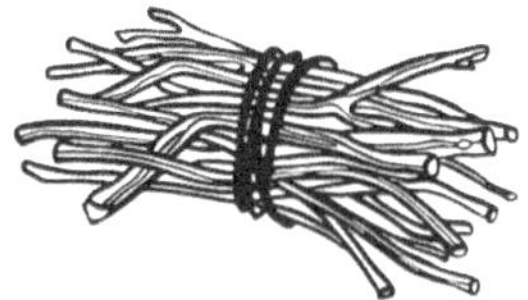

EyoMsintsi (Month of the Coast Coral Tree) September 1972

On weekdays, my parents dressed in silence to allow my sisters and me to sleep an extra hour. Umama said that hour would help us stay awake in school. But this was Saturday, a workday for me and my sisters. When Ubaba switched on the overhead light in our bedroom, I pinched my eyelids tight and held as still as the dead.

"It's dark outside," whined Onele.

I winced. She had no common sense about when to keep quiet.

Asanda and I continued to fake sleep, but Ubaba shook our bunks. They shuddered as though rammed by a water buffalo. We grumbled, rolled out, then slipped on our shorts and tee-shirts.

Onele's task was filling a burlap bag with soiled clothes and carrying it to the employee laundry room. She could be depended upon to complain the entire way. I reminded her how in Soweto, I hauled the heavy plastic bin of dirty clothes to the hydrant, then lugged them back home and hung the clean clothes on the line Ubaba strung between Ife's shanty and ours. The way she scoffed told me she was unimpressed, so

I launched into how happy and grateful I would have been to have a laundry room in Soweto instead of trying to wash our clothes at the community hydrant without dropping at least one item of clothing in the mud. She rolled her eyes.

During our three months at Ilanga, we came to take for granted many things we hadn't had previously, such as our five-room rondavel featuring a real bathroom, concrete floors instead of dirt, and a thatched roof rather than corrugated iron. Now accustomed to spinning a spigot and watching fresh water spring out, the memory of carrying heavy, leaky plastic buckets for cooking and bathing faded from my mind.

Asanda tore me from my musings by shoving our parents' bedclothes in my face. Then she smiled smugly, looped the strap of the second scratchy bag filled with bath and kitchen towels around my neck, and let it fall against my back. When I stepped away, she gave it an unnecessary yank, stopping me in my tracks as if I were a plow ox. I searched her face. Did the tiny smirk mean she was joking, or was she demonstrating her power as the eldest? Onele and I were eager to finish our chores and scoot along to the watering hole, so I let it go.

The lodge provided two washers and a dryer. Our shift began at 6 a.m. Asanda's job was to clean our new home. I believed she returned to bed because rarely had she done much by the time Onele and I returned.

Umama was a kitchen worker. Father had many duties. At dawn, my father and two other men spent hours engaged in the Beetle Wars. Ubaba wore his grumpy face. Arno and Jabu grinned until I thought their faces might fall off. I couldn't figure out why. If assigned that job, I'd be as cranky as our father.

The guestroom doors didn't reach the floor. Large black and brown beetles entered through the space. The two-and-a-half-inch toktok-kies made clicking noises that warned tourists of their approach, but the slender-legged tiger beetles slipped in silently and attacked the crumbs tourists dropped in their rooms. When guests awakened, then touched their bare feet to the concrete floor, the little devils darted across their toes. Men cursed; women squealed. That morning, as Onele and I strolled toward the laundry room, an elderly woman wearing metal pin-curl clamps in her bright red hair hopped on one foot, flailing out of a guestroom door.

Baas John maintained that tiger beetles were Olympians, running 125 body lengths per second. But they weren't as quick as my father. Sweat beaded on his forehead. Beetles crunched beneath his feet as he swished his broom back and forth. The hard-shelled creatures flew off the ceilings and walls, then the men swept them out the door. Beetles scurried in every direction while snarling Ubaba, side by side with grinning Arno and Jabu, swept furiously to clear the covered walkways.

Still, the beetles far outnumbered the men. Tourists leaving their rooms for an early breakfast expelled disgusted sounds such as ugh, ick and yuck when they stepped on the critters, smashing their broken bodies into the cracks between the pavers.

The men continued sweeping until the sun warmed the walkways and the surviving bugs crawled into their moist hideaways to await the peaceful night, only to emerge as guests slept in their beds, unaware the beetles, once again, had scuttled under the doors in search of tasty morsels.

Arno and Jabu, still grinning as though having the time of their lives, waved to my sister and me as we tiptoed over beetle carcasses.

"I hate laundry day," said Onele as we stepped inside the wooden shed.

I yanked the chain attached to the single overhead bulb. Lint balls lit up like dancing fairies. I crammed the bedclothes in the washer. Onele plopped her bottom into the plastic chair and pulled her *Go Fish* cards from her pocket. This didn't upset me. It was our system.

She shuffled while I filled the soap dispenser, then started the machine. When she thought I wasn't looking, Onele arranged the deck to guarantee her favorite sea creature ended up in her hands—the goldfish with long eyelashes and lips that looked as if she wore the same lipstick as Bini's mother when she went to Queen Alice's Shebeen—Cherry Bomb.

We'd played six or seven hands before the washer clunked to a stop. Then we worked as a team. Load after load, I pulled out our damp clothes, towels, or sheets, and Onele stuffed them in the dryer. Then each time the dryer buzzer sounded, we laid down our cards, spread the clothes on the table, and smoothed out the wrinkles. Our rondavel came equipped with an iron. But we stacked each piece neatly in the plastic bin so we could avoid the hot, tedious process of pressing our clothes.

As we left, Onele's stomach growled. "I'm starving."

The few bites of paw paw we had gobbled before leaving our rondavel had worn off, providing my opportunity to motivate her. "If you help me make the beds, we'll finish quicker so I can cook you a nice big breakfast sooner."

Standing at our two-burner stove, flipping *boerewors* in the frypan, I sent thanks to the ancestors who reminded me that only weeks ago, we worried how long it would be until we ate meat. Grease crackled, spotting the stovetop. The spicy aromas of coriander, nutmeg, and cloves were too tempting to resist. When the juicy beef and lamb sausage was brown, I sliced a bite, blew on it, and enjoyed the rich, meaty taste.

Asanda should have been there cleaning. Instead, the sink was full of dishes and the furniture coated in dust. For once, that didn't bother me a bit. It left the fat juicy *boerewors* for Onele and me to eat by ourselves. Besides, the more Asanda disobeyed, the better I looked.

Umama complained the manager had the kitchen help cook too much. Since that resulted in more than the guests would eat, employees helped themselves to food that exceeded our generous allotments. "Some tourists are greedy and careless—toss half in the rubbish. They act like they don't know what it is to be hungry."

Often, I found my mother's complaints annoying, but after the long hours she used to work to provide even our most meager meals, I understood why the waste of food concerned her so.

I eagerly awaited the breads—mixtures of mashed beans, millet, sorghum, plantain, yams or rice, deep fried, steamed, or grilled into different textures and shapes. Umama explained our breads were so different from the kinds to which American tourists were accustomed that many had no interest. Yet the manager required the kitchen help to fill the woven baskets, then place them on the tables. Not wanting to look like a ninny before the other students if Asanda and I earned scholarships as we discussed in Soweto, scholarships that would enable us to attend an American university, I asked Umama what bread they ate.

"Full of air." She rubbed her palms together as if molding a piece of clay. "You can roll it into a gummy ball. Our bread is the same as Africa, sturdy and nourishing."

That explained why the breads remained on the tables until stale. For me, the dry crunchiness was special. We stuffed our mouths until our cheeks bulged and held it until our saliva softened the bread. This extended the time my sisters and I spent, our legs dangling off the rough-cut deck, squabbling over who deserved the best piece.

From our perfect view, we watched the wild animals and pretended they were our own special pets. These moments alone with my sisters, out from under our parents' watchful eyes, were precious, to be guarded like a rare jewel.

Onele, who had become her own little eating machine, munched until the basket was empty. We had only been at Ilanga a few weeks until she complained her waistbands were pinching her. Umama snipped and added elastic. I thought I was funny when I teased her, but Ubaba said it might take a while for Onele to accept that she wouldn't go hungry anymore. Then she'd cease storing up as though the plate before her might be her last.

Onele and I shared the fat sausages and a mound of scrambled eggs, even shared a plate. I washed and dried it, then returned it to the cupboard. The dishes in the sink, I indignantly left for Asanda.

I muttered, "I don't know where our sister has gone, but we've waited long enough. We are not our sister's keeper."

Onele cheered.

We scurried out the door, eager to enjoy our daily sojourn. Since we had finished our chores, we could stay out as long as we wanted. But first, I wanted a moment alone with Rosie to ask about the underground newspaper, the one I had dug out after she tossed it in the rubbish bin.

When we reached the path that led to the big kitchen, I told my younger sister, "I'll get the breads, then meet you at the watering hole."

Umama's warning flashed through my brain. *"Your sister is so small and tender, a lion could eat her in a single bite."*

"Wait, Onele." Unease overpowered my desire to ask Rosie where the underground newspaper was published and if would she help me get an article to them. But when my little sister tsked and turned to me with *why* written across her face, I waved her on.

She skipped away, clicking her tongue and singing the tune our grandmother Hulu sang to comfort her as a child. *"Imvula, imvula. Chapa, chapa, chapa. It's raining, it's raining. Chapa, chapa, chapa."*

My sister's childlike expression, her trusting innocence, once again caused me to pause. But the sun shone bright, and the sky was clear, not a gray cloud in sight. We had left behind Soweto and the evil men who kidnap girls and sell them on back streets of Johannesburg and Cape Town. No rational explanation existed for the disquiet I felt.

I turned my back on Onele, then scampered up the steps. Umama saw me peeping in the big kitchen's window and opened the door.

"Go on in. Rosie has your breads, plus a special treat."

My mouth watered at the thought of any special food Rosie might have cooked, but first I had to ask about the paper. When I cozied up to Umama's side, an egg-white froth flipped off the whisk.

After she moved away and went back to chopping meat, I whispered, "Rosie, I have a secret question to ask."

"My, doesn't that sound delightful? Ask it quick before Jala returns from the refrigerator."

"The newspaper you think nobody sees you read…"

Rosie glared into the metal bowl as if beating the life out of whatever was in there.

"I dug it out of the rubbish."

Her eyes shifted to the doorway, then back to me. "Eshile, I don't think—"

"Rosie, you know I write. I wrote a short piece in support of the women in Soweto who risk being thrown in jail by protesting the requirement that they carry pass books. I also wrote of my impression that the women here hold their heads higher because police don't sneak up and ask to see their pass. Maybe you can tell me how to get an article to that paper?"

"Sounds important. I assume your mother approves?" Rosie's arm froze over the mixing bowl. "She doesn't, does she? Lordy, what am I thinking? Bring it, but don't let anybody see you. Now take your breads and get yourself out of here. Nosy Jala will barge in any moment and ask what we're whispering about. Once that woman knows, everybody knows."

Rosie pointed her whisk at the bundle she had disguised in a frayed dishtowel. Once down the steps and out of sight, I peeled back the corner and peeked to see which leftovers she had placed inside. To my surprise, a *vetkoek* sat on the top—not a leftover from the guests' breakfast, but a fat cake freshly fried for when the sightseers returned for lunch. I took a bite. Monkey orange jam squirted between my lips.

I bumped a row of white flowers, delicately outlined in purple. The plant marker at their base read *Belladonna Lilies*. The stamens broke loose, dusting the fuzzy curls on my legs with sticky white pollen. I had been at the Soweto Street Market when Auntie Grace bought dried belladonna leaves and flowers to create a medicine that reduced pain and helped people sleep. This was one ingredient she didn't let me grind because they're poisonous if too much is ingested. I picked a full bloom, tucked it into my curly hair, and smacked my hands together to remove any loose pollen that might have clung.

When I looked up, the kitchen manager stood a few feet away. Rosie had told me we weren't supposed to pick the flowers. The staff arranged luxurious arrays designed to convey the image that our guests had arrived in paradise. So, I ducked behind a wall covered with woody stems of Old Man's Beard. I breathed in the vine's almond scent and, once more breaking the rules, stuffed a handful of its greenish-white blooms into my pocket.

Onele as the youngest, and Asanda as the most at risk, seemed to draw most of Umama's energy and attention. But the Old Man's Beard should make me her favorite, at least for that evening. Our mother's skin cracked from stirring steaming pots and washing dishes. I planned to boil the flowers, then after Umama soaked her sore red hands, I'd massage them with Vaseline.

When the kitchen manager turned off the path, I rose from my hiding place and continued to the viewing platform. To my surprise, Asanda had met up with Onele. I envisioned my sisters turning toward me with toothy grins. But Onele was curled up, her head resting in big sister's lap. I stuffed the jam-filled *vetkoek* into my mouth.

Onele always asserted her right as the youngest to pick first. Asanda, as the elder, believed that right was hers. Moisture glistened in Onele's eyes as she scrambled to sit and stretch out her hand.

I glanced toward the watering hole to see which of our animal friends were there. The family of waterbucks stood gracefully at the water's edge. The juvenile curved its neck to drink while the larger kept watch on a snorting warthog.

"What took you so long?" asked Asanda.

Flaunting my power as the holder of the bread, I snubbed her and scanned the area for our favorites, Kuhle and her elephant calf. After his birth, we named her baby *Ingonyama*. We agreed on this name because he acted as if he was the King of Africa, throwing back his head and rolling his baby-sized trunk to trumpet warnings. The same as with Bini's complicated name, I shortened Ingonyama's to Yama. When we last saw him, he tried to walk between Kuhle's legs, but his mother's belly hung too low. When he bounced back, the stunned expression on his face sent us into a fit of giggling when he bounced back.

We easily recognized Kuhle's approach because she ripped saplings from the ground and chomped on them without slowing her pace as baby Yama tromped behind. I peered into the haze.

"I'm worried about Yama." Onele's droopy face pulled at my heart, which multiplied my guilt over hiding the *vetkoek* from her. "We haven't seen him and Kuhle for days. Did poachers hurt him?"

"Is that why you were crying, baby girl?" I squinted as the sun sliced through the marula tree. Yama's young. "No need to worry. Poachers want older elephants, ones with tusks."

Onele smiled as if she took that as a guarantee Kuhle and Yama were unharmed. I didn't elaborate. Telling her that Yama's aunties would adopt him if poachers killed his mother might only make her worry again.

Onele scooted closer to the breads in my hands. "Ow. A splinter."

I held her sweaty palm and picked at the protruding stub. But when a drop of blood rose, she jerked away. "You're hurting me."

"Do you want this to become infected? When the pus turns green, we'll have to cut off your finger."

"I need that finger."

Asanda slunk away. Perhaps I could have used Onele's wound to inflict guilt and keep our sister with us. I knew where she was going, but I was in no mood to cover for her. I was also weary of playing mother to my big sister Asanda, so I pretended not to notice and bit down on the splinter.

"You're killing me." Onele stuck her finger in her mouth, then sucked the blood while looking around for Asanda. "Gone again. Where'd she go?"

I lied. "Don't know. Let's go home and wash your hand and wrap your finger in gauze."

Onele cradled her wounded finger, turned her Eeyore face on me, and hopped down from the viewing platform. As we headed home, I decided that night was *the night*. When I got my older sister alone, I'd tell her that not acting her age, her sneaking around, would bring shame on the entire family if she didn't stop.

~

Three weeks passed, then four. I was itching to ask Rosie about my article, but it was as if Great-Grandmother Haile whispered in my ear, "*Don't. You'll jinx it.*"

Onele snuggled up in Ubaba's favorite overstuffed chair. The moment she closed her eyes, her breathing slowed, and she was asleep. I too would have liked a nap, but I settled for leaning back in the sofa's corner and propping my feet on the coffee table.

As soon as I let my eyes glide shut, they popped back open at the sound of a soft tapa-tapa. Onele didn't stir. I grumbled my way to the door. As I pulled it open, an arm reached in and yanked me out.

"*Eish,* Rosie. That kind of hurt. What's wrong?"

She glanced over her shoulder, leaned close, and shoved her hand down the front of her blouse. I knew immediately that was where she'd hidden the underground newspaper, *Inyaniso Yethu.*

"Is my story in there?"

"*Yebo*, yes." Rosie's voice was no louder than a hush as she unfolded the paper and pointed to the bold headline — **Pass Books Condemn Women To Poverty**

"The front page?"

"Three paragraphs. Much to be proud of. The rest is on page two."

Rosie flipped the page. Except for an advertisement for Caster oil to treat dry, brittle hair, my article filled the entire second page. My head swirled as if I might pass out.

"Quick! Read your article, then burn it before anyone sees it." Rosie stepped back from our door, then looked me in the eye. "Eleven years old, yet you have done more for our cause than many aged one hundred."

I braced against the doorjamb and watched Rosie scurry down the path. When she disappeared, I crept to the bedroom, leaned against the closed door, read every word, then paced. Burn it? Never! But I couldn't let anyone see it. Where could I hide it? Where would it be safe from my nosey sisters' prying eyes and Umama's uncanny sense of knowing everything a person tried to conceal? Feet shuffled toward the door. My heart stopped when the doorknob turned. I grabbed my oldest, worst looking tee-shirt from the closet, wrapped it around the underground newspaper, and crammed the bundle beneath my folded nightgown. Hardly safe—but I had no time to look for a better hiding place.

Onele toward me bunk. I spun her around, then nudged her out of our room. "We have cleaning to do. The dishes are still in the sink. Our lazy sister also didn't sweep. And Onele, if she didn't sweep, you know what else that means."

"She didn't beat Umama's rug. She's in trouble now."

Ubaba had worked diligently to earn the rand for this basket-weave jute rug in shades of brown and gold, and our mother had honored us by letting it stay in our room where our father rolled it out on our first night. If a person wanted Umama calling upon the ancestors to lay a spell on them, maybe an itchy rash, then forget to beat her rug. To keep myself safe from such a curse, I abandoned the idea of a nap.

I rolled the heavy rug and dragged it to the path. Grunting, I flung it over the wooden handrail, then returned inside to fetch the broom. Onele had crawled into her bunk. A sound like beer pouring from a thin-necked bottle bubbled from her mouth. Crying about the splinter had clogged her nose. I grabbed the broom and headed out.

Dust billowed each time I hit the rug with the straw broom. On the third solid whack, bristles broke and whizzed like miniature arrows.

Angry that Asanda left me her work, I smacked harder while fuming over her thoughtlessness.

I understood why my older sister didn't think any of this was her responsibility. While living with our grandparents, nothing had been required of her. Our grandmother Hulu did the housework and laundry while Asanda attended classes and fun activities at the Catholic school. Gone five or six days a week, she had no idea how hard Onele and I worked to help Umama. But now that we went to the same school and our duties were greater than in Soweto, I resented Asanda's privileged attitude.

I was also irked because she didn't seem to care about the risk of being found out. How could she think these secret meetings with this boy were worth the possibility of Ubaba being fired from the best job he ever had? If forced to return to Soweto, once again, there'd be no flowers to pick for our teachers on the way to school. And I'd have to leave Kalisha, the friend I'd made at school. How could Asanda put our parents at risk of being asked to leave our rondavel, abandon our own stove and refrigerator, give up running water, a toilet that flushed, and electric lights in every room? Was she crazy, or just that insensitive?

Then it dawned on me, she'd had all these things at our grandparents' house. But even so, did she think it was worth leaving Kuhle and Yama and all the other amazing animals just to play kissy-face with some stupid boy? I couldn't bear the thought of being kicked out of the first proper home I'd ever had and forced to return to the aluminum corrugated roof, plastic walls, and dirt floors of our Soweto shanty.

But most of all, the thing I couldn't face was that we'd be hungry again.

I cranked my body onto my back leg, stepped into my swing, and put my weight behind the broom. But when I drove my hips forward and launched the broomstick as if it were a baseball bat, I hit the thick porch rail. Wood splintered and pain shot through my elbow.

I glared at the broken handle. "You got me in trouble now."

Umama's voice filled my brain. *"What dimwitted thing were you doing?"*

This could put me in bigger trouble than if I hadn't cleaned the rug. I tucked the two broom parts under my arm and ran to the big kitchen. I peeked in the door and motioned Rosie to me. Fortunately, Umama had her back to me and was intent on dicing tomatoes. When Rosie stepped onto the porch and I held up the broom, she glanced over her shoulder and whispered, "Your mother won't be happy about that."

I followed her around to the back. She opened a closet full of mops and straw brooms. When she nodded, I reached in and helped myself to a broom that had obviously been used before. The bristles were worn shorter on one side, just like the one we had.

"Toss that old one in the rubbish bin and scurry back home. Your mother's shift is over in ten minutes."

I whispered, "Thank you," and hugged Rosie quickly, but firmly.

She chuckled and shooed me down the path.

While kicking straw off the walkway, I decided to find Asanda and talk some sense into her. It took a while to haul the rug inside, then roll it out between our bunks. As I worked, Onele's snore revved like when the safari jeep drivers were impatient to leave, but her face had the same sweet expression it always had.

I started out the door, then hesitated. Should I go or stay? The last time I left Onele alone, I thought it might be the end of her and me. I sat on the sofa to consider my options, only to have a spring poke me in the behind.

Only two years before, on Onele's first day of school, I had nearly lost her to those horrible men who kidnap and sell little girls. I reasoned that Ilanga was a safer place to live. The only strangers were guests and delivery men. Besides, my sister was now almost nine. She'll be fine, I told myself, unless she wandered out and got speared by the ornery warthog that wanders up from the watering hole. When my head snapped forward, I realized I had fallen asleep. A long shadow stretched from the lamp across the floor. More than an hour had passed.

I poked Onele's shoulder. "We need to finish your homework."

"Too tired."

"Get your book before I smack you." I shook my head. Not at Onele, but at myself, because I sounded like our mother.

Onele grumbled her way to the table, opened her book, then flipped through the pages. The chapter she needed was missing, more than likely ripped out by a student who previously used the book. She was better at maths than I. The only reason I could help her was I had taken the same class taught by the same teacher.

But when Asanda sauntered in, I said, "We'll do your maths later, Onele. Go listen to the radio."

She slapped the frayed textbook closed, cranked the volume high, and danced to *Hot Butter Popcorn,* flapping her elbows like an ostrich at the pinnacle of his mating dance.

I glared at my older sister. "Sit, Asanda."

"No."

"I said sit." I mimicked Umama's sternest expression, her raised-brow, squinty-eyed combination. "You must stop."

Asanda surprised me by plunking herself into a chair. "Stop what?"

"I'm not a child. I know where you're going."

"So?"

"You're lighting a fire in the wind."

"I am not. My love for Leo is different. I'll always love my family, except maybe you. You're more nosy than old Ife in Soweto."

"Plenty of nosy people here. You can bet they're chin-wagging about you and the vet's son."

"We're careful. Nobody knows."

"If I know, others do too."

"So what?"

"Asanda, you *know what*."

"Nobody cares."

"His father will when he figures out that instead of checking on the animals, Leo's sneaking off with you."

"He does his work."

"Does he? Then why don't you do yours?" I can tell Asanda's winding up to make a sarcastic comment, so I cut her off. "Besides, Baas John won't approve."

"Baas John doesn't care."

"Asanda, you'll get our parents fired."

"No, I won't. Leo and I are the same."

"No, you're not." I expected Asanda to argue, but she looked down and picked her cuticle.

"He and I are White."

"You wish you were. You're close but not as light. In Soweto, you stood out like a snowflake in a coalbin. But here, you're more the color of the bleached blonde who has been out by the pool all week."

"You're jealous."

"Listen, Asanda, if our birth father had married Umama, you might get away with acting White. But since he ditched us and went back to the Netherlands, that makes you Black, the same as us, regardless of our different shades."

"Leo doesn't care."

"He's just a boy. He may not now, but when his father finds out, the same misfortune that happened to Umama will happen to you."

"No, it won't. Leo is a man. He won't disappear."

"What if you get pregnant like our mother did?"

"Eshile, we are not doing that. You're such a child, you don't understand. So, are you going to snitch?"

"We don't do that to each other. Besides, I don't need to snitch. Umama finds out everything on her own."

Onele gave us her usual dirty look that meant *quiet-down*, then settled cross-legged in front of the radio to listen to *The Casey Kids*. Asanda sat beside her and shot me a snarky once-over—her way of telling me I was the one left out.

Weary from arguing, I dipped a washcloth in the cold soapy dish water and began working on the dishes that had sat there the entire day.

"I'm warning you, Asanda. Nothing good can come of this."

CHAPTER FOUR

Feeding Frenzy

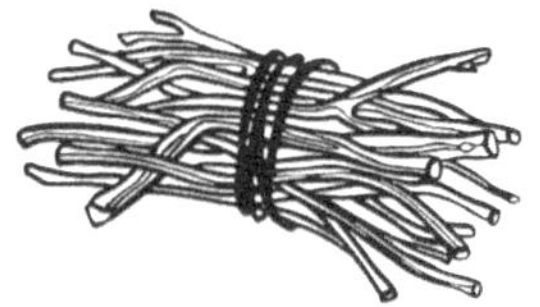

EyeNkanga (Month of Small Yellow Daisies) November 1972

First, we cleared it with Umama. After completing our assigned tasks, we could do as we pleased. Asanda, wanting to trade, offered to do laundry if Onele and I cleaned the rondavel. We scrubbed and swept as if *hose geeste* hovered over us, ready to steal our souls if we did not meet our mother's standards.

After we stacked our dishes in the cupboard and wiped the sink, Onele plopped onto the blue braided rug, hands behind her head, exposing her sweaty armpits, while I double-checked our work. We knew what Umama expected, still, our first attempt didn't always measure up. The last thing we needed was to risk Umama's wrath, putting our plan in peril.

I gazed out the window. A cluster of yellow daisies had opened their petals to show their faces to the sun, but Asanda's face was nowhere in sight. Umama would discipline her for not finishing the laundry. The problem for Onele and me was that we needed the clean sheets so we could make the beds to keep our sister's punishment from leaking onto us.

"Up, Onele. Let's head to the laundry and collect the bedclothes from big sister."

Like a piglet who ate too much, Onele patted her bulging tummy. "Too tired."

"No, you're not. It's 10 a.m."

"Let's rest. If Asanda isn't back in thirty minutes, we'll write her a nasty note."

"You know that won't work. She might not come back. Or if she does, she'll toss the sheets on our beds, then disappear again. She'll rankle Umama and take us down with her. Come on, Onele. It's a nice day. The sun is shining."

"The sun always shines here."

"It rained last night. Can't believe you slept through the thunder. Our bedroom window rattled as if it might fall out of its frame. The watering hole path will be a muddy mess."

Onele puckered her lips into a full-force whine. "Asanda never does her chores. I'm sick of her pinhead excuses. It's not fair. She never gets punished the way we do. Even Hulu didn't know how to make her mind. I told her to cut a switch from her orange tree. She said she couldn't because sister's so white. I no longer care if her skin swells blotchy red. It's still not fair. I'd get a stick and—"

"Good Lord, Onele. Stop ranting. It won't do a bit of good."

"My muscles hurt from the work we already did."

"Then you better take a nap. I've got lots to do. I want to run down to the watering hole. Baas John said Khule might be pregnant again."

"Will her baby be born today?"

"Heavens, no. If she got pregnant at the beginning of the mating season, that means she's only one month along. But he saw three baby monkeys with their mothers playing in the overhanging trees."

Onele popped up like bread from our toaster. "I'm rested."

I surveyed the room. Confident our cleaning would pass Umama's inspection, we headed out in search of our sister and the bed sheets.

Onele skipped along the pathway until something caught her eye. Then she huddled off to the side, brushed away loose leaves, and pointed at two fat slimy snails with their antennae entwined. "They're kissing."

I chuckled and signaled for her to rise. Stagnant air clung to our skin. Moist tree branches, heavy with rain, drooped toward the ground. Dewdrops sparkled from their perches on elephant-sized leaves. I repeated what I'd heard Umama say many times. "The ancestors cried tears for us."

Onele picked a handful of tall yellow daisies. "For Umama, so she'll know how much I love her."

We turned at the next fork, then entered the wooden shack. The moist air smelled of laundry soap. Off balance, the washing machine rumbled and bounced as if trying to escape with our clothes still inside its bowels. The dryer huffed and puffed. Lint swirled in puffs, a tornado of baby clouds. I couldn't inhale.

Asanda had folded shirts and pants and left them stacked on the warped plastic table.

Onele pressed her nose against the dryer's glass window. "That's our bedclothes in there."

"*Yebo*, but where's our sister? I am so fed up with her sneaking about."

Onele shrugged, and the dryer beeped. I filled my arms with warm sheets and sniffed their soapy scent. "Help fold these before they wrinkle." I dropped my armload onto the table, but Onele didn't move. I peered down my nose. "Now."

"Not my job." Onele's eyes flew wide open when she plunked her rear in the plastic chair and its wobbly legs slid on the concrete floor, screeching their complaint.

I almost laughed, but managed to hold on to my *are-you-looking-for-trouble* face. "Do you want Umama to forbid us from feeding the vultures because your other sister didn't finish her chores?"

Onele leapt from the chair faster than a springbok fleeing at the scent of wild dogs. Wrapping her arms around my waist, she bounced on her toes. "Can I help today? Please, please."

"No reason you can't, since you promised to fold these sheets."

Onele's eyebrow shot up in Umama's signature expression. I pinched my lips between my teeth to hold back a chuckle. Onele knew I was tricking her. I could almost hear her brain whir as she debated whether to go along.

She needed a bit more encouragement. "Don't ruin this and make me change my mind. So far, you've helped with every chore without whimpering or whining."

"I'm a big girl now."

"Yes, you are. And this is going to be a special day with the vultures."

Onele's eyes grew larger and larger as she bounced on her toes. "Tell me! Tell me, please!"

"Umama said two busloads of guests leave in the morning. That means a celebration tonight. The cooks will have carved the meats by now. Extra buckets of bones and gristle will be waiting for me."

Onele stared as though she needed to hear every single word I might say. "So…" I paused, making her wait for the answer I knew she wanted to hear. "I need the help of a girl big enough to carry heavy scrap buckets to the feeding ground. A girl just like you."

Onele grabbed a pillowcase and spread it smooth. She folded up the sides, neat and tight, as though it were a Christmas gift.

"Not necessary to be that careful. If we spread the sheets on the beds while they're still warm, we can fool Umama into thinking we ironed them."

"We have to make the beds?" Onele scowled. "Okay. I'll help. Let's hurry. The vultures might leave before we get there."

"Tell you what, baby girl—"

"Big girl."

"I'll carry this pile of clothes and pillowcases. Grab the sheets. Onele. I'll race you home."

Onele took off like a bullet. I pretended to run as fast as I could. She giggled and called to me that I was too slow. When we reached our rondavel, Onele, a tad too excited, burst through the door. It bumped and bounced off the wall. Fortunately, the door didn't do any damage, and I caught it with my foot before it hit me in the face.

We whipped around the beds like whirlwinds then ran out the door. Then as we approached the big kitchen, I let go of my worries about Asanda. Three loaded plastic buckets sat beneath the metal cutting table, both filled beyond their brims with bloody gristle, animal innards, and huge leg bones sticking out the top.

"Can I carry one?" Onele's expression was too eager to resist. I chuckled when I handed her a bucket and her nose curled up at the metallic reek of blood. I carried the other two.

The spot where I fed the vultures was as distant as the watering hole. Onele clenched the wire handle in both hands and heaved her heavy bucket forward with each step. The motion propelled her down the winding path. I expected her to stop, plunk her bottom down, and demand to rest, but she charged on without complaint. When we approached the patch of dirt where vultures lurked overhead, Onele squealed, "Lookie, look!"

Baldheaded birds darkened the sky. Hundreds of eager scavengers had claimed their spots in nearby trees. Clasping branches with gnarly claws, vultures flapped and squawked at others who landed close. Then hundreds more swooped in. A deep buzzing, like an airplane dipping too low, filled the air. The sky rained branches and leaves, feathers and bird shit. When we moved to where I always emptied the buckets, the most aggressive vultures dropped to the lower branches. Our flying dinner guests stretched their scrawny necks and hissed, making so much noise we didn't hear Baas John walk up.

"Stupid tourist attraction. Empty-headed Americans think they've come to a zoo. More trouble than they're worth."

I nudged Onele and pointed overhead. "They're hungry. And you're about the size of a water buffalo thigh, so you'd better stay behind me."

Miss Yeboah, my new teacher at Ilanga Community School, had taught us how dangerous South African vultures could be. Still, my desire to have this job was greater than any nervousness. In Soweto, when Mr. Cromwell unjustly fired Umama, I lost my job of mending for his wife. A colossal disappointment. While Asanda shunned jobs of any type, I worked hard to earn money.

Most importantly, Baas John trusted me. His words from when he offered me the job rang in my ears. "Some tourists are idiots. Their brand-new Canon cameras dangling on their necks, don't let these fools move closer than where the trail forks off toward the pool."

Baas John explained that after their first safari through the knob-thorn and marula veld to see leopards, lions, and other animals that could eat them alive, these folks thought they were invincible. So, he charged me with scaring them with vulture tales that frightened them into staying behind the line.

"Eshile, tell the crazy ones these vicious birds' favorite food is a juicy human ear."

I snickered because I knew from Miss Yeboah's class that wasn't true. These lazy birds only ate what someone, or something, else had killed.

But Baas John saw nothing funny regarding my new responsibility. "Wilson will stand by to be sure nobody gives you trouble. But remember, lose a tourist, lose your job."

Last week, when I dumped my bucket into the clearing, an American man leapt in and snagged a three-foot bloody bone. Five, maybe six, vultures screamed while diving at his head. The American dropped the leg bone, but the birds, at war to secure every scrap, slapped the young man with their powerful wings and pecked his hand until Wilson scared it away with his broom.

This big baboon fool, as Baas John called him, ran as fast as Abebe Bikila, the first African to win an Olympic gold medal. The rule-following guests howled as if cheering Abebe to victory.

Several newly arriving guests walked the path toward us. I welcomed them, then began my speech. "In Zulu culture, a vulture is called *Inqe*. We honor them with this title of purifier or the one who cleans off the land. Known as birds of the King and respected for their great strength, tradition honors vultures as the reincarnated souls of Zulu hunters and warriors. Many grind the bones of a vulture who dies of natural causes into a powder that protects them from their mortal enemies. And now you are about to see some impressive warrior behavior by these birds."

Proud that Baas John chose me to introduce our international guests to this bird that was so important to African culture, I held my chin high and continued my speech using the exact words he had taught me. "These vultures leave when the meat and bones are gone. If you need a souvenir, you may gather feathers when the last bird leaves."

I scraped a line in the dirt with the heel of my white canvas *takkie*, and closed with, "But stay behind this line. Vultures will attack you." I cast my most serious glare up one tourist and down the next. "Humans are not a vulture's first choice, but these giants battle over every piece of meat. Anyone too close might get hurt. At least, battered by their massive powerful wings. If they mistake your arm for a waterbuck leg, they'll claw it off."

I waited for my warning to penetrate their brains. Wilson had said most tourists are too afraid of vultures to attend this event, but five showed up that day. Of the five, three stepped back from the line in the dirt and the other two stayed where they were but shifted from foot to foot.

I spoke again. "My goal is not to scare you. It is to educate. The vulture is a valuable member of African animal society. I think of them as the cleanup crew. A single flock can clean an antelope carcass in twenty minutes. This prevents its decay from seeping into water sources. As well, these birds limit the spread of disease because their digestive systems kill bacteria such as from plague, anthrax, and botulism. So please stand back and keep your arms to yourselves while the vultures do their work."

Abnormally aggressive that day, hundreds swooped to lower tree branches before I took a single scrap from my bucket. Another twenty-five or more, rather than taking a perch, sailed above the treetops. Not because they were timid or afraid; they had a combat strategy.

Eyes wide, lips stretched into a fearful grimace, little sister tipped her bucket, ready to throw its contents as far as she could.

"Now, Onele."

As animal parts flew from our buckets, circling vultures dive-bombed, shrieking their way to the ground. Graceful flight transformed into violent and frantic beating wings. The birds clumsily perched in trees dove to join the fight. The finest of the airborne brigade snatched the best body parts for themselves, tearing the flesh with their beaks and claws. Within seconds, they created a giant dust ball of feathers, dirt, and strips of gristle.

And seconds were important; the most important being the one in which I snatched Onele out of the flight path. Umama's punishment would be extreme if I brought my little sister home covered with bloody claw marks.

The larger vultures grunted like rabid pigs and snatched meat scraps from the beaks of smaller birds. So majestic in the air, these creatures became ripping, shredding, eating monsters on the ground. They threatened each other with the sound our dog in Soweto made when he barked and sneezed at the same time. While we had laughed at Dinga, nobody laughed at these warrior birds.

December is generally the hottest month, but that late November day, the thermometer hit 91 degrees. Vultures carry a dusty, chalky smell, but the stink of urine told me the birds were pissing themselves to cool their bodies.

When the flapping and squawking ended, the tourists stood stunned into silence, yet no one's eyes popped out of their sockets more than Onele's.

I helped guests gather souvenir tufts of soft gray feathers, long sleek quills, and the few shards of bone left behind. Wilson, standing by holding a rake, smoothed the soil. When my sister and I picked up our empty buckets, her eyes sparkled with excitement and sweat glistened on her forehead. I picked a clump of gray vulture underbelly fluff from her hair, then took her sticky hand in mine.

Onele babbled while we tromped up the path. She recounted every detail of the vulture feed as though she had forgotten I was there. While climbing the kitchen steps to return the buckets, she asked, "Why doesn't sister stay with us? We wouldn't get stuck doing her chores if she did."

I wondered if Onele had overheard our big sister talking about leaving. The two of us, we did fine without Asanda, but there was still the issue of our sister going to America on a scholarship. She was thirteen, two years older than I, and had four years of school before she matriculated. Still, I didn't care to be caught unaware and left behind.

Auntie Grace said the ancestors communicated with Onele the way they did her. Perhaps they messaged her in a dream. I found it more likely Asanda had discussed her plans with Umama again, and big-ears Onele had been lurking around the corner.

But I didn't ask. I had this sense of dread that if Onele thought Asanda was leaving for America, just her saying it out loud might make it come true.

Healing Touch

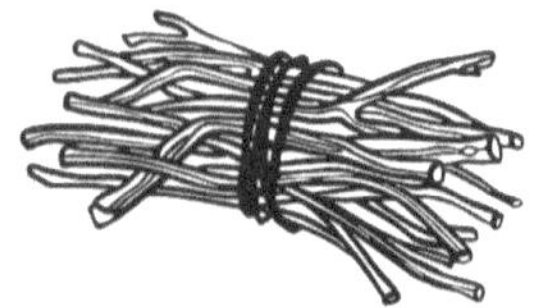

EyoMdumba (Month of the swelling grain) February 1973

Yesterday, I snapped around in my seat and knocked Anthony's lunch pail off his desk. I would have knocked his head off, but my arms were too short.

Seething with anger, I recited my disgust with his behavior to Miss Yeboah as politely as I could.

But she said, "Be that as it may, I told you to pick up your books and get back to your assignment, but you and Kalisha disobeyed me and crawled on the floor instead."

Anthony's big talent was that he spat slobbery paper wads with a deadly aim. Yesterday he bounced one off my neck. Startled, my arm flew out, sending my books across the table Kalisha and I shared. When they slammed onto the cement floor, Miss Yeboah leapt out of her desk chair, then scowled at me. I pointed at Anthony, who shrugged his shoulders. The cream on top was that before I uttered a word of defense, he out-and-out lied and claimed he did not know what caused me to knock his lunch pail off his table.

My friend Kalisha and I dropped to our hands and knees and searched beneath our desks to find the slimy evidence.

It was gone.

As unfair as it seemed to me, I was told to apologize to Anthony instead of him to me. I was *kwaad*, as angry as I could be, because in this single spit-wad incident, he ruined my efforts, all my hard work, to gain the position of Miss Yeboah's favorite.

She marched us to the office, where I failed to present evidence of the spit wad. Without that proof, the lead teacher remained unconvinced I was innocent, and after listening carefully, deemed me the troublemaker in this incident, but excused Kalisha to go home since all she did was crawl on the floor.

The lead teacher glared the entire hour she held me in detention. When she set me free, I worked out my anger by playing rugby with the boys on the field next to school. I was sorry Anthony skipped the game, cheating me out of my opportunity to inflict revenge on him instead of his unsuspecting best friend, who tumbled and rolled when I stuck my foot out, preventing him from tackling the ball carrier.

That night I fell asleep as quickly as a shea nut hits the ground. Being a light sleeper, I usually heard Asanda when she sneaked out in the early morning, but the day's stressful activities wore me out. I slept as soundly as a puppy dog until Umama woke me because we planned to bake a cake for Rosie's birthday celebration.

I hated getting out of bed before the sun came up, but Rosie was worth the sacrifice. We were close. Not quite as tight as I was with Auntie Grace, but they both had special powers. Rosie wasn't a *sangoma* like my auntie, but she used many of the same herbs, flowers, and greens that my Auntie did, all from nature to treat illnesses—from broken legs to smallpox. But more than the herbal tea and poultices she made, I believed her curative powers came from the love in her heart that flowed down her arms and healed through her tender touch.

If my mother had come into our room instead of calling my name from the kitchen, she might have noticed the flatness of the upper bunk across the room from me. Then she would have sent me in search of Asanda. I sorely wanted my sister caught and punished, but not at the personal cost of missing out on baking Rosie's birthday cake. So, I took out my annoyance on the batter by whipping it with such a vengeance that my elbow hurt.

As I slid the pans into our oven (a luxury that still caused amazement and gratitude to well inside my chest), Umama removed her apron and headed for the door.

"I'll be back in an hour. I must help cook breakfast for a European group that paid extra for special meals. Wake your sisters and do your chores."

When Umama had awakened me, I expected to find Onele in the kitchen waiting for me to warm her *putu pap*. Ever since we moved to Ilanga, with access to an unending supply of milk, sugar, and fresh-churned butter, she couldn't seem to get enough of the crumbly cornmeal porridge. I considered calling her to help, but decided I'd rather keep all Rosie's praise for being such a good daughter by helping my mother the way I did, rather than sharing it with Onele.

But now that it was time to tackle our chores, I returned to our bedroom. I'd left yesterday's clothes hanging on my ladder. I shoved them aside, but Onele's bunk was also empty. The house was silent, yet I checked the bathroom just in case. Of course, she wasn't there.

I stepped out our front door mumbling, "What? They both snuck off? Left me to explain to Umama where they went! Selfish. Ungrateful. I need new sisters… or no sisters at all." Then it occurred to me, perhaps my sisters left me behind and went to collect our daily basket of discarded breads. I was halfway down the path to the big kitchen when Onele screamed.

I ran.

Our mother cradled Onele in her lap and pressed an ice-filled dishtowel against her forehead.

The lead weight in the pit of my stomach told me I'd be blamed for Onele slipping out behind my back. The lecture on how I nearly lost my sister in Soweto was surely sitting on the tip of my mother's tongue, waiting to be hurled at me.

Now I was angrier than before. "Enough crying, Onele. You just fell on your rock-hard head. If you'd stayed home with me, the way you were supposed to, you wouldn't have hurt yourself."

Umama's evil eye augered me like a tree-killing, shothole borer beetle. "I'll deal with your smart mouth later."

Premonitions of my early demise overpowered me so much I almost didn't hear the softening of my mother's next words. "This wasn't your fault, Eshile. You were busy whipping the batter when I told Onele to come with me. Take her home and put her in bed to rest while you complete the chores."

Relieved about not being blamed, my anger subsided. I even forgave Asanda for disappearing, though it meant I'd be doing the rest of our chores by myself. I held out my hand. "Okay, baby girl. Tell me what happened while we walk."

"The breadbasket wasn't ready, so I hung over the porch rail on my belly and pretended to be an airplane flying across all of Africa."

"Sounds fun, but I can't be everywhere making sure you're safe. Now that you're nine, you must think situations through before you act." I patted her head the way Umama did, as if I were an adult. But the handrail was a thick, smooth wooden post, plenty sturdy to hold a kid. When I visualized her shaping her body like an aircraft and making engine noises, it made sense to imagine flying as she did. After all, I planned to fly to the American university of my dreams in a plane so enormous it could hold a hundred people.

Once inside our rondavel, Onele supported her sore arm while I wiped the dirt from her face, then tucked her and Monkey into bed. As I closed our door so she could rest, she whimpered, "Eshile, my arm hurts."

I assured her she'd be fine and set about speeding through our chores. Moments later, I heard her soft, snuffy snore.

But I was beside myself when Umama stomped in the front door at the exact same moment Onele staggered from our bedroom, holding her arm, which was then red and swollen to the size of the porch rail. Umama paled. Each passing second left me feeling worse about my abilities as a big sister. Umama swooped up my sad-faced sister, and we rushed to the women's dormitory as quickly as we dared without jostling Onele's arm.

I was comfortable apologizing. I'd had plenty of practice. This time, I meant it. I couldn't say sorry enough. I should have checked on Onele sooner.

Umama handed Onele to Rosie. When she laid my sister on the cot and kissed her cheeks, I was jealous. I also felt ashamed.

Rosie pulled a dented metal trunk from under her cot. "Rosie's gonna fix your arm. She'll make you well." She lifted the lid and pulled out a string-tied cloth bag and a clay bowl. "Eshile, fill this at the tap."

Rosie poured the contents of her bag into the water. I sniffed the rich scent of fertile dirt that rose from the bowl. "What's that?"

"Healing mud. When my family left Nigeria, they moved to a village called *Mmotla* in the North West Province of South Africa." Rosie kneaded the damp soil as if it were bread dough. After spreading the mixture on the puffiness, she wrapped a clean, but stained roll of gauze—obviously reused many times—around Onele's arm to hold the mudpack in place.

"What does the mud do?"

"Sweet Eshile, it drinks the swelling and consumes Onele's poor luck."

"How can dirt do that?"

"A star fell in the Soutpan Mountains a thousand years ago. It shattered on the banks of the Mmotla River and burned the soil. This released its healing powers to flow in the river's waters and continue to enrich the earth. People travel from other countries to bathe in her holy waters. *Sangomas*, prophets, and religious leaders throughout Africa proclaim it heals both the body and mind."

"Do you believe that?"

"My brother's leg was crushed in a slide in the diamond mine."

Sadness washed over me. "Rosie, my uncle died in a slide."

"Oh my, I am so sorry, Eshile. I should not have spoken of it."

"It's okay. I want to hear what happened to your brother."

"Ah, yes. My sister and I carried him to the river. We held his head so he could float for hours each day. Three days later, with our support, he took two steps. At the end of six days, he hobbled home." A wistful smile washed across Rosie's face. "He still suffered with pain. I heard him cry at night when he thought we were all asleep. But at least he could move well enough to plant a garden—the most abundant I've ever seen. The healing waters allowed him to rebuild his dignity by feeding his family and selling the rest of his fruits and vegetables in our village."

"Rosie, will the power ever run out?"

"Never. The gods blessed the soil and the water. Once the gods bless you, it's forever. These muds also healed my mother. A witch cursed her mind before she left to join the ancestors. God bless her soul. One day she recognized her family, the next she screamed they were evil spirits sent to kill her. But after bathing in the waters, she lived her final years in peace."

"Is this the last of your soil?"

"Yes, Eshilc, but do not worry. Baas John grants me leave to visit my family in the low tourist season, July or August." Rosie tucked the ends of the gauze inside the wrap. "Does that hurt, Onele?"

"No, it's better."

"I will return to repack your arm every few hours until the mud absorbs the swelling."

"Rosie, I thank the gods for your kindness." Umama turned to me. "Eshile, you will stay home from school today and watch over your sister."

"But Umama, I promised Kalisha I'd eat lunch with her today." That wasn't quite true. Kalisha and I ate together every day. However, I didn't think my mother knew this, and since she was the one who drilled in our heads that one should always keep their promises, I thought it was a compelling argument, until her killer-eyebrow rose.

"That may be so, but I know it is more important to you that your little sister not be alone when she's in so much pain."

I may have rolled my eyes because Umama shot me *the-look*. I didn't say another word, but I was thinking, doesn't anybody understand how important my best friend and my classes are to me?

Unlike the healing of the baby *kudu* Ubaba and Dr. Vorster discovered in the veld, which took a solid week of Rosie's loving touch, Onele's swollen arm shrunk to normal by bedtime. Since Onele seemed grateful not to be alone, plus later that night my mother made a big fuss thanking me, I didn't complain about missing one day of eating lunch with my best friend.

Ubaba had told us the circumstances of Dr. Vorster finding the kudu after leaving the Veterinary Wildlife Services meeting regarding the increase of bovine tuberculosis among white rhinos. While traveling the road between Kruger National Park and Ilanga, the veterinarian noticed signs of poachers less than a kilometer from the lodge. That afternoon, Ubaba drove him back out to scout the area.

Dr. Vorster expressed surprise when they came upon a male and female kudu within the borders of the protected lands. Vultures can detect the smell of death from more than a mile away. Why they hadn't eaten the kudus' remains was a mystery. Dried blood caked the antelopes' chests and pooled where their gracefully curved horns used to be. Poachers killed male kudus because powerful spirits dwell in their twisting, spiral-shaped horns. They also prized the horns since they brought a high price from those who used them for musical instruments or ritual symbols of male potency.

Kudus were frequent visitors to our watering hole. Earlier, Ubaba had joked that the white fur encircling the kudu's tail looked like a target on its butt. After finding the slaughter, he never made that joke again.

We saw more females than males because the males tended to hide out until mating season. Now Dr. Vorster questioned why the male and female were traveling together. The veterinarian and my father set off to track the poachers but stopped when tall strands of wild wheat quivered just a few steps from them. Ubaba said the doctor moved as silently as a black stork on the hunt until he stood over another kudu—a miniature replica of its mother.

Dr. Vorster scooped up the calf, wrapped her in a blanket so she couldn't kick, and held her as Ubaba drove. After they arrived at Ilanga, the doctor carried the kudu toward the wooden pen for animals, my father hurried to the kitchen and told Rosie to collect her herbs.

When I saw Rosie running, I followed because I'd never seen her run. She had trouble getting one thigh past the other even when ambling leisurely. Now my father seemed to struggle to keep up, so I knew this was big.

Baas John stood in the center of the pen. In his arms, he held the kudu, wrapped in the soft blanket the color of a fawn, the same as this infant's fur. Large pink ears flickered at every sound.

At first, Rosie waited and watched. When she stepped inside the pen, the frightened kudu thrashed and kicked Baas John's hips. As soon as he set the tiny antelope on its feet, it tried to leap the fence. But its spindly legs were weak, so the poor animal crumpled to the ground. Rosie sat in the dirt, then lifted the flailing kudu onto her lap. She caressed the shivering animal's back and neck until it stopped fighting her strong but gentle clutch.

"You're safe, little one. You're Rosie's now." Rosie rolled up to her knees and supported the kudu beneath its belly. Three tries later, it balanced on its wobbly legs. Wild-eyed, ears flipping like a frightened rabbit, the tiny kudu stood.

"Okay, Rosie's baby. Try to walk."

Bolder by the minute, the kudu barked. I laughed. "Ubaba, that's the same scratchy sound Rufaro makes when he smokes too much."

"Come to me, little one. Rosie needs to find out if her baby kudu is hurt." Rosie's voice was calm and smooth like my Auntie Grace's when she coaxed out the *idemoni*, the demons, who had driven a shriveled old man in Soweto to wander the street market, calling for his dead wife.

I hardly believed what I saw. The kudu staggered, then dropped her head in Rosie's lap. Rosie massaged the base of its ears, then worked her large fleshy hands along its neck. "Your name will be *Usana*, my baby girl," cooed Rosie while moving her fingers down its legs, inspecting the tiny black hooves.

Dr. Vorster whispered, "She let Rosie lift her feet. The kudu has no greater sign that it trusts her touch."

As the weeks passed, I helped Rosie wean Usana off the bottle and entice her to eat leaves and shoots. Her favorite treat was watermelon. Baas John, pleased with the kudu's progress, announced, "We will reintroduce her into the wild within a week."

Rosie turned to me, snorting under her breath, "I'll tell Baas when Usana is ready to be free."

For our first year at Ilanga, Ubaba's primary work assignments were to sweep the pathways, combat the giant beetles, and trim the bushes that scratch the tourists' delicate skin while they walked on our paths, as well as an endless stream of other odd jobs assigned by Baas John. Our father didn't like all these jobs, but Umama was grateful her husband was home every night. But his good work changed that.

My mother was proud of his achievements, yet she couldn't help but grumble a bit after twelve black rhinos were delivered from the Zambezi Valley in Rhodesia. Dr. Vorster needed to track the rhinos for several days and nights to ensure they were well and settling into their new terrain. Since his regular driver was ill, our father took his place. I'd never seen my father so excited as when he described how stealthily he drove, careful not to frighten these spectacular and massive ebony animals.

Dr. Vorster told Baas John our father was the best driver he ever had. He cited as evidence the rescue of Usana and the skill my father demonstrated when tracking the black rhinos. Then he requested Ubaba's reassignment as his assistant who would drive him whenever he traveled through Kruger National Park to survey the wellbeing of the animals and treat those that were ill. My father beamed when he announced Baas John not only agreed but also promoted Ubaba to Lead Driver of the Sunrise and Starlight Safaris.

With each safari, my father's popularity grew among the lodge's guests. Ubaba became renowned for finding hippos clambering out of the river to graze on reeds and delicate shoots of creeping grass long after the sun sank below the horizon. Tourists prattled happily while snapping pictures of these tank-sized animals and themselves. But that didn't satisfy everyone.

Ubaba instructed his charges to be silent, to listen for haunting owl hoots and nightjar high-pitched chirps. These warnings the birds scnt, telling each other to stay safe, helped him track the other animals' movements, especially in the dark, which enabled him to drive the tourists to the sights in which they were most interested.

He told us that when a spotted leopard leapt onto an antelope's back, then dragged it up a tree, the lucky safari-goers were thrilled to witness the survival of the fittest. But no visitor believed they received their money's worth unless they witnessed a pride of lions on a fresh kill.

My father's only complaint was that no matter how high the anticipation, safaris seldom left on schedule. Ubaba explained he could count on the women to create a delay. One evening, he flapped his ears to imitate the giant dangly plastic earrings worn by a woman on that morning's Sunrise Safari. He clomped his feet like she did in her platform sandals as she hurried toward the jeep. We girls laughed out loud when he wiggled his butt and cupped his hand against his chest as if holding two large *spanspek* melons to imitate this voluptuous blonde who kept everybody waiting until her painted nails dried, but Umama did not find it the least bit funny.

The night before last, after a Starlight Safari, Ubaba surprised us by saying a man delayed the group. His traveling companions remained patient for a while, until one jumped out to investigate. He found the man asleep under a thatched umbrella by the pool, an empty bottle of Three Ships whiskey clenched in his hand. Instead of waking him, he left his friend, but they still lost safari time.

Given my father's long and erratic hours, I hadn't had the talk I wanted to have with him. So, I set my mind to roll out of bed and ask his advice before he left for the next morning's Sunrise Safari. I had tried discussing with my mother how Anthony veered out of his way to poke me in the waist every chance he got.

She shrugged me off. "He's just a boy. He doesn't know how to say he likes you."

Likes me! He was torturing me. Clearly, Umama had lost her mind, and I needed a man's advice on what to do to stop Anthony from pestering me in class.

When the yelping and woofing of a black-backed jackal awakened me, our bedroom glowed a hazy gold. I'd slept too long. My father had been gone for hours. Asanda was also gone. No surprise. But it still made me hotter than Rosie's red chili sauce.

Judging by how high the sun was, I expected Ubaba's return within the hour. But he wouldn't be in the mood to talk until he took a much needed nap in preparation for driving Dr. Vorster to check on the twelve black rhinos and taking tourists into the savanna on the Starlight Safari. So, I descended my bunk, careful not to cause the rungs to creak and wake Onele. I suspected Asanda had stayed out all night, and she was in trouble now. Given the oily burnt smell of Umama straightening her hair for church, there was no way my sister could sneak back in unseen.

It was my practice to remove the tangles before Umama got her claws on me, thus saving myself a bunch of pain. Eager to witness the spectacle our mother would launch when she caught my sister, I grabbed my wide-tooth comb from the dresser and pulled it through my curls while tromping toward our kitchen.

Our shiny new silver oven for heating our straightening combs sat on the kitchen counter. I had begged to buy this heater with a cord that plugged into the wall, so we wouldn't have to warm our irons on the stovetop burners. Because the description on the box said this new device wouldn't overheat the pressing irons, I was confident Umama wouldn't burn our scalps as badly. That turned out to be a fallacy.

When I entered the kitchen, my mother smiled as though I was the only person in the world. I loved that about her.

She pulled the brass comb from the heated stove, and tested it on a white towel, leaving a burnt imprint behind. "Sit. I'm ready for you."

The oily odor reminded me of when ole George's truck engine burst into flames. My mother waved the heated comb in the air, then blew on it. I cringed when she pushed it into my tight curls, near my scalp. Intent on pressing my nape curls, she didn't notice when the front door creakcd, so I said, "Somebody came in."

She held the hot comb like a weapon, sliding across the floor in her backless slippers. A prickle rose on my neck, a warning that I should get out of this chair and prepare to defend our home and family as if we were back in Soweto.

"Asanda, what the *duiwel* were you doing outside?"

"Just went out for a moment to meet Leo."

From Umama's tone, it was obvious Asanda was in for the extended rendition of *you-know-what-this-boy-wants-from-you-and-how-getting-pregnant-at-fourteen-ruined-my-life*. I was okay with that until, thirty minutes later, Umama was still waving the now cold pressing iron in my sister's face, and it appeared she had much more to say.

I tried to bring her attention to me. "Umama, I can't attend services with my hair half straightened and half frizzy."

When Onele rubbed her sleepy eyes and staggered in, Umama ripped a metal clip from my hair. Since she would never discuss the details of Asanda's disappearances in front of Onele, the scolding ended, but her hand shook as her anger flared.

Umama grabbed a thick strand and pushed the overheated, smoking comb into the hair next to my temple. I slid lower in the chair, shrinking away to save my tender skin.

As Umama worked her way toward my ear, her breathing calmed. Mine did too, until at long last, she slammed the brass pressing comb into the stove so hard it slid back against the wall. "Eshile, press Onele's hair. I need to explain to your not-so-smart big sister why she'll be missing church and staying in her room except to go to school."

I wanted to protest, but Onele acted so relieved when Umama stormed from the room that I kept quiet, sprinkled Madam Jones Hot Comb Oil in my hand, and rubbed my palms together.

"Why is Umama angry?" whispered Onele.

"I'll tell you when you're older."

"How much older?"

"Four years."

Onele groaned and jutted out her lower lip. "I won't remember what I wanted to know by then."

Onele was terrible at holding still. She also didn't care if her hair frizzed or lay silky straight. But I gave the best head massage, so she settled when I pressed my fingers against her scalp and rubbed in tight, firm circles. Then I pulled my hands down each strand to spread the oil from her scalp through the ends. I lavished my sister with this relaxing treatment because the straightening went faster when Onele stayed calm.

A whiff of gray smoke rose when I touched the comb to the towel. The heat was perfect. I slid the comb through the first section, then gently worked my way around my little sister's head. My mind wandered to my problem with Anthony and how I might make him realize that punching a girl is not a sign of affection—until smoke curled up and tickled my nose. I was going too slow.

Onele sniffed the rotten egg stink. "You're burning my hair!"

"Sorry, sorry." Since her hair was so thick, she'd never notice, I slipped the melted strand into my pocket.

"Eshile, Baas John says the big bull is leaving Kuhle alone."

"Hold still or I'll burn your ears."

"He says Kuhle's swishing her tail and staying close to her sister."

I put a finger to my lips. Onele took my cue. Umama's stern tone was growing louder. Her lecture to Asanda had lasted longer than I expected.

Onele squirmed. "Done?"

"Not yet." I gave her hair an extra yank. "Hold still."

"Baas John told me this means Kuhle's preparing to give birth."

"She could be, Onele. Or maybe she's just glad the bull moved on to other females."

"Can we check? I want to see if her tummy has grown."

"Elephants are so huge we won't be able to tell. Baas John only knows because he's watched her for years. Still, if we hurry, we might have time for a quick visit to the watering hole before Umama finishes setting Asanda straight."

CHAPTER SIX

Into the Savanna

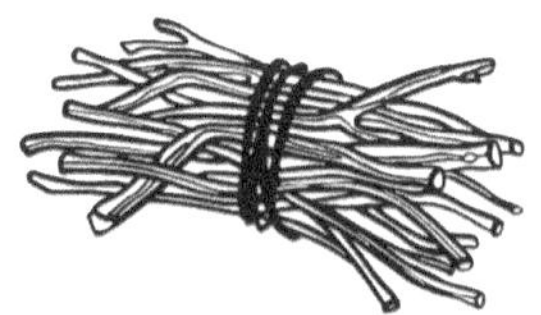

EyoMnga (Month of the Acacia Thorn Tree) December 1973

On the days Ubaba drove Ilanga's guests through the savanna of Kruger National Park, he left hours before Umama awakened us girls for school. I was a light sleeper, so I knew he never went to work without tiptoeing in and kissing our foreheads. I'd wrap my arms around my father's neck and wait for the warmth of his love to seep from my forehead to my toes.

When I released my grip, he whispered, "*Jonga amantombazana am.* Watch over my girls." The few times I failed to hear him because I didn't wake up, I worried how my day might go.

That summer morning, I was flitting through a happy dream. Bini and I walked to the watering hole. Just as I promised my best friend for life she would see the most amazing animals, Umama's voice broke through.

"Girls, get up. Your father has a treat."

"Did he bring sweets?" mumbled Onele.

"Better than that. Wear long-sleeved tee-shirts and jeans. *Khawuleza!* Be quick. Bring your cotton jackets. It's chilly out."

I waited for the trick—that there was no surprise—probably an extra chore Umama wanted done. Maybe Asanda and Onele were thinking the same thoughts because none of us moved.

"Girls! I said, be quick!"

Umama's grin spread as she motioned excitedly toward the door, so I hopped down from the top bunk and whipped the bedclothes off Onele.

Onele stretched her arms out to me, then giggled as I dragged her out of bed. "Where are we going?"

Asanda remained flat on her back, arms crossed over her chest. "I'm not going."

"Two guests fell ill and canceled for this morning's safari. Your father has permission from Baas John to take you in their place."

I slipped into my lion cub screen-printed tee-shirt, the one Ubaba bought from the souvenir shop for my twelfth birthday. "We'll miss school."

"This opportunity may never come again, Eshile. We want you girls to go."

Asanda turned her back to us. "I said I'm not going. I'm meeting Leo this afternoon."

Umama shot Asanda her squinty-eye, killer-eyebrow combination, the look everybody knew not to mess with. "Leo went with his father. Rangers reported a sick herd of buffalo—bleeding sores in their mouths and on their feet. Your father thinks they'll be at the park all day. You might see them there."

Asanda grumbled down from her bunk. You'd have thought she was descending into a deep, dark cave full of snakes. Onele, skipping toward the bathroom while pulling on her jeans, tumbled to the floor. I scurried after her, dabbed toothpaste on my finger, and rubbed it across my teeth. That would have to pass for brushing. I was excited to go. As we hurried out, Umama handed us each a banana. "Have fun and mind your father."

We ran to the lodge entryway to find Ubaba holding open the van's sliding door. "*Shesha*. Be quick, girls. Squeeze in. Only two seats left, but you are small enough to fit."

We were greeted by a chorus of "Hello," "Good morning," and "Climb aboard." Ubaba turned the key. The engine groaned, sounded as if it would stall, but when it roared, the passengers cheered. Tires spun and gravel flew when he pressed the gas pedal. The van leapt forward and started around the circular driveway. We all cheered again.

"It is an hour drive to Kruger National Park," announced my father in his official tone. "Once inside the Phalaborwa Gate, we'll stop for a restroom and coffee break. The sun comes up about the time we arrive. Rest, enjoy a nap if you can. You'll need your energy for the adventure that awaits."

Onele peeked out from where she sat, smashed between Asanda and me. "I'm keeping my eyes open. Lions hunt at night."

"Go to sleep, dopey," said Asanda. "It's dawn, not night. Besides, lions don't come near this busy road."

Jealousy crept up my neck when Onele snuggled against our older sister. Never had I called Onele dopey, yet she snuggled up against the sister who did. I leaned against the window and must have fallen asleep because only seconds seemed to pass until we stopped beside an enormous sign.

Welcome to the

Kruger National Park

PHALABORWA GATE

It's mine it's yours • Xa mina I Xa wena

My father turned toward us. "Stay in the van. We're early. The gate doesn't open until 5:30."

Third in line, we waited until the guard inside the shack motioned for the two trucks to enter. Ubaba pulled forward while cranking down his window. The men passed papers back and forth. When the guard waved him along, Ubaba parked the van alongside the jeeps near picnic benches.

He announced, "Prepare to witness animals in their natural habitat like you have never seen in your own countries."

The grinning man in the front seat scanned the area. "Lions?"

"I prayed to the ancestors, asked that they guide me to the Big Five."

Ubaba never told the passengers what he had explained to us. The more lions, elephants, leopards, water buffaloes, and black rhinoceroses he found, the more generously the guests tipped. My father prided himself on knowing which person would reward him the best, and he primed that person to take the passenger seat up front. That day it was a short muscular man wearing a khaki safari shirt so new the fold lines were still crisp. He shook my father's hand and introduced himself as Joe.

My father had also told us the guests rated the rear seat as second best because as the highest seat, it gave them an unrestricted view. Joe helped a small woman wearing large tortoiseshell sunglasses climb into the jeep. When he patted her knee and told her she'd be able to see everything just fine, I assumed she was his wife. A redheaded woman and a burly blond man, who apparently hadn't shaved since beginning his vacation, joined her on the rear bench seat. I grasped Onele's hand until Ubaba motioned to where we should sit, then the three of us climbed in, squeezing into the shorter, middle bench seat designed to accommodate two adults.

Ubaba announced, "My ancestors visited my dreams. They favor us today." And when the guests broke out in applause, he rose and took a bow, smiling so wide I saw all his teeth.

The sun shone deep gold but hovered only inches above the horizon, too low for its heat to warm our bodies. Onele shivered when our jeep moved forward. I wrapped my arm around her shoulders to share my body's warmth.

Kruger employees work hard to maintain the dirt roads. Still, we hit dips and ruts. We yelled, "Hang on!" and hooted with every air-catching bounce. We drove another fifteen minutes before Ubaba slowed the jeep to avoid startling a giraffe that stepped from behind an acacia tree. Leaves fluttered at the sides of his mouth as he chewed. He peered at us with big, soft eyes. I couldn't help but bat my eyelashes back at him.

Cameras clicked.

Ubaba said, "The male giraffe, the tallest animal on the planet, grows to five meters and the females to four. The males weigh in the range of 1,200 kilograms, while the dainty ladies, 800 to 900. For our American guests, that would be approximately 2,600 pounds for the males and upward from 1,700 for the females. Like you, giraffes are social and bond in groups. Others are nearby. When you have enough photos, we will seek this one's family and friends."

Ubaba drove the jeep along the bend in the path. The burly blond man pointed. "Two more!" He lowered his voice as though the giraffes might hear him and flee. "His fur looks so smooth. Wish I could pet him."

When Ubaba stopped, a second jeep pulled up close enough to hear him speak. "Giraffes eat seventy-five pounds of food a day, mostly leaves. Acacia, the tree these are feeding on, is their favorite. This particular acacia earned the name of giraffe thorn tree because the unique shape of the giraffe's tongue enables it to avoid the thorns. You might also find it interesting to know that his tongue is approximately fifty-three centimeters, or twenty inches long. The giraffe also grazes on grasses, but you can imagine how difficult it is to bend that long, arching neck to the ground."

The walkie-talkie hooked to Ubaba's belt emitted buzzing static.

"That's Leo's father," whispered Asanda.

Ubaba lifted the device and a man's voice crackled. Asanda slumped.

"*Mholo*, man. Where you be?" After Ubaba told him our location, the friendly, but croaky voice said, "Ahead of you, half kilometer to the north, a pride rests. They don't appear eager to leave. Go now and you have time."

"Thanks, my friend." Ubaba stood so everyone in both jeeps caught his words. "I will drive quickly until we come close. When I slow and raise my hand, please be quiet. Do not speak above a whisper. It is not good to frighten the King of Beasts."

Our jeep lurched forward. We slammed against the seats. The guests jabbered, loud enough to hear each other over the wind and engine noise. But when Ubaba braked to a crawl, then raised his hand, we fell silent. Both jeeps stopped twenty meters from a male and three female lions lounging in the shade of a grove of mopane trees. The male yawned and crossed one paw over the other, the way women sit. His black-tipped golden mane rippled when he shook his head.

"He's old and wise." Ubaba spoke only loud enough to be heard over the idling jeeps. "I know this because of how long and dark his mane is."

The driver of the second jeep leaned closer to my father and pointed to a herd of elephants a short distance off the road. An enormous male, his ears flapping like palm fronds in a breeze, approached, angling his five-foot ivory tusks as if threatening an enemy.

"Don't move or talk," whispered Ubaba. "December is the first month of the mating season. From now until the end of March, these bulls secrete *musth*, a hormone high in testosterone, from between their eyes and ears. During this period, we must be careful because the males are especially aggressive."

Guests raised their cameras in slow motion. Click… Click… Click.

My mouth hung open. Onele's eyeballs bugged. She grabbed my arm, then pointed beyond the road. A second, smaller bull trumpeted his battle cry. The older, larger elephant curled his trunk and proclaimed acceptance of the challenge. The force of his bellow caused the jeep to shimmy.

"Nobody move," warned Ubaba as the distance closed between the raging goliaths. "Stay quiet. We must not call attention to ourselves."

The bulls met in the middle of the road. "He's too little," whispered Asanda. "He hasn't got a chance."

The female elephants, some with calves at their sides, stopped to watch the bulls rage and stomp their feet. Dust flew. The younger elephant tried to gore the powerful bull. But the elder bull tolerated none of that. He rammed his head against the smaller elephant until they were eye to eye and pushed the little guy closer to the jeeps. Onele scrambled into my lap.

The redheaded woman screamed so loud my neck hairs prickled. "We're going to die! Get us out of here!"

I couldn't stop staring at her twisted fire-red lips and the lipstick smeared on her teeth.

Joe turned in his seat beside Ubaba and snarled, "Woman, what's wrong with you? Our driver warned us to be quiet."

"Get me out of here!" Screaming Redhead's high-pitched cry was more irritating than nails on a chalkboard. "They'll kill us."

Joe ground his jaws. "If they do, it's your fault."

Screaming Redhead threw one leg over the jeep's railing.

Her husband, the burly blond, grabbed her pink and yellow paisley shirttail, yanked her back in, and growled, "Damn it. Shut your mouth." They continued to bombard each other with heated words while Ubaba signaled the other driver to back away.

The lions, too comfortable to move out of the shade made by the large butterfly leaves, watched from between the straggly mopane tree trunks. When the male narrowed his golden eyes, I felt it as if his glare pierced my chest. Then his brow rose, much the same as Umama's killer-brow, but he didn't move.

Was this lion entertained or irritated by the commotion in our jeep? I sent a quick prayer to Great-Grandmother Haile. *Please make him stay where he is.*

When the bull turned and glared down upon us, Ubaba jerked the gear into reverse, then floored the gas pedal. "Sorry to throw you about." But nobody protested. Humans and animals alike retreated from the big bull.

Ubaba's walkie-talkie buzzed again, and the croaky voice asked, "Say, man, did you find the lions?"

"Them, plus much more. Tell you of it later. Taking our group for a coffee break. But it's me who needs the break."

Ubaba drove the short distance to a camouflage truck parked in the patchy shade of an umbrella thorn tree. A cheery-faced man, wearing a brown long-sleeved shirt with *Volunteer* embroidered over the pocket, stood at the end of a long folding table pouring coffee into paper cups. I didn't like the taste of coffee, but the roasted nut aroma made me think I should try it again sometime. A young woman, beaded braids piled high on her head, filled other cups from a large metal thermos. My sisters and I helped ourselves to the sweet mango juice, then pulled out the bananas our mother had given us.

Joe chugged a cup of coffee. "Needed that after waking up so early. What's next?"

"I want to go back. Now!" demanded Screaming Redhead.

Ubaba's voice held greater sincerity than I'd ever heard from him. "*Miesie*, I'd love to return you to the lodge, if only I could."

"Me, too," muttered Joe.

My father passed among the passengers while they nibbled fresh sliced seeded bread and American-style muffins packed for the trip by Ilanga's cooks. "Kruger is one of the largest game reserves in Africa. It covers an area greater than 19,000 kilometers. That's the size of Israel or the state of Massachusetts. The Big Five are sometimes elusive, so we'd better get on our way."

The cheery-faced volunteer who served the coffee strolled among us toting a plastic litter bucket. We deposited our cups, then clambered into the jeep. The guests shared tales of fear and excitement as if their fellow passengers hadn't experienced it themselves.

Twittering birds filled the trees, singing their morning songs. Glossy starlings, foraging for insects, took flight from their feeding spot. Screaming Redhead crumbled her muffin and tossed it into the air. The beady-eyed blue birds swooped in, then pecked at others of their flock to keep them from snatching the tasty morsels.

"I guess she forgot Ubaba said not to feed the animals," whispered Asanda.

The jeeps rolled past woodlands of mopane, acacia, and clumpy red bushwillow trees. The sun warmed my shoulders. My head bounced with the rhythm of the road. Since the coffee break, we'd seen only birds. I learned enough about them from Miss Yeboah at school. My mind was fuzzy, half asleep, when Ubaba stopped.

I opened my eyes to a skinny-necked creature with an enormous chest, or maybe it was his belly, who looked to be even taller than Baas John. "Now, that's a bird."

"Ahead is a flock of black-necked ostrich."

When my father paused, I considered asking why the bird's neck wasn't black, it was gray, but he continued too quickly.

"These birds, the largest in the world, cannot fly, but they run very fast." My father let the jeep roll closer. "Males' bodies are black. When they spread their white-tipped wings, the contrast is quite spectacular. Females, less flashy, are brown and white. While the ladies grumble about the unfairness of this trait in nature, I believe the gods gave the females colors that blend with their surroundings so as not to attract those who might harm their offspring. Ostrich eggs, especially those painted with the Big Five, are the most popular souvenir in Ilanga's gift shop."

As we left the wooded area, Ubaba told the tourists, "The African savanna is vast. Rolling grasslands like those we now enter are found in the southeastern section of our continent. The arid landscape, between the tropical and desert areas of Africa, features both sweet and sour grasses and shrubs, in addition to isolated trees."

I had never seen my father in this light. He was the expert. People listened to him. My chest expanded with pride, filling my lungs with the earthy fragrance of dry wheat as Ubaba drove us deeper into the savanna.

"Important to know today is that the mopane trees and bushy shrubs are favorites of the elephant. Fifty percent of its population lives in Mopanveld. Many argue that this magnificent creature should hold the title of King of Beasts." Ubaba swept his hand in a wide arc. "We identify this region for its granite *koppies*, hills sprinkled with boulders and bushes."

Ubaba cranked the steering wheel to a sharp right. The jeep swayed. "Sable Waterhole is ahead. Its name comes from the spotted sable antelope. Please keep your voices low. These shy animals prefer the safety of denser thickets, so they may be difficult to spot. Only when they feel safe, do they come out in the open to visit this watering hole."

"Won't the jeeps scare them off?" Joe asked.

"No, I will approach slowly." Ubaba's glare seemed to bore into Screaming Redhead's eyes. "Sudden noises will cause them to flee quicker than you can snap your photographs."

Ten of the antelope herd clustered on the ground a few meters from the watering hole. Feet tucked up to their bodies, they perked their nervous ears our way. The white that lined their long-pointed ears and slim faces was dramatic against their dark fur coats. They were more incredible than I had realized from the photos in my schoolbooks. Seven sable antelope stood at the water's bank. Four waded knee-deep to fill their bellies with cool water. They arched their thick necks, throwing their semi-circular horns over their shoulders, then returned to drinking.

The walkie-talkie vibrated against Ubaba's hip.

Asanda smiled smugly. "Leo's father."

Ubaba pushed the button. My sister frowned when the voice with which we had become familiar squawked out of the black plastic case. "My man, what distance are you from the Olifants?"

"Five kilometers. What have you got?"

"Buffalo and hippo. Come quick."

My father hooked the walkie-talkie on his belt. "We usually take another break at this time—meat pies, cold juice, and mango slices."

Joe pointed toward the road. "Forget the food. Let's go!"

My mouth watered. I could almost taste the buttery flaky crust of Rosie's Nigerian meat pies. But the passengers, even Screaming Redhead, who thought the bull elephants would kill her as they fought for dominance, echoed Joe's cry. "Go! Go!" Startled sable antelopes leapt and fled.

"Hold tight," cautioned Ubaba. "Keep your cameras inside."

The scorching air dried my skin and lips. My eyes watered. I imagined the guests were just as uncomfortable. When the van hit chuckholes, they squealed, "Hang on!"

I turned to look for the second jeep. It was invisible in our dust. We were lucky to be leading.

Ubaba slowed to climb to the peak of a sloped hill. The second jeep rolled beside us and stopped. Amid "Oohs" and "Ahhs," cameras clicked. Six hippos cooled themselves in the Olifants River. One sank, disappearing beneath the water's surface. When his mass rose, he twitched his miniature ears, then sprayed muddy water out his nose.

"Crocodile at three o'clock, sliding off the bank."

"Will he attack the hippos?" asked Screaming Redhead.

"No, he's smarter than that. Might go after a calf, but this herd is adults." Ubaba rolled the jeep to the riverbank until we were face to face with a submerged hippo.

All we saw were tiny twitching ears and large bulging eyes above his fleshy, wet nostrils. When the hippo stood, water streamed off his back. Ubaba gripped the gearshift. He needed not say a word of warning. Instinctively, we all braced as he prepared to throw the jeep into reverse. But the hippo didn't move toward the riverbank. He raised himself until half below, half above the waterline, then released a giant spray of hippo shit.

Onele squealed. Joe's wife, the petite woman with shiny ebony hair, placed her delicate hand over her slender nose and rosebud mouth.

Joe howled. "You got to admire a male who can do that."

When Screaming Redhead stated, "Now we know why the water is so brown," even Ubaba and Asanda laughed at her joke.

Water buffalo sauntered on the far side of the river. The massive lead buffalo acted as though he hadn't noticed us. Perhaps he didn't care. He was larger than our jeep. The breeze blew towards us, so he may not have detected our scent. But I smelled him and the others that followed. The odor reminded me of the shredded, filthy oriental rug Umama made Ubaba return to the rubbish dump where he found it.

"The water buffalo is also called Cape buffalo. His heavy horns form a continuous bone shield called a *boss*. Some argue for the buffalo to be recognized as the King of Beasts because he gores and kills over two hundred people every year, many more than our lions."

In contrast to Screaming Redhead's frantic high pitch, her husband spoke with a measured and gravelly voice. "Still, the lion deserves to be king."

"Most agree, but consider this fact. Mosquitos kill more humans than the mighty lion."

The exotic woman with the long shiny hair spoke for her first time. "Who is this buffalo's enemy?"

I'd watched her the entire trip. Imagining myself being born with hair that hung straight and smooth against my scalp and down my neck, I tossed my head as if it were true.

"Man is his greatest enemy," said my father. "Yet this animal is clever and protective of the members of his herd. Buffalo circle, then mount a counterattack when hunted. Earlier this year, we watched a lioness take down a calf."

"Who got the worst of it? The lioness or the buffalo?" asked Screaming Redhead's husband.

"The buffaloes gathered as if to watch," answered Ubaba. "But that's not what they do. They join forces to attack their enemy. The largest buffalo charged the lioness and threw her aside, then the herd chased her up a tree."

"Was the baby hurt?" asked Screaming Redhead.

"Stunned and bleeding but appeared okay. Stumbled up, then ran. Four of the largest, older males stood guard under the tree until their herd and the wounded calf were out of sight."

Screaming Redhead's burly husband grinned. "I'd like to have seen that."

"I'd like to see a leopard," declared Joe.

"You shall. I understand your group is leaving Ilanga tomorrow for the Lower Sabie Rest Camp. You will see leopards on the night safari. Now, we return to the vans for the drive back to the lodge. An opportunity to shower, perhaps a quick nap, before the farewell feast the staff has planned for you."

Asanda tapped Ubaba on his shoulder. "Where are Leo and Dr. Vorster?"

"North. We can't go there."

My big sister looked like she was winding up to throw a fit, so I leaned close to her ear. "Our father can't allow tourists near sick animals."

She crossed her arms and slumped in the seat. Ubaba backed the jeep from the river's edge, then motioned the other driver to follow. The passengers chattered about what they had seen and the photos they'd taken. Ubaba slowed our speed in order to miss the deepest ruts.

At the Phalaborwa Gate, we climbed aboard the van. The sun had shifted, so it was no longer shaded. When we climbed inside, the heat hit us as if we'd opened an oven door. Onele curled up, head in my lap, feet in Asanda's. Screaming Redhead rested against her husband's shoulder, then fell asleep as if the day had been harder on her than anyone else.

That December summer was hotter and drier than normal for South Africa. When we exited the Kruger National Park, the thermometer attached to the post read 32 degrees centigrade. The wind was too hot to cool us. Dust clung to our sweaty skin. We stank like one giant armpit, but nobody uttered a single complaint during the trip home.

I was eager to shower, but my sisters rushed past me and scooted into the bathroom while I slipped our leftover meat pies in the oven to warm for our lunch. I gave them what I thought was a reasonable amount of time, then banged on the door. Onele padded out, leaving a trail of wet footprints as she walked to the living room. Asanda, hair wrapped in a towel, strutted out wearing an expression that conveyed her irritation at me for rushing them.

When I emerged, clean and refreshed, Onele was curled up on our red and white flowered sofa telling Monkey about every animal she had seen. She added a few untruths to her description of our lion encounter, as if she must exaggerate to hold the attention of that ratty, one-eyed stuffed animal. But she looked so sweet and innocent in her new flowered nightgown that watching her warmed my heart.

I called my sisters to the table. Onele bounced in with Monkey riding on her back, his arms tied in a knot around her neck.

"Shouldn't have gone," muttered Asanda. "We didn't find Leo. He'll wonder where I am."

I considered reminding her Leo was with his father tracking hoof-and-mouth infected buffaloes, and I was pretty sure he was so busy treating sick animals and devising a plan to stop the spread of this disease that she hadn't entered his mind. Fortunately, I was bright enough to keep my mouth shut.

When we finished eating, I filled the sink with soapy water. Asanda pushed away from the table and mumbled her way out of the room. Onele, with Monkey still hanging from her neck, was in a merry mood. And just when I thought she'd finished telling him every detail of our adventure, she hopped up and grabbed a dish towel without being told, then began retelling Monkey everything from the start.

I tried to block her chatter from my mind, but soon gave up and asked, "Onele, I need quiet time to do my homework. Can you color for a while?"

Mr. Nnadi traveled from Phalaborwa to teach mathematics to students in Standards 7 through 12. He had warned today's lesson was to multiply monomials. Since the government required that he teach maths in Afrikaans, I only understood half of what he said. Since I had gone on safari instead of class, that left me to figure out how to do the computations by myself. I opened my workbook and read the equation printed in bold ink.

```
a to the m power x aⁿ = a to the m power + ⁿ
```

I stared. Intent on willing the numbers and letters to rise off the page and tell me how to calculate the equation, I jumped when Asanda said, "I'm going to the rock and wait for Leo."

I muttered, "Good riddance," as she sashayed out. When I finished my homework, I wanted to record this amazing day in my journal, maybe even write a story for the school newspaper. I didn't need her grousing around, spoiling my mood.

Field Trip

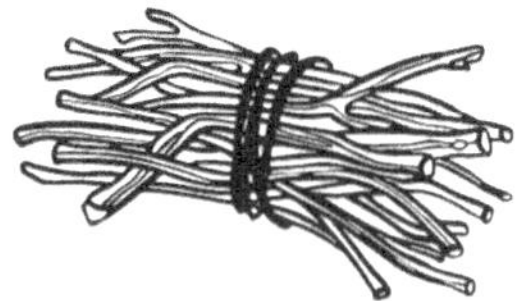

EyeDwarha (Month of the Lily Pad) October 1968

The bedroom was pitch black. Normally, I'd have fallen back to sleep, but for two reasons, I was too excited. Even though safely tucked inside my school notebook, the sheet of lined paper on which I had written an article for the school newspaper popped into my brain, causing me to jolt up in bed at least three times from a sense of dread.

The great majority of those who taught or attended my school were *nie-blanke.* As non-whites, not only did we hail from South Africa, but also from Ethiopia, Namibia, Mozambique, Nigeria, and Zambia, as well as far-off places such as India and China. However, the owner of Ilanga and the village school were Dutch. So, I worried Miss Yeboah would not approve the article I had written for publication in the school newspaper.

I had been inspired by a two-page story in the underground newspaper about Onkgopotse Tiro, the university student I admired for his vocal protest of apartheid. Tiro had set aside his work on an application form, requesting to continue his studies, to open a parcel labeled as from the International University Exchange Fund. The bomb exploded, instantly killing him.

I kept my bookbag near my feet as I slept. Perhaps that was too close and what allowed its contents to keep me awake. But more than my article disrupted my sleep, and I could no longer still my excitement of what the day promised. I scrambled down my bunk ladder, then scurried toward the dim light in our compact kitchen, thinking that very moment was my big chance to tell my parents of my intent to share what I was coming to understand about the depth and extent of apartheid on the lives of Blacks. And to tell my father about the classroom adventure that I hadn't had the opportunity to do, something I knew would delight him. But I found Umama alone, sitting at our kitchen table.

"Is he still asleep?"

"Your father's gone."

"But I wanted him to know about the field trip Miss Yeboah is taking us on today."

"Ubaba's aware you're going. He said you didn't stir when he kissed you goodbye, so he didn't wake you. He left early because Dr. Vorster knows where those poachers are."

"*Eish*, I wanted—"

"This is better, Eshile. I have fresh eggs and ground curry, so tonight, we'll make his favorite *bobotie* for dinner. You know how he gobbles up my meatloaf. Rosie, such a generous woman, brought us ripe *paw paws*, the first of the season. If you slice these papayas and drizzle honey on them, your father will sit at this table and eat until his belly can hold no more. That should give you plenty of time to tell him about your adventure before he falls asleep."

I was disappointed about having to wait to talk to my father, but it didn't dull my anticipation.

I loved Fridays. It was the best day of school, not because it was the last day before the weekend, but because our teacher always had a surprise. And I expected today's adventure to be the best yet.

All month long, Miss Yeboah spent many hours taking photographs of birds using the Kodak Pocket Instamatic her father sent for her birthday. Sun filtering in the window glinted off the camera's stainless-steel body as she ran her finger over the rangefinder while explaining it enabled her to focus more accurately and produce clearer photos than with her old camera.

Our teacher couldn't have been more excited over this five-inch-long gift that she could slip into her pocket (thus its name—Pocket Instamatic) for easy access when a bird flew into her sight. Her most recent photo was of a yellow-breasted Sharpe's Longclaw standing watch over the eggs in her nest. Miss Yeboah rearranged her bulletin board to accommodate the new photo while explaining that her favorite thing to do, except for teaching us, was to hike through the bushveld in search of a bird she hadn't yet photographed. In particular, endangered birds and the circumstances of their demise were her favorite subjects.

With this adventure, Miss Yeboah had designed a combination art and science project for us. My classmates and I had saved our old homework until we had filled the rubbish can. Earlier that week, we cut the paper into thin strips, then mixed flour, white glue, and water to create a big mushy mess. We formed the slimy strips into three small eggs each instead of playing kickball at recess. Then she announced every student had returned their permission slips, so we could all go on the field trip to gather long grasses and roots to make nests for our eggs. This made her so crazy-happy we hardly learned a thing in class that day.

Now that the day arrived, I was pretty happy with myself, perched in the front seat, being chauffeured in the lodge's white kombi bus. My sisters sat behind me. I pretended they weren't there, that it was just me and Baas John delivering eighteen brown paper lunch sacks. Besides being my first time riding to school in the eight-seater van, my status in the class had moved up a notch. I may have led my fellow students to believe I played a role in providing these sack lunches for our outing.

Umama had gotten wind of my deception and warned me, "Eshile, the worst you can do is clothe the truth in lies."

I shrugged, acting as though I didn't understand. But it was clear from the lift of Umama's eyebrow, she wouldn't buy any explanation I might create as to why I led everyone to believe I was responsible for the free sack lunches.

I shrugged and kept my mouth shut, but she had more to say.

"March is a busy month at the lodge. More tourists than stinky ants. Think about it, Eshile. Baas John wants to impress Miss Yeboah as much as you do, maybe even more. Do you think he'd have the kitchen help make lunches for the children and deliver them himself if he wasn't sweet on her?"

Romance between my teacher and Baas John? I would save that revelation and reveal it on another day, another opportunity to be the center of playground conversation.

We students chattered excitedly as Miss Yeboah took her place at the front of our classroom. She tapped her ruler on a new poster taped to the wall to get our attention, then spoke with a voice that bubbled with cheerfulness. "What can you tell me regarding this bird?"

I hurled my hand over my head and waved frantically, but Miss Yeboah called on Anthony. Made me so mad. Half the time he answered before she called his name, and he usually babbled the wrong answer.

Our small school served the children from surrounding villages and Ilanga Safari Lodge. Clustered by age, I was in Class 10-11-12. Miss Yeboah named us The African Oystercatchers. I was twelve, soon to be thirteen. I didn't think I was arrogant because it was true that even though Anthony was also twelve, anyone as annoying as him and his friends should have been in group 7-8-9 and called The Dodo Birds.

Anthony puffed his chest, then pointed to Miss Yeboah's new poster. "That bird is the blue bustard."

If I had been Miss Yeboah, I'd have thumped him on the top of his dim-wit skull.

But Umama had recently complimented me on being more patient with Asanda, so I tried to treat this annoying male child the same. I smoothed the skin my eyebrows had pinched into a frown and bit down on my tongue.

"Very good, Anthony."

Very good! Miss Yeboah, are you kidding me? The bird on the poster had a blue neck and chest, and the print read Bustard. I raised my hand to point out that Anthony was as big a fool as the boy who let his sheep run away twice, but my teacher ignored me again.

"Anthony, what else do you know?"

"The blue bustard is dying."

I couldn't stand it any longer. I had to speak out. "Dying! Miss Yeboah, the existence of their genus is threatened across Africa."

"Exactly, Eshile. That is why we are excited. While taking my after-dinner walk, I came upon a hopeful sign that this bird might survive. Today, in the name of science, we shall photograph a blue bustard and her chicks.

When Miss Yeboah told us to rise from our seats, we popped up like toast. We scrambled to be first in line and snatch the brown lunch paper sacks and an empty bag for collecting nesting materials as we filed out of the classroom. Two students held up their lunches. "Thank you, Eshile." Miss Yeboah cocked her head as if wondering what I did to rate the praise. I skipped out before she could ask.

I waited outside the door for Kalisha, who walked out at a normal pace behind the other girls. Miss Yeboah directed us to form a nice straight line, but soon into our journey, we bunched with our friends and chatted merrily. Anthony challenged Ralphie to race to a tree, a hundred meters off the path. Miss Yeboah hailed them back, but they kept running. They were neck and neck when they hit the leafless knob thorn tree. Both boys screamed in, then hobbled back with long scraggly scratches and bleeding cuts.

Bini giggled. "You know he's showing off for you. Your mother is right."

"How can a boy be so dense to think that running into a tree impresses a girl?"

"My father made a flying leap over a rock to get my mother's attention. He didn't know a cow had left a fresh dung pile on the other side."

"That should have been enough to tell your mother not to marry him."

Miss Yeboah gave the boys a look of well-deserved disgust. "It was not enough to run into the thorns? You had to get in the bristle grass, too? Wipe off the blood. You'll be fine. Perhaps now, gentlemen, you will follow my instructions."

Kalisha and I covered our mouths, but when Miss Yeboah turned her back, the boys glared and snarled so we knew they heard us laugh.

After following Miss Yeboah for an hour along a winding footpath through a veld selecting the best twigs and low grasses to make our nests, Anthony snatched my lunch. I smacked him on the shoulder. When he howled like a wounded dog, Miss Yeboah snapped around and scowled. Sheepishly, Anthony handed back my sack.

"Quiet, students. We are close." Miss Yeboah raised her hand in the air, her signal we should halt.

"Krok kau, krok kau," called the blue bustard.

We crept closer. Who would believe seventeen students could step so carefully they didn't make a sound? Even the crickets and cicadas silenced their music. Miss Yeboah pointed to a large nest resting in a circle of separated and flattened foot-high grass.

A female bustard rose to stand two feet tall and swelled her chest. Our school poster was of the male with its blue neck and underparts. This female had a gray neck and a striking black crown atop her head. When she crouched and stretched over her nest, up popped a fuzzy version of that mother bird.

The click of Miss Yeboah's camera broke the stillness. Click, click— echoed inside my head like an ax chopping a tree. The bustard spread her wings. I held my breath in wonderment. Was she going to leave her chick?

"Krok kau, krok kau."

Slowly, quietly, we stepped back until mother and chick were out of our sight. Miss Yeboah didn't need to tell us to be silent. Nobody spoke until we stopped under a flattop acacia tree that shaded us as well as the thatched grass umbrellas surrounding Ilanga's swimming pool.

Sitting cross-legged on the ground, we dug into our sack lunches, chattering the way students do, mouths full of seed bread, boerewors, and paw paw slices, until Miss Yeboah asked for our attention. She was not the type to let a teaching moment pass. "The blue bustard has relatives. Where do they live?"

I shot my hand skyward.

A thumb-sized sausage sailed past my nose and hit Kalisha. Miss Yeboah wasn't smiling then. She pulled Anthony to his feet and marched him a few meters away. Watching her shake her finger in his face brought me satisfaction. As his head sunk lower on his chest, I felt justified. But then the strangest feeling came over me, a mushy warmth like when I held Bini's newborn kittens.

Previously, when I told Umama I had detention at school because Anthony nailed me with a spit wad, causing me to knock my books off my desk, she said, "That's what boys do when they want a girl's attention."

I whispered to Bini, "Umama will say stealing my lunch and bombarding me with sausage is proof Anthony's sweet on me."

"I'm beginning to think she's wrong," replied Bini.

I snorted my agreement. "Can't you just see Baas John throwing food at Miss Yeboah?" I must have spoken louder than I intended because Ralphic snickered.

When Anthony snarled at his friend, Miss Yeboah gripped his arm so hard her fingernails left red indentions when she lifted him up and propelled him away to sit by himself. "Eat up, children. Five minutes until we leave. That will give you time to paint your own posters with the watercolors my auntie sent from Cape Town."

Kalisha and I gobbled down our last few bites and were first to form a line again. Several times as we walked, I reached down to pick another handful of soft grass for my nest. But when the thatched roof of our five-room schoolhouse came into sight, everyone broke from the line and ran wildly to be the first back to our classroom.

Everyone, except for me. I stopped and stared. The Ilanga Safari Lodge van had returned. When we brought the lunches, Baas John told us to walk home as usual. I hoped Umama was right about Baas John's attraction, that he was here to see Miss Yeboah again, not to retrieve my sisters and me. I had no desire to raise a fuss and refuse to leave before I painted my poster. It was to be my father's birthday gift.

Baas John stood by the van, looking at his feet, leaning his head close to the lead teacher as if discussing a serious topic. Onele and Asanda had already settled in the rear seat when Baas John saw me and opened the passenger door.

"Thank you, Baas John, but I can't go home. I need to paint my poster."

"Sorry, Eshile. Umama told me to bring you girls to her."

I looked through the kombi's window at my sisters. They shrugged.

"Why? Please, Baas John, I really need to stay."

"There was an accident."

I jumped into the center seat. "Is Umama okay? Was it those pots of boiling water? I told her they were too heavy."

Baas John turned the key, cranked the steering wheel, and revved the engine. Onele puffed her lower lip. "I want my mother."

"Girls, your mother is fine."

The van hit a bump and bounced my bottom off the seat. "Then who's hurt?"

"Sorry, can't talk. Must concentrate on my driving." Baas John yanked the steering wheel to the right.

I slid across the seat. Gravel shot out from beneath the tires and peppered the bushy shrubs growing at that corner of the road.

Timidly, I said, "Baas John, you're driving awfully fast."

He pinched his bushy eyebrows together and gripped the wheel until the blood vessels bulged on the backs of his hands. When he made another sharp turn, I slipped across the seat again. "Baas John, this is the wrong street."

He gunned the engine. The van lurched.

I slammed back against the seat.

Onele squealed, "You're scaring me!"

Asanda leaned in. "Where are you taking us?"

"The hospital. Your father was injured."

"My Ubaba got hurt," whimpered Onele.

My heart pounded. I struggled to catch my breath. "What happened?"

"Your mother will explain."

Onele made the squeaky noise that always preceded her sobs.

"How long until we get there?" Even Asanda's voice quaked.

Baas John pushed harder on the gas pedal. "One hour. Your parents are in Phalaborwa."

Neither my sisters nor I had been to a hospital. This building was the largest I'd ever seen, immense when compared to the clinic where we took Auntie Nofoto when her husband broke her arm and beat her until her chest welted up purple, green, and blue. Two stories tall, the hospital was the same height as the lemon meringue house but was as long and wide as if ten of Hulu's former beloved home were pushed together to make a rectangle. Three people stood on the sidewalk, watching a tattooed teenager struggle with the door. A white bandage covered the boy's left eye, and his right arm was suspended in a blue cloth sling. Nobody made a move to help.

Baas John screeched into the parking lot. I pointed to a metal sign perched atop a pole.

Doctors Only

He jammed the gear into reverse. The tires squealed when he spun the steering wheel and careened into a parking space farther away from the entrance. My knees shook as I climbed out. Asanda rushed toward the hospital door. Baas John grabbed her shoulder, then pointed at a yellow sign.

```
These public premises are reserved for

   the exclusive use of White Persons.

  By Order of the Provincial Secretary
```

Baas John nudged Asanda toward a large arrow that pointed to the building's back corner. The lettering on the arrow's shaft read:

```
       Non-European Hospital.
```

We halted at a glass door with black printing centered above the frame.

```
              Nie-Blankes

             Non-Whites

            Waiting Area
```

I bolted past my sister, yanked the door handle, and stepped into the crowded room. The stink of sweat, blood, and disinfectants gagged me. I stepped back to allow Baas John and my sisters to enter, then released the metal door to clang shut behind us.

"Follow me, girls," commanded Baas John.

We hurried down the long hall. Onele bumped my leg to avoid being hit by the metal bed on wheels that rattled when it came too close to her. The orderly pushing it had blood on her scrubs.

Onele's chin trembled. I swayed when I hefted my sister onto my hip. At age ten, she was too heavy for me to hold like that, but she needed comforting. "It's okay, baby girl. We'll be fine as soon as we find Umama."

My sister tucked her hot sweaty face into the crook of my neck, then rubbed her runny nose against my skin. I would have liked to cry myself. She crumpled my collar and clenched it tight for balance as she leaned out of my arms to look in every room we rushed by.

I croaked, "Onele, loosen your grip. You're choking me."

Baas John stopped at the last door. "Wait here, girls. Let me ask your mother what we should do."

I sneaked a quick peek inside. Unlike the dingy hallway, this room was a sea of white. White walls. White ceilings. And white curtains hanging from a metal bar attached to the ceiling separated the room into six smaller areas.

The first curtain was open. The only color I saw was a man's black face peeking out from under white bedclothes. He moaned when a white-coated man, with gray at his temples, pushed against his stomach. The pressure seemed to send a sweet sickly smell out of the man. The nurse, whose uniform nipped tight at her waist, made what looked like squiggly marks on her clipboard.

Onele pointed a stubby finger. "Who are those people?"

"The doctor and nurse." My chin quivered.

"What are they doing to that man?"

"Not sure, Onele." I placed my hand on her shoulder to steady myself.

"Where's Ubaba?"

Asanda motioned down the row of beds toward Baas John. His face disappeared through a split in the curtain. "I have your girls."

When Umama pushed open the curtain, the metal rings made a slight scraping noise against the metal bar. Her voice was too faint for me to make out what she said to Baas John, so I inched closer. The nurse standing at the head of the bed rapped the end of her pencil on the clipboard, then glared at Baas John. He backed away. When he reached my sisters and me, he directed us into the hall. "Umama will come out after the doctor speaks with her."

"Baas John, was she crying?" I swallowed hard trying to not break into tears myself.

"Your mother is a strong woman. She'll be okay." He breathed in jerky puffs as though he was holding back. That scared me more.

People lined the hallway. Some stood, leaning against the walls. Others slouched to the floor. I sat Onele on the cool cement, then slid my body down the wall. Only then did I notice the rubbish scattered on the floor and dirty smudges on walls that might have been painted green in the distant past. Still, I felt comforted when Asanda squeezed in between Onele and me and pulled us close.

A boy near my age stepped out of the room across the hall. One pant leg cut off, his foot and calf were wrapped in a white substance similar to the papier mâché we used to make our bird eggs in class. He clomped with every step and jutted out his chin as if proud. I was thirteen, almost a woman, but I still thought boys were nincompoops, and watching this one strengthened my belief.

A squeaky sound stole my attention. A tall, thin Black man, silver hair like a steel wool cleaning pad, pushed a wheelchair holding a teensy woman, scrunched against the arm rail, taking up so little space another person could have ridden alongside her. She mumbled while waggling her finger as if scolding someone. I thought I should warn them the wobbly wheel might fall off, but I couldn't speak.

Individual sounds melded into a low, steady buzz. I was too tired to hold my eyes open. But when my head jerked, I returned to watching every person who passed by me in the hall. Everyone looked either hurt or sad.

Asanda and I stood when a doctor and nurse came out of the room Ubaba shared with nine other patients. I didn't know whether to be happy or worried when they headed toward another family.

"Here comes your mother," said Baas John.

We hurried toward her, but long-legged Baas John reached her first. "I brought them as quickly as I could. This never should have happened.

I am to blame. I should not have let him come. Too dangerous."

"This is not your fault. My husband was proud to be a part of your efforts to save Africa's animals." Umama blinked her bloodshot eyes. "Girls, let's go outside."

Baas John motioned toward Ubaba. "I'll stay in case he wakes."

When Umama hefted Onele from the floor, her untied canvas *takkies* bumped against our mother's knees. Onele patted Umama's back. "Don't cry. I'll take care of you."

Asanda and I followed our mother to a wooden bench in the shade of the evergreen canopy made by a large white milkwood tree. When Umama sat, a flock of finches fluttered past us. Onele stared in awe.

I asked, "Is Ubaba okay?"

My mother drew in a deep breath that seemed to fortify her strength. "Don't know yet, Eshile. He was shot."

"Shot! By whom? Why?"

"Not so loud, Eshile. You're scaring baby sister."

"Wasn't he with Dr. Vorster?" asked Asanda.

Umama nodded.

"Why did they bring Ubaba here? So far from where we live?"

"His wounds are too serious for the clinic to treat." Umama gazed upward as if searching for a sign from our ancestors. "Sammy visited me in a dream and told me he was sorry he couldn't protect me from the dangerous event that would happen." A tremor ran down her body. "I begged your father not to go."

"Ubaba should do what you tell him, like we always do."

The shadow of a smile crossed Umama's lips. "Yes, Onele, exactly like you girls always do."

"Umama, did Ubaba wreck the jeep?" I was ashamed but couldn't stop myself. "Could he get fired? Will the owners force us to leave the lodge?"

"No, Eshile. Your father is not to blame. The liquor store owner overheard poachers bragging about where they planned to hunt today.

So, long before dawn, Dr. Vorster picked up your father to drive him and Baas John to the location.”

Umama's jaw quivered. I hated to ask more. All I wanted to do was run away and hide, but I had to know. “Then what happened?”

“Baas John says they found the poachers where the store owner said they'd be. Normally, poachers speed off when they see someone coming. But this morning, when Dr. Vorster and Baas John stepped out of the jeep to confront the poachers, they held their ground. The men yelled and threatened. One pointed his rifle at Dr. Vorster.” Umama's voice faded to a whisper. “The guide knocked the gun from the shooter's hands, and it went off.”

Umama's lips moved, but only air came out. Onele broke into a full-out bawl. Asanda leapt up and held our mother when she crumpled forward on the bench, small and helpless, as though she were the child. My heart shattered into a million pieces. My brain and body stopped working. I couldn't even comfort my mother.

“Dr. Vorster didn't realize the bullet hit your father until he cried out.” Umama's voice caught in her throat. “There's… there's no way to explain why it… it happened. He was still sitting in the jeep.”

“I hope they shot the poacher,” stated Asanda.

“No, no one shot.” My mother trembled. “Your father was their first concern. Both Dr. Vorster and Baas John ran to Ubaba to stop the bleeding. So, the men jumped in their jeep and raced away.”

“So, they're gone for good?

“They're… they're looking, Asanda. The police and park rangers… everybody's searching for them. Surely, they'll find them.”

My mother's expression told me she was thinking the same thing as I. *So many places to run… so many places for them to hide.*

We sat in a daze on the bench under the milkwood tree. People paraded by—most paid no attention—except for the woman who stopped, dug in her pocket, then held out a packet. Finally, my arms moved. I accepted the tiny tissues, saying, “Thank you, thank you,” to her kind face.

Asanda stood and wrung her hands. "What did the doctors do?"

"They operated on your father and removed the bullet from his head."

"His head?" I swallowed the foul slime that rose from my gut. "He'll be okay, though? Right? They didn't shoot his heart…"

Asanda pressed against her forehead and swayed.

Umama reached to steady her. "Your father has faced many problems. He is strong. He'll be fine."

Our mother was always honest with us girls, but from the jerky way she turned and glanced away, I knew she was holding back important information. I wanted to know the truth, only I was too afraid to ask.

A breeze rustled through the tree branches overhead. A single leaf that had turned red with age fell and clung to the curly hair on my arm. "Umama, Auntie Grace uses milkwood to treat broken bones and bad dreams. A bullet in your head is kind of like a broken bone. I'm sure Ubaba will have bad dreams about this, but her potion will help him."

Umama pressed her hands against the back of her neck and looked up to the sky. Then she braced against the bench to stand. "Let's go back to your father's room. He needs us at his side."

We stepped into the waiting room that was now more crowded than when we initially arrived. We walked past rows of metal chairs. Some people coughed wet juicy hacks; others groaned in pain. Mothers bounced babies on their laps or rocked them in their arms, but not a single child quit crying. A girl, blood running from her nose, weakly wiggled her fingers at me. I smiled as best I could and waved back.

Umama opened the waiting room door, only to be confronted by a nurse who glared at Onele, then me, and tapped her clipboard with her pencil. I lowered my gaze and scooted into the hall. It seemed to be the same long hall we'd been in before, but I wasn't sure, so I peered into each door we passed. Room after room, they all appeared identical to me. I doubted we'd find my father again, until Umama stopped outside room 104.

"Wait in the hall."

Asanda reached for Onele and me. Her palm was cold and dry; mine hot and damp. Once again, tears rolled down Onele's cheeks. I removed a tissue from the packet the nice lady had given us and wiped my little sister's face.

"We must be brave, baby girl."

Onele sniffled, then rubbed her nose on her sleeve. We leaned against the wall until Umama returned.

"Girls, we'll go in now, but you must be strong. No crying. The doctor wrapped your father's head in gauze and put a breathing mask over his nose and mouth. And there are wires attached to his chest that are hooked to a machine that lights up and beeps. He looks rather scary, but don't let him see your fear. Ubaba needs to see your sweet faces smiling back at him. He's unconscious, but the doctor believes your voices might help awaken him."

Onele blinked hard to hold back the fresh tears welling in her eyes. "What's unconscious?"

"Asleep… a very deep sleep. The surgery made your father very tired. He hasn't opened his eyes yet, but he needs to hear your sweet voices in his dreams. One more thing, Ubaba is pale, and he isn't moving. He lost too much blood, but they are giving him more. So don't get upset about the blood bag above his head. And don't be frightened. It seems like a lot, but the treatments ordered by the doctors and nurses will help him get well."

Umama opened the curtain. My father didn't turn toward us.

"Ubaba, it's me." I expected him to awaken, to open his eyes, but he didn't move.

His arms lay atop the sheet. A thin tube ran from the clear plastic blood bag overhead to the back of his hand. The white tape was stained red where the needle penetrated his skin. My chin quivered when he didn't smile as I rubbed his shoulder.

Onele stood on tiptoes and leaned close to him. "Please wake up, Ubaba." She looked puzzled when he failed to respond.

Umama nudged. "Tell your father how much you love him."

"I love you, Ubaba, more than Monkey or apricot jam. I love you even more than Dinga, and you know how much I loved him."

Like a tiny chorus, Asanda and I spoke at the same time. "I love you, Ubaba."

"Onele, tell him about the beauty you saw outside," urged our mother.

"Ubaba, we sat on a bench under a big green tree. The tiniest birds flew right by my face. I wish you could have seen them. Their chests were the same rusty red as that cat who begs outside the lodge's kitchen door." Once again, tears rolled uncontrollably down Onele's cheeks. "Umama, he's not answering me."

"He wants to, baby girl. He's just too weak. The surgery took a lot out of him."

Asanda crouched until her lips were next to Ubaba's ear and sang softly. I recognized the song as "Many Rivers to Cross". When she got to the part about not being able to find the way, Umama choked on a sob.

My mother trembled when I cupped her shoulder in my hand, a small gesture to comfort her. "Umama, we need Auntie Grace. Her herbs and chants will make Ubaba well."

"Oh, I wish… but Eshile, we can't get her here in time. We can't call. She doesn't own a phone. Letters take days, then more days to travel so far."

"But we must try. I'll write a letter. Abel can get her here quickly in his truck."

"First, we must pray."

I mumbled, "Pray? Yes, we must pray… but who first? Jesus or uThixo? Or Auntie Nofoto? Who, Umama, who can do the most?"

Onele sucked in a huge breath, then used what Miss Yeboah called an outdoor voice. "Great-Grandmother Haile!"

I pressed against my forehead to relieve the throb and scolded my poor little sister. "You don't need to scream."

"Hulu said to call on Great-Grandmother Haile when a question is extra important, or a problem is too hard to solve. Making Ubaba well is the most important thing in the world."

"Onele, I'm just saying it's not necessary to shout."

Umama's eyebrow rose. "Quiet, girls. No fighting. Jesus first, then uThixo. Later we'll pray to our ancestors, but they watch over us, so I'm sure they're already doing everything they can."

Onele stuck out her lower lip. "I'm praying to Great-Grandmother Haile, the way Hulu showed me."

I rolled my eyes, but Umama caressed Onele's face. "Hulu will be happy you are doing as she advised."

When the curtain slid, Baas John poked his head inside. "Sorry to be gone so long, but I brought the local *inyanga*. His powers are strong."

The dwarf-sized man, face as dark and wrinkled as a raisin, moved to the opposite side of the bed. He inspected Ubaba's face so closely they shared the same air. Still hunched, his hand hovered over Ubaba's chest. The *inyanga* requested a glass of water as he removed small containers from his *muti* bag. The powders he sprinkled smelled like cowhide. After he swirled the glass, he lifted Ubaba's head. When my father didn't even groan, my head filled with a dreadful thought. It must be too late.

The *inyanga* motioned for Umama to remove the mask, then separate Ubaba's lips. Light brown liquid trickled from the glass. I saw no sign of my father swallowing, but the mixture disappeared. After administering a final chant, the *inyanga* slipped outside the curtain. Baas John followed him. The rapping of footsteps faded as they left.

"Umama, don't let them go."

"No need for him to stay, Eshile. All we can do now is give the potion time to work."

When Onele climbed onto the hospital bed, I expected Umama

to pull her off. I watched with wonder as Onele curled into a ball at Ubaba's feet, and in seconds, made the snuffy sounds of sleep. Asanda scooted the only chair closer for Umama to sit. She dropped heavily into the seat as if the weight of the world had knocked her down. The plastic legs creaked when our mother bent forward to kiss our father's hand. She made the sign of the cross, then rested her head on his arm.

I prayed silently. My sisters closed their eyes, so I assumed they were too. Fifteen, maybe twenty minutes, passed before our mother's lips moved.

"Umama," I whispered, "who are you talking to?"

"Great-Grandmother Haile."

"Is she answering?"

"This must be beyond her. I'm talking into a deep dark well."

Umama's words of prayer became softer and softer until her chin bobbed, and she joined Onele in sleep. I glanced at Asanda. Her expression was as devoid of hope as I felt.

The nurse entered the unlit room, switched on the overhead light, and checked some boxes on the form attached to her clipboard. The eerie shadows cast on her face reminded me of the dancers' painted masks at Uncle Sammy's funeral.

Asanda whispered, "His breathing is slower. He hasn't moved."

The nurse tapped the clipboard with her pencil, then scribbled something else on the form. "The doctor is at dinner. He should return within an hour."

I gulped down my fear and met Clipboard Nurse's eye. "Please, can you check my father's heart?"

"Yes, dear. That's why I'm here. I'll check his vitals then record the results on his chart so the information will be there when the doctor returns."

Her calling me dear made me suspicious. It seemed out of character or as if she was preparing me for bad news. So, when she set the clipboard on the metal table, I scooched closer. The pencil scratches inside the boxes printed on the form made no sense.

Neither Umama nor Onele stirred when the nurse squeezed the empty bag hanging above Ubaba's head. "I'll return with more blood."

I asked, "Ma'am, isn't there more you can do? Shouldn't we wake him up to eat?"

"Trust me, dear. He's getting the nourishment and medicine he needs from these pouches. When he wakes up in the morning, we'll bring him a fine breakfast. But what about you girls? Have you eaten?"

Umama raised her head. "Thank you, ma'am. There's nothing we need."

"Thank you, ma'am," I said. "We're waiting for our father to wake up." I worried that I'd hurt my father if I touched him, so I leaned closer. "Ubaba, I am terribly sorry I didn't wake up when you kissed me goodbye this morning because I needed to tell you about our school trip. If you like, I'll tell you now." I startled when he heaved a deep breath, but then decided that was his way of saying he wanted to hear my tale.

"Ubaba, the sun was gentle, warmed my head and shoulders, but it wasn't hot enough to make me sweat. The long soft grasses shimmered like gold and tickled my ankles as we walked through the bushveld. We walked very quietly—even the boys—then we came upon them! A mother bustard and her newly hatched chick!"

Excitement rose in my chest the same as it had hours earlier. Aware I was talking faster, louder, I concentrated on keeping my voice low. "Miss Yeboah nearly jumped out of her sandals, that's how excited she got. But we couldn't get too close. Mother bird was having none of that."

My father's eyes moved from side to side beneath his moist eyelids. I took that to mean he was hearing me. "Ubaba, all the kids are spending the afternoon painting a poster of the bustard and her chick. I planned to hide mine and save it for your birthday present, but now I've decided not to wait. I'll paint your poster my first day back at school and give it to you right away."

A hand from outside slid open the curtain. Clipboard Nurse

returned carrying a tray of sponges, needles, and a new bag of blood. A young man holding more white plastic chairs slipped in behind her. While Clipboard pierced my father's skin and pushed the plunger, emptying a mysterious liquid into his arm, the man unstacked the chairs and motioned for us to sit. Like the young Sotho man who stood near the entrance to Ilanga wearing a conical hat, pulling small hand-carved animals from his pockets to sell to tourists, this man pulled treats out of his baggy pockets. I hadn't realized I was hungry until a yellow box of Rowntree's Fruit Pastilles, several Cadbury Chomp Bars, two small bags of cheese curls, and a package of saltine crackers magically appeared.

"Couldn't carry the juice," he said. "I'll return with it."

Clipboard Nurse exchanged the empty bag on the IV pole for the one filled with fresh dark blood. Then she dipped the sponge from the tray into a bowl of water and wiped the dust from driving through the veld off our father's arms and neck. I prayed he would open his eyes and thank her, but he didn't stir. I hoped she saw the thanks in my face. The light above Ubaba's head cast greenish shadows across his eye sockets and cheekbones. When Clipboard gently followed the lines and hollows of his face, I expected the sponge to wipe away the olive pall. But after she patted his skin dry, the color remained unchanged.

Onele awakened when the young man set a metal pitcher and a stack of small white paper cups on the side table.

Umama poured the guava juice. "Eat up, girls. We're staying the night." She didn't touch the snacks, but my sisters and I each snatched up our favorites. I ripped open a Chomp Bar wrapper, then took a huge bite. As I licked chocolate off my fingers, Umama placed her palm over Ubaba's heart, cocked her head, then bent until her ear touched his chest.

Red lights flashed on the small screen attached to my father by black rubber-coated wires. Umama straightened up, swaying as if about to pass out. Asanda rose, but not fast enough to stop our mother from crashing into the table. I reached out to catch the pitcher. Pink juice splashed against the white wall.

My mother screamed, "Help! We need help!"

"I've got it, Umama." Thinking she wanted help cleaning up the mess, I grabbed the towel the young man had draped over the foot of the bed.

The machine behind Ubaba's bed beeped frantically. Clipboard Nurse ran in, followed by a swarm of people wearing white who circled my father's bed. A doctor I hadn't seen before pushed me out of his way. I stumbled backward as he slid his stethoscope beneath Ubaba's hospital gown. He frightened me more by calling out numbers and words I didn't understand. Then the doctor tossed his stethoscope over his shoulder, pressed one palm against my father's chest, and pounded it with the fist of his other hand.

Umama fell against the wall. Her hand flew up to cover her open mouth, then her eyes darted from one medical person to another, and lastly to Ubaba.

"You girls must leave," barked the doctor. "We have work to do."

I followed my sisters toward the door, then looked back. A hole opened in my heart when the curtain slid along the metal pole, separating me from my father.

The following night at Ilanga, lying in my top bunk, I skipped my prayers. There was no point. I forced my swollen eyes shut. In my sleepy haze, I saw the doctor run up behind Clipboard Nurse. People rushed, talked in brisk sentences, shouted commands. Suddenly, it all stopped, and Umama cried, *Hayi, Hayi. No, no, don't go.*

The next thing I was aware of was Umama shaking me awake, telling me to get out of the kombi van. Asanda scooped Onele into her arms and carried her to our room. She still had orange powder from the cheese curls on her lips.

My body felt so heavy I struggled to pull myself up the ladder and roll into my bunk. In the other room, Baas John lowered his deep voice until it was as soothing as a bubbling stream. A heavy darkness enveloped me. The last sound I heard was Umama's shaky voice.

"I don't know what to do."

Bring My Father Home

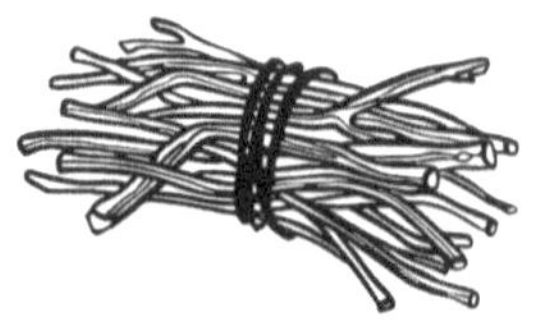

Two days later, *EyoKwindla* (Month of
the First Fruits) March 1974

Instead of speeding and skidding around the curves the way he had when he picked my sisters and me up from school, Baas John drove the van slowly, carefully. We had returned from our trip to bring my father home, only, after hours of waiting, to be turned away by hospital staff.

I think the ordeal exhausted all of us. When we arrived at Ilanga and entered the rondavel we loved so much, I was eager to settle in my own soft, safe bed, but I flopped like a fish, never finding a comfortable position. After my sisters fell asleep, I left my bunk and walked toward the glow of the kitchen light.

Umama, hunched at the table, held her head in her hands. When I caressed her shoulder, she pulled me onto her lap. I had grown almost as tall as she, so the two of us balanced awkwardly on the kitchen chair.

"Can't you sleep, Umama?"

"Too worried."

"About Ubaba?"

"No, my heart is broken by the loss of your father, but he has joined the ancestors. Death is a robe. Everyone must wear it. Your big sister worries me most."

"Why, Umama?"

"When I sat Onele on the rear seat, she rolled into a ball, reminding me of Bini's kittens. And you, you'd sleep a few minutes, then wake up crying—just as I expected of you two. But Asanda sat ramrod straight, her eyes glazed as though she saw a vision that was invisible to everyone else. That's why she scared me the most."

"What do you think she was seeing?"

"Don't know, but I've seen that expression only once, on Hulu's face after Sammy died in the rockslide—when his friends slid his body from the wooden cart."

I nodded knowingly, remembering the vacant expression and the hollows that mysteriously formed below my grandmother's eyes, never to leave. I remained in my mother's lap, clinging to her as if only she could keep my soul from also leaving this world, until she kissed my cheek, then nudged me up.

"Best you go sleep now. I need you to be strong tomorrow."

The following day, we walked around like zombies. Baas John checked on us, each time having whispered conversations with our mother. The day passed in a dull blur. My sisters and I clambered into bed the moment the sun fell from the sky.

When I awakened in the early hours, our room was dark. Onele and Asanda were still sleeping, so I didn't switch on the light. I ran a hand along the wall until I came to my mother's room. I longed to curl up next to her the way I did when I was a little girl.

"Umama?" She didn't answer. I crawled into her bed.

The bedclothes were cold and unwrinkled, as if my parents had never slept there. I hugged my legs to my chest but found no comfort, so I rolled out of their bed. I couldn't imagine any pain would ever be greater than what sat in my heart until I thought of what Umama must feel.

My feet padding across the floor made the only sound as I approached a shadow. Umama had buried her face in the cushions of her red and white flowered sofa, the one she never allowed us to put our feet or sit on with dirty hands. I thought she must hurt too much to be alone in the bed where Ubaba slept every night, his hand resting on her stomach.

"Umama?"

The shadow groaned. "Eshile, it's me. Rosie."

"Where's my mother?"

Rosie patted the big white flower peeking out from under her large behind. "Baas John woke me a couple of hours ago. He said the hospital called, and he was taking Umama back in the truck to carry your father home. He didn't want you girls waking up alone."

"Bring him home?" Was this home? I didn't know. After two years, I should have, but maybe home was our old shanty.

While our grandparents still lived in Soweto, Umkhulu claimed he would never call it home. Laws must change before they would be allowed to move back to Johannesburg, yet he swore the big city would always be his home. I never lived in the lemon meringue house, so it couldn't be my home. When Sammy died, Umama argued the family should take his body to Umkhulu's tribal village on the North Coast of KwaZulu because that was our heritage, our true home. I'd never been there, so I had no way to judge.

I listened to the midnight songs. The crickets, even the cicadas, fell silent when an elephant trumpeted. Was Kuhle announcing the birth of her second calf? Or perhaps warning off a threat?

"What should we do, Rosie?"

"Nothing now, Eshile."

"Rosie…"

"Yes, dear."

"I was supposed to paint my blue bustard."

"You can paint it when you return to school."

"My poster was to be a birthday gift for Ubaba."

"He'll see it. He's watching over you."

I leaned into the comfort of Rosie's body. I closed my eyes and tried to place what I had been doing when that awful man shot my father. Walking through golden grasses? Resting in the shade? Tattling on Anthony for stealing my sack lunch or doing some other childish thing? Could it be that the exact moment the sausage sailed past my face was the same instant the bullet flew toward my father and entered his skull?

Rosie nudged me. "Climb back in your comfy bed."

"Can't sleep."

"Try, sweetheart. Death is a thief. It will steal the strength you need for what is yet to come."

As I stood, Rosie pulled her feet back up on Umama's sofa. "We'll all feel better when the sun rises."

As smart as Rosie was, I knew she was wrong. The sun coming up wouldn't make me feel one bit better. But there was no point in arguing. I climbed my bunk ladder and escaped the nightmare we were living by returning to the field trip on the morning of my father's death.

But in my dream, no other children were there, just Miss Yeboah and me. We wore no shoes. Short brown grass prickled my toes. A wide-eyed ostrich twisted his skinny neck to watch which route we would take. I recognized the raspy "raak, raak," of the lilac-breasted rollers overhead, but they were not the birds for which we searched. We were seeking the blue bustard mother and her chick. As we walked deep into the veld, the birds ceased singing, and the air was silent.

Then the repeated jab of a finger poking the soft spot below my shoulder blade awakened me. "Umama's not in bed, and Rosie's on the sofa snoring like a hippopotamus."

In the dusky light, I sensed the warmth of Onele's large soft eyes, more than saw them from where she perched at the top of the bunk ladder.

I kissed her nose. "Listen to the owl."

Onele's stale breath assaulted my nose. "Rosie has her feet on Umama's sofa."

"Hungry, baby girl?"

Onele stared like I'd gone softheaded. "Rosie's feet are on a white flower. Umama won't be happy about that."

"We'll wake her in a minute. Asanda, too. But you didn't answer. Are you hungry?"

"No, don't want to eat."

"Me neither, baby sister. But if we wake Rosie, she'll cook. That's how she fixes people when they're sad."

"Same as Hulu. I wish she was here."

I hung my feet over the side of the bunk. Onele gripped Monkey in one hand, wrapped her arms around my neck, and swung onto my back. "Loosen your grip. You're choking me." Awkwardly, I descended the ladder. "Shall we get Asanda up or let her sleep?"

"Wake her lazy butt."

"Onele, that's not nice."

"You say it."

"This is different. She's dead tired." I gasped. The word I used echoed in my head. *Dead, dead, dead.* Thankfully, Onele didn't seem to notice.

"We're up. She should be too."

"You do it. She gets less angry with you." Onele released one arm from my neck and shook Asanda until she shooed us away.

As I turned toward the bedroom door, I remembered Umama sharing her fears over the way Asanda seemed to stare off into nowhere. Guilt washed over me. We should have let our sister sleep. Onele, Monkey clenched in one hand, still clung to me as though she were my baby monkey. I hooked my arms under her rear.

"Do you smell food cooking?" she whispered.

"I think we woke Rosie. Let's go see."

Rosie pointed a wooden spatula at the kitchen chairs. "Heard you girls stirring. Sit and eat."

I cut the fried egg, then distributed tiny pieces across my plate so Rosie wouldn't notice I wasn't eating. I couldn't swallow the lump that filled my throat, and nothing could get past it. But nothing gets past Rosie either. She waved the spatula at my plate and nodded encouragingly. The glitter of meat juices and grease from the boerewors caused my stomach to roll, so I slid a forkful of egg into my mouth. When my stomach growled loudly as if to say, "Thank you," Onele giggled and spit yellow streaks of half-cooked yolk.

After we finished, Rosie washed the dishes. Silently, I dried, then put them away while Onele sat at the eating table coloring a dog that looked like our old Dinga. A stranger watching would not have realized how sad we were.

The front door creaked. We bolted, so fast and hard, Umama staggered from the weight of us crashing into her, hugging, tugging, to gain her attention. Like a flock of Willie Wagtail, one chirping louder than the other, Onele and I vied to be heard.

"I missed you, Umama."

"I went to your room, Umama, but you weren't there."

"We'd have gone with you if you woke us up."

"Rosie cooked breakfast. Eggs and boerewors."

Rubbing her eyes, Asanda emerged from our bedroom. "Did you bring Ubaba home?"

Onele and I stopped jabbering.

Our mother appeared barely able to muster the energy to speak. "The hospital said I could, but the police started an investigation."

"When can you?"

"Not sure. Soon. I'll bring your father home soon."

I struggled to find the right words. Once again, I worried whether she meant to bring Ubaba here or take him to the distant place she said was our ancestors' home? Or Soweto? Before I shaped these thoughts into words, Umama rubbed her eyes with her trembling hands. "I must lie down."

Rosie steered us girls back into the kitchen. "Let's make beef stew and fresh mielie bread. Eshile, where's your mother's largest pot?"

"But we just cleaned up the breakfast mess."

"Got to have leftovers, Eshile. We don't want your mother worrying if you're going hungry while she has important arrangements to make."

The mielie bread steamed, and the stew bubbled in the pot. The room smelled heavenly until Rosie pulled out the Dettol and poured a generous amount into the cleaning bucket. We scrubbed until the room stank like a hospital, swept then mopped until Rosie gave the okay to stop. Then she crossed her arms over her breasts and tucked her hands in her armpits. "You girls okay if I go to work?"

"Yes, ma'am," we answered, Asanda more eagerly than Onele and I.

"And not a peep until your mother wakes."

Seconds after Rosie closed the door, Asanda opened it again. "I'll be back."

"Can't you stay away from your boyfriend for a single day? Did it ever enter your puny head that Umama needs us here?"

"I'll come back before she wakes up."

"What about Onele?"

"She's got you. Besides, I want to tell Leo what happened to Ubaba."

"Don't you think his father already told him since he was there when Ubaba got shot?"

"Oh, Eshile, you're such a know-it-all."

Asanda slammed the door, and I returned to our room. Onele was on the lower bunk dressing the Gerber doll Ubaba bought the last time he drove Dr. Vorster to town to buy supplies. Onele called it her baby girl. It was the first doll she ever had that looked the same as her, so I guess that explained why she loved it so much.

❧

I couldn't say what occurred most of that day. Years passed before the recollection of Rosie's eggs and meaty boerewors links returned, and even longer for the memory of Asanda's swollen red eyes after her meeting with Leo. What I did remember was sitting between my mother and Asanda at the table for a late meal, staring at Rosie's mielie bread, but I couldn't recall why Onele was not with us. Yet I have a vague picture in my mind of a tear slipping from my mother's eye as she patted my hand.

"Eshile, you may leave the table."

I found Onele on the sofa, her face buried in a pillow. She had her Gerber doll and Monkey bunched together, crushed beneath her as she clenched them to her chest. I wanted to pick them up and hug them all. But she tensed when I came near, which I took as her sign she needed to be left alone.

I tiptoed from the room, reached up to the top shelf of our closet, and retrieved the book Miss Yeboah had loaned to me. Then I climbed the ladder to my bunk. After punching the pillow to fluff it, I snuggled in and carefully turned the pages.

"It's old. One of my favorites," Miss Yeboah had said. "I share it only with students who can be careful, those who will value it in the same manner I do."

Written in 1946, this book was almost as old as Umama. The cover was bumpy, possibly leather. I traced a finger over the gold print. *The Birds of America.* Confidence rushed over me. With the facts I would learn from studying this book, I would convince Miss Yeboah that I was her favorite and watch that annoying Anthony sink to the bottom of her list.

Opposite the title page was a portrait with John James Audubon printed below. Mr. Audubon appeared to have seen a ghost rather than a bird. Beady eyes peered back at me. His skin was as white as the enormous collar surrounding his face. My skin crawled at the sight of the black cape trimmed with fur from some poor dead animal. Mr. Audubon looked more like Dracula than a nice, bird-loving man.

A pounding knock rattled the front door. I jumped down from my bunk, didn't even use the ladder, but Umama was faster. She opened the door and invited Baas John in before I exited my room.

I heard "truck" and "not until." Too few words for me to decipher what was being said. Baas John's voice was the deepest, strongest of any man, so I was amazed he spoke so softly. Since the way they put their heads together told me my presence was unwelcome, I hid behind the wall, listening.

"A police officer called… The investigation may require reinspection… His body… Friday at the earliest."

Umama's voice rose. "Too long, Baas John. His soul wanders." My mother's voice dropped to a murmur. "This is not right. My husband needs me to help him into the afterlife."

"The officer understands, sends his apologies, yet swears he's serious about locating the poachers. He vowed they would pay."

"You'll take me Friday?"

"Yes, I'll drive. The officer will call again to confirm, but we should be able to collect your husband then. I explained to the kitchen help that you'll be off work for a while."

"But that large group coming in?"

Baas John stepped toward the door. "Not your worry. Everyone agrees. They volunteered to cover your duties. Try to rest."

After closing the door, Umama turned to me. "We should have given more."

"To whom, Umama?"

"The Lord, Eshile. To the Lord."

"I don't think that's why Ubaba died." I held her and whispered, "You give every Sunday."

My mother was the strongest, fiercest woman I had ever known. Auntie Grace said Umama had been that way since age fourteen, when she became pregnant with Asanda. But now she quivered like a baby bird. As strong as everyone knew her to be, this load was too much for her to carry alone. At that exact moment, I pledged to set aside my childish ways.

CHAPTER NINE

A Hero's Farewell

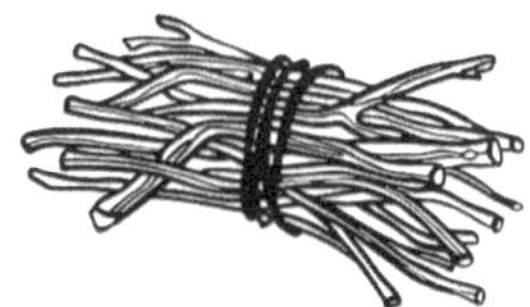

UTshazimpunzi (Month of the Withering Pumpkins) April 1974

Throughout our mother's absence, Rosie cared for my sisters and me as if we were her own. She inspected our uniforms before we left for school, then each afternoon, greeted us at the front door of our rondavel as if she'd been waiting all day for our return. Rosie scrutinized our homework with the attention to detail of the head schoolmaster of a private British school, then cooked us a nutritious, albeit overly abundant, dinner. Among all this, the thing I was most grateful for was that she stayed and slept in Umama's bed so we wouldn't be alone at night.

Rosie spent so much time with us that it didn't surprise me when she sang her three chickadees wake-up song, sleepy Onele stretched out her arms. "Umama, I'm happy you are home."

"*Hayi.* No, baby girl. It's just me." Beyond the embarrassment, pride flashed across her face. "Hop up and eat the breakfast I cooked. Scrub your faces. Put on nice clothes. It's going to be a good day. Baas John and your mother should be home soon."

Two weeks had passed since Baas John received the call from the Phalaborwa Police Station, and the lead investigator explained they obtained sufficient evidence to prosecute the poachers and imprison the shooter for many years. Therefore, he would release Ubaba's body to the next of kin.

Before they left for Phalaborwa, a town long known for its mining of copper and iron, Umama promised to return in two days. Two turned into three, then four, then two full weeks before I found out why they stayed gone so long.

Upon receiving the investigator's call, Umama had been so eager to bring Ubaba home that Baas John drove through the night. Early the following morning, he dropped off Umama at the Phalaborwa coffin maker's shop to select the wooden box to house her husband beneath the ground, then he went alone to the police station. But the moment he told the officer that Umama would claim the body, things began to go wrong.

The safari guide was a local Black man employed by a company that specialized in hunting the king of Africa's prized five. New to this job, he swore nobody informed him of the laws defining territorial boundaries inside which authorities allowed raising lions for the sport of killing. Sympathetic to the claims of the guide, investigators blamed the safari company rather than this local family man and released him to return home.

By using the discharge of the safari guide as their argument, the attorneys persuaded the judge to grant a temporary discharge for their clients, the shooter's friends and fellow poachers, on the condition they return for a hearing at noon, one week from that day.

Two attorneys, one representing the tourists and another the safari company, caught the duty officer by surprise. Delivering official-looking papers in their own blustery manner, the attorneys intimidated the officer until he unlocked the cell door and released their clients.

Baas John reported that the investigator barked at the duty officer for not calling him. But in the end, even though the officer's release of the prisoners constituted a failure to follow the chain of command, the judge ruled that regardless of the attorney's bullying behavior, the officer had no choice but to comply with the court order.

Nobody ever saw the men again.

The poacher who murdered my father was from Japan. His lawyer reminded the judge that apartheid classified Japanese citizens as White and convinced authorities this earned him the right to spend the night in the local hotel instead of a cell. One officer guarded the door. Another, posted in the lobby, tracked everyone as they entered and left. Still, my father's murderer disappeared from the second-story room. He knotted bedclothes and then hung them from a drainpipe outside the window. The officer reported that Ubaba's killer slid the length of the sheets and dropped to the street.

Asanda said, "Too bad the fall didn't break his legs."

The police wasted time searching every hotel and nearby restaurant. Later Umama would redden when she said, "Only an idiot would expect a killer who jumped out of a two-story building to go across the street to eat a meat pie instead of running for his life."

After squandering precious hours in town, investigators raced to the airport, only to recover the poacher's abandoned rental car. The airline manager confirmed that all three men bought tickets to leave South Africa. The clerk claimed the anxious travelers couldn't wait for a flight to Japan. The next available was to Rio de Janeiro, so that's where they went.

I overheard Baas John tell Rosie that Umama tore into the investigator assigned to convey the unwelcome news. She pounded his chest, cursing him into an unpleasant eternity for not securing the justice Ubaba deserved. Yet the investigator did nothing to stop her. He only protected himself with his arms until Baas John took Umama by the shoulders and pulled her off.

Rosie glanced at the ceiling. "Thank the ancestors that investigator was Black. Otherwise, we'd be bailing Umama out of *ijele*."

Then the police chief canceled the release of the body. Which made no sense, as though my dead father was the sole person they had the competence to control. Officers and investigators scurried from one place to the next, asking questions nobody could answer. There was nothing additional to learn except that the police let my father's murderer escape.

Six days after Umama and Baas John arrived in Phalaborwa, police finalized the charges. Five days later, the case came before the court, even though my father's killer, along with his attorneys, had left the country.

When telling us this, Umama's eyes glinted like steel. "A sham to soothe their guilt for what they did not do. A man who beats a drum for the mad to dance is no better than the madman."

Baas John said the police and the judge postured as if they had done their job, congratulating each other. They felt they had achieved a fair and just outcome because if Ubaba's murderer returned to Phalaborwa, a warrant for his arrest was on file.

Baas John described how the police investigator tried to comfort Umama, but she screamed, "*Amaxoki*, liars, all of you. You promised punishment."

The investigator patted his chest as if he was the owner of the final response. "Ashes fly back in the face of he who throws them. We will catch the man who shot your husband, then see he receives the sentence he deserves."

"But your mother refused to be placated," Baas John explained. "She stood eye to eye with this man and drilled her finger into his chest."

Heat rose in Umama's face. "I told him he was wrong. I asked how he could believe my husband's murderer was ignorant enough to return to South Africa to receive his due punishment?"

Baas John had Arno and Jabu, Ubaba's former beetle-sweeping friends, set up a table in our living room to hold our father's coffin. The shadow of it loomed across Umama's flowered sofa. The air was heavy. I sensed my ancestors watching over my father as other spirits swirled with evil intent, seeking to pull him off the path to the afterlife.

When the men left, Umama cooked an American breakfast, which we normally considered a great treat. Yet I experienced no joy or gratitude. I rammed my buttered toast into the soft egg yolk, then jabbed again as if it were to blame for my misery. My sisters, forks midair, stared bug-eyed at me. Umama placed her hand atop mine to stop my attack on this poor defenseless egg. But her sturdy grip didn't stop the anger burning up my neck and lodging in my jaw.

"Eat, girls. Nutritious food fortifies our minds and bodies. We need that for what lies ahead." Our mother nodded her approval when my sisters filled their mouths. I took a bite of toast, but the bread turned to putty, choking me, making it impossible to swallow.

Rosie had appeared earlier and covered the windows with ash from the firepit. This blocking out of the sun left our rooms hazy dark. Yet enough light sneaked through that I could see my sisters holding as still as the Queen's Guard outside Buckingham Palace, so as not to add to Umama's distress.

My mind wandered back to when late the previous night, Umama's mournful voice had awakened me. I had tiptoed to the door and listened to Rosie reassure her. "Your husband was honorable. His spirit will cause you no trouble. He understands you can't take his body to his ancestral birthplace for burial."

"But Rosie, my people—my brother, my sister, our grandmother— all of them we failed to deliver to their birthplaces. How much will the gods tolerate?"

The clink of silverware drew my mind back to what was now happening at the breakfast table.

"Don't fidget," hissed Asanda.

My little sister positioned her fork to scoop up a bite of fried egg, but Umama pulled Onele's plate right out from under her nose and dropped it in the sink.

"Umama. I wasn't—"

I shot Onele a look. *Not-a-good-time-to-complain.*

"Girls, go sit on the sofa." Umama didn't tell Onele to wash the streak of yellow yoke off her hand before sitting on her sofa, a sure sign a huge thought was on our mother's mind.

"Your father brought his family to this beautiful place. He was proud of that. Spoke of it as his single true accomplishment."

A roaring filled my ears. Umama's voice was faint, as if far from me, as if I was fading into the past, pulled by an unknown force into memories of two years earlier. In my mind, I heard her urge my sisters to catch up. Several paces ahead, my father and I walked side by side, following the curve of the path. For a moment, I felt the joy we shared when we were the first of my family to see the Ilanga Safari Lodge.

Had there been a sign? Something I missed—we all missed? I searched this memory, but all I saw was myself slipping my hand into my father's, then feeling his warmth in my palm. When I thanked him for bringing us to this place, he had hid the dampness in his eyes. The force of this colossal loss coursing through my body rendered me unable to contain my tears. I should have told him we needed to go home, but I was tricked by the beauty that surrounded us. While I now saw the deception, deep in my core, I still craved to remain.

I rose from the sofa but sat back down when Umama pulled the tissue I so desperately needed from her pocket and handed it to me. "This is upsetting for us all, but we must make a decision. Great-Grandmother Haile agrees with me that we should bury Ubaba at the lodge. Your Uncle Sammy disagrees. He came in a separate dream and demanded I bury Ubaba in Braamfontein Cemetery, in the family plot alongside him and my sister, Nofoto. However, I do not believe this is what your father desires."

Umama crossed her arms over her chest as if daring either my sisters or me to disagree. I searched my sisters' faces but saw no hint of their thoughts. The three of us held our breath and our words. A smile fluttered in my heart. If Umama buried our father in Ilanga, surely, we would continue to live in Ilanga.

Umama stared at me and my sisters until we squiggled in our seats, then returned to the kitchen. The instant she turned her back, Asanda slipped out. I took the broom from the closet and swept, slowly and quietly. Then Onele and I spent hours making paper bracelets, coloring them with our brightest Crayons to resemble African prints. When my little sister yawned and rubbed her eyes, I motioned toward our bedroom. She crawled into her bunk and curled herself around Monkey. I lifted a book from the dresser, but before I asked Onele if she wanted me to read aloud, her snoring began. I exchanged the book for my journal, then climbed into my bed. But not to sleep. I had serious thinking to do.

What if I was wrong? What if Umama chose to move back to Soweto to be near her mother and sister? Would our ancestors send a sign? Which decision would ensure our future? The wishes of my heart were hard to ignore. Each beat seemed to say, *Be ready. Be ready. You must persuade her to stay. Stay at Ubaba's side.*

I had just finished writing thirteen plausible arguments in my journal when Baas John's deep voice broke my concentration. I tiptoed to our bedroom door. He and Umama lifted my father from the coffin, then placed him on the kitchen table. Ubaba, mottled with shades of greenish purple, looked like he was beaten to death rather than shot in the head. His body emitted an unpleasant odor that brought to mind a strange mix of garlic, rotting cabbage, and cheap perfume.

Too much time had passed.

At age seven, I had asked to help clean Sammy's body, but Hulu needed to be alone with her son. Six years later, I was more mature, yet the thought of touching my father called a burning slimy residue of last night's dinner up into my throat. I crept backward as silent as a cat.

My mother was facing away from me when she said, "Eshile, I am glad you're here."

I never understood how my mother did that. I hadn't made a sound.

Baas John said, "Ladies, I must leave, attend to my duties."

I gazed at Baas John's retreating back, my mind whirling, trying to devise an excuse Umama might accept as a reason I should go with him.

My mother brushed Ubaba's mouth with her lips. "Do not worry, *sithandwa sam*, my love. Eshile and I will prepare you to travel the long road into the afterlife."

Her words woke memories of the arduous road Ubaba traveled to his job at the goldmine, a trip so long we saw him only on the weekends. But this sadness turned to anger when I recalled how the foreman had caught my father drinking, then fired him on the spot. I wondered if Umama now regretted how angry she became, throwing her wooden spatula at him as Ubaba scurried out of our shanty. This was the fight that led to our leaving Soweto. Did my mother feel the weight of blame?

The image in my brain of my father cowering away from my mother was enough to make me decide never to hit my husband. While Great-Grandmother Haile taught her daughters not to let men take advantage of them, she also recited the African proverb that reminds us a broken man is a man to no one.

Later that evening, I had overheard Ubaba beg for my mother's forgiveness, then her soothing him, telling him he was her only love. That left me uncertain whether he left of his own choice to find a job or was Umama to blame. I couldn't stop thinking that if the foreman hadn't reported my father, he'd still work in the mine. And he'd still be alive.

Umama slid fresh-cut *inzinziniba* twigs into Ubaba's nostrils so he would smell the lemony fragrance of the white flowers and green leaves rather than the odor of his deteriorating body. She also ground *inzinziniba* roots and soaked them in a bowl on the counter. Soft and distended, they surrendered their powers to the water. She caressed Ubaba's forehead with a washcloth dampened in the fragrant potion. With the tip of her bare finger, she caught water droplets running from his eyes like tears. I wiped mine on my sleeve.

My mother cleansed inside the folds of skin below his chin, then murmured as she rubbed in small circles on his cheeks and neck. "Great-Grandmother Haile, prepare the way for my husband. He is good, albeit his decisions sometimes were not. He needs you to guide him." Umama doused the cloth repeatedly, then massaged the infused water onto his shoulder and underarm.

"Uncle Sammy, you are strong," I intoned. "Please come. Don't let my father's spirit stray."

On the opposite side of the kitchen table, I dipped my cloth and duplicated my mother's movements as she worked down Ubaba's arm.

"Sister Nofoto, I send my husband to you. He is my love. As with your death, his was also violent, at the hands of another. You told me of the difficulty of letting go of your hatred. Please help him find forgiveness and the peace you have found for yourself."

Umama lifted his stiff hand and kissed each knuckle. I fought the urge to scream, *Jesus, uThixo! Are either of you our loving Father? Or are you both filled with hate and spite? Why would a compassionate god take my father from me? You could have stopped this, if only you cared.*

Umama cleansed between his puffy fingers and under each nail. I choked down my sobs while duplicating her movements and struggling to remain intent on cleansing my father of malicious spirits that might prevent his entrance into the afterlife.

The importance of family during times of loss had compelled me to write to my Auntie Grace the day we returned from the hospital. I told them they might miss Ubaba's burial, but Umama needed them to come, anyway. With all that went wrong, this single effort turned out right. My aunties Grace and Buhle and Uncle Abel arrived the evening before we laid my father in the ground. Jabu saw them pull into the parking lot and ran to collect us only moments after the last mourners finished paying their respects and left our rondavel.

Auntie Grace was larger than I recalled from two years ago. She drew my mother to her breast. Her ample body welcomed Umama's thin frame as though the women were melting into one. Neither sister moved a muscle nor made a sound. Uncle Abel, Auntie Buhle, my sisters, and I stepped back as if we feared breaking the spell or perhaps being absorbed ourselves.

Several long minutes passed before my mother raised her head, taking in air like someone who had been sucked to the muddy floor of Olifants River and had broken free and risen to the water's surface. When Auntie Grace released my mother from her embrace, Umama pulled herself to full height for the first time since my father's death. "Thank you, sister. I needed that."

Only then did the rest of us greet each other. And only then did Ubaba's parents climb out of the bed of Abel's truck.

As I gazed from one sad face to another, each attempting to smile as if glad to see the other, it occurred to me—I took my family for granted. It had always been that way. I didn't realize how my aunties and uncle raised my spirits and shared my load. When we hugged and kissed, the weight lifted as if each had taken a brick off my shoulders. Like my mother, I stood up straight.

Yet I longed for my grandmother's counsel; her gentle touch to lift the final burden from my sagging shoulders. "I wish Hulu had come, too," I said to our guests. Instantly, I felt shame for my whiny tone.

"Your grandfather isn't well. The trip would be too much," explained Auntie Grace.

Thankfully, before I blurted what was on my mind, that their trip was nothing compared to what we experienced first coming to Ilanga, Uncle Abel asked, "Where's my friend? I want to see him."

Umama motioned to an opening in the lush vegetation at the far end of the parking area. As we walked toward our rondavel, I breathed in the almond scent of Old Man's Beard vines and studied my family's faces, wondering if they were comparing this walk to the streets of Soweto, particularly the constant stink of *kak*. How could anyone choose to go back?

As a line of nine, our movement created a breeze that loosened golden dust from the Amaryllis Belladonna clusters. Even the slightest scent brought Auntie Grace's senses to life, attuning her to the healing properties a plant possessed. Her gaze darted, then locked onto Rosie's garden of greenish-yellow, pointy-toothed Kranz aloe. Its orange blooms caught the moonlight. I read Auntie's thoughts on her face. She wanted to ask for cuttings to take on her return home. I opened my mouth to answer her unspoken question. Instead, I swallowed hard to keep from crying. All I could think of was how badly I wanted to stay.

Baas John was waiting outside our door when we returned to our rondavel. Umama introduced him to everyone, but it was the handshake between him and my Uncle Abel, the kind in which men bond immediately, that gave me much to think about. What is it about a person, what is it we see in another, that lets us know we have met a friend?

After Umama and I dressed my father in the suit Baas John had brought by, she spread the oxhide on the floor of the casket and over the sides, readying it to be wrapped around Ubaba. Baas John helped lift my father off the table and return him to his coffin. Umama guided our other family members from the kitchen into our living room to pay their respects and offer gifts for his successful journey. I couldn't endure another wail or call to the spirits. So, I stepped outside, leaned against the wall, and tried to block out all sound as if that would release the painful tension in my neck and shoulders.

Still, I heard Auntie Grace. "A lovely photograph of you and the girls. Even though he will never forget you, it's proper to put this in his coffin, to have you all by his side."

I stepped back inside as my uncle asked, "Whose blue suit is this?"

"Woman, what were you thinking?" Uncle Abel unbuttoned the top button of the white dress shirt, the one Umama had buttoned so carefully, then pressed the fabric away from my father's neck. "You know he'll be miserable spending his eternal life wearing a suit instead of his favorite flowered shirt."

My mother's laughter, not heard for weeks, was a welcome sound. "My husband shall not meet the gods in that old rag."

Auntie Grace tucked dried pumpkin seeds beneath Ubaba's hand. "For you, brother-in-law. You may look down from your heavenly home and see struggles and periods of disharmony that disturb your peace. These seeds will calm you and promote good rest."

"Hulu and Umkhulu sent two gold rand." Uncle Abel pulled a leather money bag from his pocket and loosened the twine to reveal its coins. "And I brought homemade wine." He placed the bottle between my father's hip and the coffin wall, then patted his shoulder. "You are fortunate, my friend. Surrounded by green satin and a bottle of my best *tembo*, you'll have no problem finding contentment in the afterlife."

Umama nodded her approval. "I could use a glass of wine myself."

Looking proud of himself, Uncle Abel said, "You are in luck. I brought a second bottle."

My mother took the bottle from his hands. "You are a generous man,"

As Abel beamed his thanks for the compliment, Asanda reappeared. I thought Umama would call her up short, but she acted as if she hadn't noticed her eldest daughter's absence.

"Girls, please set the table. Our refrigerator is full of food. Rosie saw to that."

Umama had eaten sparrow-sized meals for the previous two weeks. Now, surrounded by family, she said, "A large plate for me, please." This simple sign of normalcy told me Umama would regain her former strength. Another brick fell from my shoulders. We will be all right.

Our conversation carried me back to Hulu's Sunday dinners. We filled our plates and chattered as though gathered for some reason other than my father's burial. Auntie Grace told everyone Abel's boss, who claimed her husband was the best employee he ever had, gave him two weeks off from work. My aunties and uncle had arrived in a shiny *bakkie* pickup truck, used, but new to Abel, that made their journey to Ilanga faster and less complicated than ours two years before. Still, they had stories to tell, and Abel was a storyteller.

"I drove the roads as fast as any Black man can without getting thrown in prison but had to stomp on the brakes when we came to a parade of elephants." Abel held out his arms. "The biggest female I've ever seen stopped us like a policeman blocking the road."

Auntie Grace squinted at her husband. "You know my Abel. He wouldn't wait until the matriarch saw that the other females and their calves crossed safely. Oh, no. He urged her to move by taking his foot off the brake and letting his truck roll."

"But that old cow had other thoughts." Abel puffed his chest, squared his shoulders, then waggled his arm like an elephant trunk. "Biggest I have ever seen, that ornery cow walked straight toward my new truck."

Auntie Buhle wiped *tembo* from her chin. "Fool, I tried to stop you. Did you think I slapped your leg for fun?"

Abel threw back his head. "I wish you had seen Buhle. Thought her eyeballs might pop out of her face when that old gal braced her head against the hood. Pushed my truck out of her way."

Auntie Grace snorted indignantly. "She scared you too."

"The ancestors teach us the elephant brings good luck. But all that old cow brought me was trouble."

Ubaba's mother whispered, "I wanted to jump out of the truck and run."

"I had to hold her down," added his father.

Auntie Buhle spread her arms wide. "Bigger than a school bus, that elephant could have crushed the front of Abel's truck, but that wasn't what she had in mind. She simply wasn't letting any threat near her family."

"More men should be like that." Auntie Grace gave Abel a disapproving look that, in my opinion, he did not deserve.

Abel ignored his wife. "Strangest thing. When that elephant bent her neck and pushed with her head, I looked straight into her eyes. Instead of golden brown, hers were silver, outlined in bluish-black. Lordy, I swear it felt like she was peering into my soul."

Rosie had told us the story of a silver-eyed elephant who had led her great-great-grandfather to safety long ago when his tribe was attacked. Umama refilled her wine glass and confirmed the power of a silver-eyed elephant. "She delayed you. Took you off the course of *ububi*."

Yet this notion of *ububi* and the elephant's ability to stave off evilness unsettled me even more. Ubaba believed we had arrived in paradise, and he could keep his family safe from the *idemoni*. And I believed my father when he claimed this, but now my heart is filled with doubts. While Ilanga was a different world than Soweto, it was clear to me a demon's reach was greater than my father had known.

Later in the evening, after everyone was talked out, Umama spread a sheet over the red and white flowered sofa. Onele changed into her knee-length pajama shirt, then curled up with Monkey tucked under her arm. I offered to sleep on the floor so my aunties and uncle could use the bunk beds. As I retrieved my old sleeping mat from the closet and rolled it out between Onele and Ubaba, my thoughts returned to the morning following my third night in Ilanga. After sleeping in the amazingly comfortable top bunk, I carted my handwoven mat out to the rubbish bin, experiencing a sense of achievement as if this represented a final act of my former life.

But Umama stopped me from dropping in my mat. "You can't know what waits ahead or what you might need to survive."

Once again, back on my mat, I smelled the dirt floor of our Soweto shanty mingled with the smoke of the metal cooking brazier we had used to grill meat. I had sworn I would never lie on this mat again. I hated to admit Umama was right. Circumstances change, not always for the better. As it turns out, I needed this thing I thought I was done with forever. How many more times would that be true?

My arms and legs felt heavy. I couldn't hold up my head. I was so tired I thought I might sleep for a hundred years on the floor between two loved ones—my breathy little sister, snoring like a newborn piglet, and my beloved father, silenced forever.

Tradition dictated that to prevent Ubaba's ghost from wandering and causing harm, we must remove him from our home, feet first, through a hole in the wall. Baas John didn't even ask permission because he knew the owner wouldn't allow it. The open door would have to do, so we spun the coffin until my father's feet pointed out.

Baas John, Uncle Abel, Arno, and Jabu lifted the coffin. To confuse my father and keep him from returning to our rondavel, they zigzagged on the path to Ilanga's small burial ground.

Umama pinned a black cloth to the neck of her blouse, so it draped down the back of her flowing, long-skirted *dashiki* printed with the Tree of Life. Auntie Buhle braided my mother's hair and twisted the strands into a knot on her crown. The beads she wove in each braided strand were the same deep royal blue and pure white of the necklace that covered Umama's chest. Wrapped from her wrist to her elbow, the beaded bracelets Rosie made covered the rich coppery color of my mother's arms.

Head held high, Umama walked along the winding trail behind my father's coffin with the bearing of an African princess. Ubaba's mother trembled and stepped uncertainly. His father squared his shoulders, then raised his chin as if to pull himself up to his full height even though it was easy to see that he was a shrunken man. My sisters, Aunties Grace and Buhle, Uncle Abel, Rosie, and I followed like a string of ducklings dressed up in Easter Sunday wear.

At Umama's request, the women of our family wore *pagnes* of bright African patterned cloth wrapped to hang below their knees. Though Abel was Xhosa, he wore Ubaba's gold and black tribal print shirt in honor of my father's Zulu heritage. My uncle looked so handsome I regretted not suggesting we bury Ubaba in that shirt. Since we wore comfortable clothes made of soft fabrics printed with bold geometric or lush tropical designs, I thought it unfair that my father couldn't be laid to rest in his favorite flowered shirt.

"The gods must see your father as a man worthy of their respect." My spine tingled when my mother spoke as if she had read my thoughts. "Wipe that frown off your face. Your father wants you to be happy and rejoice in his burial as a natural phase of life."

I gritted my teeth to hold back my words. *But his death was unnatural… unnecessary… wrong!*

Sun glinted through the spreading branches of the marula tree, danced on leaves, and cascaded toward the path. A whiff of sweet violas floated on the breeze. As we stepped into the clearing, Asanda and I supported our mother by cupping her elbows in our palms.

Unlike Uncle Sammy's funeral events, my father's ceremony was humble and unpretentious. He deserved more. For Hulu and Umkhulu not to be here was a slight I didn't know how to process, even though my grandfather was not at the top of my list of people to celebrate my father's life. I'd grown to believe my parents' poverty resulted from Umkhulu's unwillingness to release his displeasure of my father. Now, the ultimate insult, my grandfather hadn't come to the funeral. I hurt as much as if it were me he had no wish to see.

On the other hand, my grandmother had never let me down. The time and distance that separated us made me realize she had been there for me, even when I didn't realize I needed her. Auntie Grace explained Umkhulu was ill, but how sick would he have to be to keep my grandmother away when we needed her so desperately? Why hadn't she ridden along with Auntie Grace and Uncle Abel?

Yet Umama appeared to be fine with their absence. Perhaps the slight I felt was personal. Was I thinking only of my own feelings?

My mind drifted to identifying the exact moment I forgot to think of Bini, the girl I swore to be my best friend for life. When had I become comfortable sharing my problems, thoughts, and dreams with Kalisha the way I did with Bini before? The loss of my father, powerful as a lightning bolt, cracked my outer shell and burned through my chest. I craved Bini's company, her warmth, her sympathy. I needed the comforting way she explained that no one escapes the cruelty and unfairness of living in this world.

If we still lived in Soweto, many more people would have come to say goodbye to my father. When we buried Sammy, it seemed as if all of South Africa turned out. Relatives I'd never seen or heard of showed up to honor his tribal name. Since my uncle died before apartheid stripped my grandfather of his business, his home, and his standing in the community, lines of customers from his International Imports Emporium paid their respects. Whites and governmental officials attended out of fear of insulting my grandfather and losing the special deals he offered, as well as the gifts he slipped them. Many more—our nosey neighbor Ife, and friends like ole George, Rufaro and his wife Matilde, and the women who gathered around our brazier every Friday night—came out of love.

Here, my mother and father's friends were the kitchen help, the men who had worked alongside Ubaba, and other Ilanga employees. Since the lodge was fully booked with guests, the owner allowed only those closest to my parents to leave their duties for the funeral.

We gathered around the shadowy hole in the earth. Rosie shook a gourd hand-painted with the outline of a large open eye that reminded me of those used by *Anathi,* Soweto's fortuneteller. She said it helped the dead find their way. Three men dressed in leopard skin chanted, then leaped and spun, performing what appeared to be the same tribal dance they did to welcome guests at the lobby entrance. Was the Zulu dance for *mholo* the same as for goodbye?

Auntie Grace filled a pottery bowl with dried chopped *imphepho*. It burst into flame the instant she touched a lighted match to the leaves and branches. Lifting the bowl above her head, she circled the gravesite. Mourners breathed the fragrant smoke, quieting until the only voices heard were those of the lilac-breasted rollers calling to each other. "Raak, raak."

Ubaba said his Zulu grandparents tested their compatibility by tying themselves together with ropes woven from roller feathers. If the bond had broken, the marriage would have been canceled. Just thinking about it made me chuckle. I doubted Umama would have called off her marriage to Ubaba just because a bunch of bird feathers fell apart. Once made up, she rarely changed her mind.

Following a moment of silence, our priest, Father Chipo, offered both Zulu and Catholic prayers. Rosie's arms rose like Jesus when He called sinners to his feet. When she sang the Zulu hymn, "*Sidedele singene*," her voice floated like soft clouds overhead. I joined in the refrain, a prayer to God to let my father in.

The coffin's golden wood sparkled under the scorching sun. Uncle Abel, Dr. Vorster, Baas John, Wilson, Arno, and Jabu lowered the ropes. The coffin slid as smoothly as rain off an elephant's ear until Arno lost his grip. When the wooden box thunked to the bottom of the earth's opening, we gasped.

Umama wiped away the sweat beaded on her forehead, then swooned in the warm fall breeze. I stepped closer, ready to seize her arm. A sunbird's teal feathers caught the light. A shimmering jewel, he swooped over the black pit. Everyone held their breath when the miniature bird flitted toward Umama and hovered before her face.

Then he was gone.

I met Umama's glance. She detected my father's presence, the same as I.

Father Chipo recited Psalm 23:4. I had memorized that verse in Bible School. It meant that Jesus pledged to be Umama's rod and staff.

But I'd seen no sign of Him since the poacher shot Ubaba. I wondered who would give my mother strength and protection in His absence. Was it up to me?

I knew other thirteen-year-old girls, some married, some not, who already had babies. They were old enough to be the head of their households. Surely, the least I could do was bolster Umama when she was down and protect her from whatever else might come, even step forward in moments when she was unable to carry on.

Uncle Sammy died when I was seven. The noise, the smells, throngs of people, tribal rights and traditions—there was so much I didn't understand. Though older now, I experienced a wisp of that same fear. Most alive in my memory was the sound of Hulu's shovelful of earth hitting the coffin. I had cringed because the rich dark dirt landed where Sammy's face would be.

Now I braced myself as my mother stabbed the shovel into the pile of loose dirt, then stretched her arms over the coffin. Her hands shook. Dirt rained down into the gaping hole and tumbled across the golden wood, spilling into the crevasses at its sides. I sprinkled my scoop, careful not to drop dirt on my father's face. Asanda, then Ubaba's parents, went next. My aunties, Abel, and Baas John followed them.

Onele cowered behind Rosie. I understood. It had scared me too when I was her age—the thought of dead people lurking while their loved ones completed the rituals that allow the spirit to ascend to its heavenly home. At Sammy's funeral, I hid beneath a folding table, then peeked out between the tablecloths. For weeks after, everyone suffered from my screaming nightmares waking them in the darkest part of night.

Shovel in hand, Arno stood before my mother and lowered his gaze. "The foot pains in sympathy with the toe. Your husband's death is a loss to all." We stepped away as he and Jabu filled the grave.

Umsuzwane leaves and flowers floated in a large wooden bowl of water sitting on a small table beneath the marula tree. We cleansed our hands to remove spirits that might have slipped in unseen, bringing bad fortune to the day or to anyone in attendance.

A dry leaf in the wind, Umama moved through the mourners, thanking them for the honor they had bestowed on Ubaba. The lone instance she faltered was when Dr. Vorster approached. Umama's shoulders shimmied as if she was chilled on such a sweltering day. She offered her hand, then recoiled. Perhaps she didn't want to touch him because she blamed him for Ubaba's death.

Dr. Vorster behaved as if he hadn't noticed and introduced the woman at his side. Umama responded with the hint of a smile. I knew the doctor's son Leo well, but not his wife.

Catherine was her name. Slight and willowy, she took Umama in her arms. My mother's hands hung limp, yet Catherine held her until their bodies rocked as if one. Later I learned Catherine had also suffered a great loss, a baby who was never born. I've witnessed this a few times more since that day, a woman who absorbed the pain of another and replaced it with her own strength. When they released their embrace, moisture glinted on my mother's eyelashes, but her chin was up. She stood taller than she had in weeks.

Leo, like a puppy drooling in anticipation of a treat, watched Asanda pull Onele from behind Rosie's legs, never taking his eyes from them as they moved toward him. I swear that boy wagged his tail.

I pictured Leo and Asanda and the positions I'd caught them in, perched atop the rock where they liked to neck. Was Catherine aware of this romance between her son and my sister? If so, what might transpire when they came face to face? As if I had the ability to move people, Leo's mother approached Asanda and greeted her with a hug. They continued talking in low tones while everyone else left.

Clearly, there'd been events I knew nothing of—relationships to which I was not privy. I itched to learn what this was all about. Asanda would never tell me. I'd have to find out myself.

I stared at my sister, trying to read her thoughts. When Leo touched her shoulder, she turned her back to me. He raised one hand to caress the side of her face. She leaned into the one-handed embrace. It was the most intimate touch I had ever witnessed. A warmth spread down my neck and across my shoulders. I felt as if instead of reading Asanda's mind, I had heard from her soul.

Trees and shrubs, evergreen leaves and brown twigs, glowed in the slanted rays of the setting sun. Yet my emotions were akin to anger and hate. It was not right that the path we walked to return to our rondavel sparkled as if sprinkled with gold while my spirit was dark with sorrow.

Baas John had left orders for a rolling bed to be delivered for Uncle Abel and Auntie Grace. While we were out, it had been set up against the living room wall. I was relieved to reclaim my bunk. After my first night in the rondavel, I had childishly thought I would never sleep on the floor again. But who could predict…?

There seemed no end to the kindnesses offered by Baas John. Uncle Abel mentioned that our customs dictated a deceased person's bed be removed from the home, so Baas John offered to exchange the one my parents slept in for a bed from another rondavel.

Umama thanked him but shook her head. "Not yet. His scent on my bedclothes is all I have left."

Baas John nodded, then excused himself, saying he had work to finish.

Umama went to the refrigerator and brought out a pitcher filled with an amber liquid. Auntie Buhle followed carrying four glasses. Unlike Sammy's celebration, beer did not flow like water in the River Limpopo. The owner of the lodge had not allowed alcohol to be served to his employees during the service. My relatives followed his wishes then, but in the privacy of our rondavel, they were not about to forgo their traditional funeral beer.

Abel poured while Auntie Grace pulled sticks of sandalwood incense from her bag and lit the tips. The warm, woodsy fragrance comforted me. It was the same incense she had used at Sammy's burial to purify the air and sanctify the ceremony. Onele curled up on the sofa, resting her shoes smack dab on a large white flower. I nudged my sister to save her from Umama's killer-eyebrow, then motioned her to our bedroom.

Onele gazed at me with her sad Eeyore face. "Eshile, may I sleep with you?"

Even though it was still light outside, I found myself unable to say no to my sister. We slipped into nightgowns, then I stretched out my hand to her.

Onele asked to sleep in my top bunk, but I wanted her in her own bed so I could sneak back into the living room after she fell asleep and listen to whatever stories the adults would tell. At ten years old, she wasn't a baby anymore, yet I fretted she might roll off and break an arm after I left. Since none of us could handle another tragedy, I ignored Onele's whine, nudged her into the lower bunk, and crawled in beside her.

She snuggled against me. Her muscles released the tension they had held. She lay so still that I hardly recognized this creature of constant motion. The puckering between her eyebrows smoothed and the corners of her mouth turned up. Her angel face returned. For this moment, as she fell asleep, I had my baby sister back.

Still, I worried about the day to come. Would it hit as hard as today? If so, for how many more days? Would our lives ever be the same? What might happen to us? Fearing Onele would suffer the effects of this uncertainty more than anyone, I kissed her pug nose.

Even though daylight filtered through the separation between the curtains, I was done with this day. Staying awake to listen to the tales my relatives might tell was too much of a struggle. My breathing slowed to the rhythm of Onele's baby-kitten snores. As I drifted toward sleep, my father appeared, wearing his worn khaki slacks and the flowered shirt Umama had asked him to take back to the rubbish dump. I contemplated how he managed to change into his favorite shirt until a falling sensation pulled me into another world.

My father and I were sitting on a grass mat in the shade of a giraffe thorn tree. Sunlight bounced off its light-gray thorns. We rested, side by side, against the reddish-brown tree trunk, then gazed across the savanna. An ear-shaped pod had fallen beside me. I took it in my hand and picked at the seam. I feared Ubaba would leave if I spoke.

"Daughter, it is good to be here with you. I am happy to find you well."

When I set the brittle sand-colored pod aside and gazed into his eyes, his smile faded.

"I have come to talk seriously. As the middle daughter, you might expect me to speak of this with Asanda rather than you, but you are the person whose judgment I most trust, whose strength I rely on. You must care for your mother. But do not fear. I am with you. I bring you good luck."

My father took my hand, but an unseen force pushed against my chest, pushing me away. I couldn't hold on.

Restless in her sleep, Onele squared her bare feet in the center of my spine and straightened her legs. I flailed my arms, then grabbed the bedpost to break my fall. The early morning sun peeked through the curtains. Whispered voices caught my ear. An argument. I needed to hear without them seeing me, so I picked myself up and tiptoed toward our kitchen.

"Sister, I tell you it's unsafe."

"But Grace, that's what my husband wants."

Auntie Buhle peeked out over the refrigerator door. "Eshile, you're awake. Been wanting to get breakfast on the stove."

Auntie Grace stood and smoothed the wrinkles from her skirt. My appearance had startled my aunties and interrupted the advice they were giving my mother.

Louder than his normal voice, and unrelated to the conversation going on, Abel announced, "I'll do Ubaba's work until we leave."

These snippets made me think of how the whispering fifteen-year-old girls at school, who thought they had important topics to discuss, raised their voices and acted as though they were discussing homework or some other stupid chore when we younger students came near. And in this moment, like those at school, there was a secret to be discovered, something being hidden from my ears.

Auntie Buhle bustled from the room, mumbling that she needed to change clothes. Ubaba's mother hopped up from the table, grabbed a dishcloth, then busied herself wiping the counters. I glared questioningly at Auntie Grace. But no matter how severely I squinted, she carried on, cracking eggs into the frypan and pretending not to notice my piercing stare.

❧

A short ten days later, in the early morning, we walked Ubaba's parents, Abel, and my aunties to the car park. Ubaba's father opened the crew cab door for his wife, who looked frailer and more lost now than when they arrived. After many kisses and goodbye tears, my aunties clambered into the truck. Abel stood holding the driver's door open as if waiting for someone to tell him what to do.

Of course, Auntie Grace obliged him. "Abel, get in. We have a long drive."

We waved until their truck was out of sight. I wanted to chase after them, beg them to stay. Instead, I followed Umama back to the path. Her step was brisk, as if on a mission, so she left me behind. I sensed eyes on me, or maybe the heaviness of a spirit. The shrubs seemed to whisper in the breeze—*Sticks in a bundle are unbreakable. That is your family's strength.*

Once in our bedroom, I stuffed down my sadness as I watched Onele wriggle into her Sunday dress. Rather than our flowing pagnes, we put on the dresses Umama ordered from the Sears catalog. I had done my best to talk Onele out of picking the bright yellow. She wouldn't hear of it. She loved yellow. The thick bow I tied at her back waggled when she walked. The scratchy crinolines underneath held the skirt out from her body and bounced with every step she took. She looked like a chickadee strutting about, much the same as I did when Ruthie Bekker, the Catholic priest's daughter, made fun of me.

As we entered the church, people turned our way, then quieted. Umama nudged my sisters and me along the aisle to sit in the front pew. As we took our seats, the first hymnal notes escaped the choir's mouths. "All creatures of our God and King, lift up your voice and with us sing."

My mother joined in the harmony of the praises as though she'd never held a single doubt about God's loving care. I wished I believed so wholeheartedly, trusted without question, but my anger still burned hot.

Father Chipo stepped up to the pulpit. "Our Lord looked down on what He had made. Displeased by man's wickedness, his corruption and violence, He commanded Noah to take action." Father raised the Bible and opened to the page marked by a red ribbon. "Genesis 6:14. 'Make thee an ark of gopher wood; rooms shall thou make in the ark, and shalt pitch it within and…'"

As Father Chipo continued to read, I wondered how large three hundred cubits was that it could hold so many creatures. But as my mind sank into its own murky thoughts, I no longer cared about the size and shape of the ark. It appeared that Noah and his family were the only people on earth who lived up to God's standards. All the others had to die. The Lord charged Noah with the greatest responsibility I could imagine, the saving of every species while He wiped out all other animals with His torrential rains. And God saved Noah and his family because he did as the Lord asked.

I wanted to raise my hand and ask Father Chipo why my father was not given this same act of grace. Since Ubaba died protecting the creatures the Lord worked so hard to create—two entire days and everybody knew that back then a day might have been equivalent to a month, possibly even a year, so it was a lot of work. Days might be shorter now, yet my father worked alongside Dr. Vorster to save God's animals from disease, starvation, and poachers. Albeit one creature at a time, but wasn't my father's work as important as Noah's?

Father Chipo closed the Bible and held it to his breast. "Then our Lord dried the rains and promised through His everlasting love, never to flood Earth again. And through this promise, we learn to forgive, as he forgave us."

Heat burned up my neck. If God loved us and had the power to do anything He wanted, why didn't He save my father's life? After all, He let Noah live to the amazing age of nine hundred and fifty in appreciation of his efforts. Until somebody explained why my father had to die so young, I was of no mind to forgive anyone—not his murderer nor the police who let my father's killer escape without punishment, much less the Lord himself who sat in the clouds watching all this transpire, without lifting a finger to protect the most caring man I knew.

I clenched my fist in my lap, ready for a fight. Umama set her hand atop mine. Once again, she seemed to read my mind and know what to do, all without me saying a single word. She shook her head, slowly and deliberately, as if to warn me not to do what I meant to do. Only this time her motherly powers didn't work. I stood.

Umama's hand fell away. I bumped Asanda's knee as I squeezed by. She shot me a startled glare. Onele tugged on the hem of my skirt. I yanked it out of her hand and moved into the aisle.

I felt the force of Father Chipo's words against my back. "Bow your heads. Pray with me, each in his own separate way."

Pray! Pray? Lot of good that did me. My father's dead. I stomped down the aisle. I felt my fellow churchgoer's eyes on me, watching, wondering what I was about to do. The only sound was the soles of my sandals smacking against the floor as I charged out the door and stomped along the path to the watering hole, hoping Khule would be there. She was not, so I sat on the rough-cut platform and listened to myself breathe, rapidly, madly. After an hour or so, my shoulders slumped, and tears ran down my face. I was still alone. It was time to go home.

I couldn't help but smile as I approached. Onele, glass jar in hand, leapt through the air trying to capture a butterfly. I watched until my mother spotted me. "Eshile, have tea with me."

Her darkened eyes signaled me that this was to be a serious conversation. I had questions, yet no idea how to begin. I'd tiptoed around, trying to keep our home free from upset and everyone calm so my mother could heal. And now, while I'd lost control of my emotions in church, of all places, I didn't want to upset Umama more than I already had.

She kept her back to me while filling the teapot, setting it on the burner, and removing two mugs from the shelf. I glanced around, hoping to find a clue of what was about to happen. Should I sit or stand? Nothing seemed the right thing to do. Then I spied the trail of breakfast milk stretching from our refrigerator to Onele's chair, so I reached for the damp rag hanging over the waterspout.

"Leave it, Eshile. Our talk is more important."

Umama's eyes used to sparkle for several hours following each church service, sometimes late into the night. She claimed it was God's joy bubbling inside her. That look had returned when she sang along with the choir that morning, but now her eyes were dull and hooded. She poured the boiling water over the rooibos tea bags and sat, resting her elbows on the eating table, her head in her hands, and stared into her cup. I slipped into the chair beside her and drizzled a spoon of honey into my cup.

Umama turned from her untasted tea. "Eshile, I've never felt so alone as when selecting your father's coffin. I ran my hand along each display in search of the smoothest of all those made of golden wood, then squeezed the padding inside each, wanting him to be as comfortable as I could afford. I did the best I could."

My mother's sunken eye sockets and downturned lips had me wondering why our ancestors were not at her side to guide and comfort her while she made this difficult choice. Had they lost their way?

"The coffin was perfect. I'm sure he's comfortable. Umama, now I'm worried about you. Are you okay?"

"I will be. But for now, I can't sleep." My mother reached up and caressed my cheek. "And you? You were the closest to your father, his strongest ally—recognizing the best in him, testifying to his qualities when others failed to see what you saw. My concern is you are not as strong as you pretend to be. Grief cannot be hidden forever. It eats from the inside out. You must release it, let your mind and body heal."

"He visits my dreams, wearing that flowered shirt you wanted him to throw away."

"And what does he say?"

I hesitated to speak, worried she might misunderstand and think Ubaba considered her weak.

"Is it private?"

"No, Umama. It's not that. He holds no secrets from you. He tells me I must watch over you, calm and support you because he no longer can."

"Eshile, that burden is not yours to carry. It is *my* job to care for *you*."

A heaviness lifted from my soul. We would care for each other, and my sisters too.

"He visits me also, Eshile. Please tell your father that his coming comforts me. It's the other dream…."

"What other dream, Umama?"

"The same every night. I can't fall back asleep." Umama sipped her tea. "I walk among many rows of coffins without touching them. *Okubi*, evil, waits in their shadows. When I reach the last row, it moves, bends and curves, reshapes into a labyrinth. I am trapped, never to find my way out."

"What does it mean?"

"An ancestor, I don't know who because they haven't yet revealed themselves, tells me I am lost, that I have strayed from the path that leads home."

"But Umama, isn't this our home?"

"We thought that was true, Eshile, but I sense it may not be so."

"I love it here. Ubaba did too. Look at our house—even nicer than the rental Hulu and Umkhulu moved into after the government took the Emporium from them. We'd never have such a house in Soweto."

"Your father believed he delivered us to paradise. Yet in last night's dream, he had much to reveal. When finished, he splayed his hands toward me, palms up, as if in apology, then faded into the clouds saying, *Ngenze iphutha*, over and over, softer and softer, until I could see him no more."

"But we can't be sure why he's sorry or what he regrets. He shook off his bad luck and brought us here to improve our lives." I felt ashamed of the whining in my tone. A million reasons to stay raced through my mind. Was Ilanga not our home? If we had never come here, would my father still be alive? But what if this unrevealed ancestor was right?

"Our family was whole while Ubaba lived." Umama pressed her fist against her chest and slid it down her ribcage. "But now, my heart is shattered. I am broken inside."

My father had deemed me responsible for this woman sitting across from me. She'd never been so fragile. Was I selfish in begging to live in Ilanga? Was I thinking purely of myself? Or was my thinking correct? It seemed too dangerous for us to go back to Soweto. I dreaded returning to the constant fear of police action intent on breaking apart my mixed-race family. I felt torn. We experienced no such threat here in Ilanga, yet I sensed darkness lurking. Or was my foreboding a lack of confidence that I could live up to my father's desires?

"Eshile, your grandfather had a stroke. Grace said Hulu didn't write of it because she feared we would leave all we had found here. But now she worries his life is at its end, that he might die without seeing us again. I hadn't realized how much I missed my family until I saw my sister in the car park and felt her arms around me. Now, my emotions are raw—as if my heart has ripped wide open. My body craves their healing strength."

I missed them too, but not the agony of my belly craving food. "It will be even harder now, Umama. Hulu can't help as much as she did before."

My mother quit fidgeting with her teacup and stared at our refrigerator. It was small, the same height as Onele. Yet I experienced wonderment and the warmth of gratitude each time I opened its door because we never had a refrigerator of our own in Soweto.

The worry on my mother's face told me she shared my fear, so I added a point that I thought she could not deny. "We can't leave Ubaba here alone."

"Your dad was an exceptional man, loyal and kind. You girls were more precious to him than a mountain of gold. The ancestors say if you are a good person, your grave is loved even after death."

"But Umama, we won't be here to sweep his grave or bring flowers to remind him how much we love and miss him." As those words spilled out of my mouth, I knew I should have held them inside.

"His spirit follows us. Last night, your father urged me to go."

My heart sank. As much as I longed to live here, I could argue no more. Umama was speaking the truth. My father had told me that his worry would be great if we did not return to the family. I had prayed he'd change his mind, but at this instant, my hopes seeped away, only to be replaced with pain.

"Your father wants us to live near your grandfather. He claims it no longer matters that they never saw things the same."

"But Asanda says she'll never leave Leo."

"In many ways, your sister is a woman, but she is still my child."

My thoughts swirled in foolish contemplation of declaring I wouldn't leave either, only I'd use the excuse of remaining with Ubaba. But I didn't need to wait for another dream to know how disappointed my father would be if I denied his request to return my mother to her parents.

Onele was young enough that if I told her I was excited to return to Soweto, she'd follow my lead, making it the biggest lie I would ever tell. I realized I would need to be so convincing that even Asanda would come in peace, for our mother. A chuckle gurgled up my throat. I'd need divine intervention to pull that off.

Since the Lord and I were no longer on speaking terms, I walked to the sink and finished washing our breakfast dishes. *Great-Grandmother Haile, Auntie Nofoto, even you Uncle Sammy, I need your help.*

CHAPTER TEN

Dead Butterflies

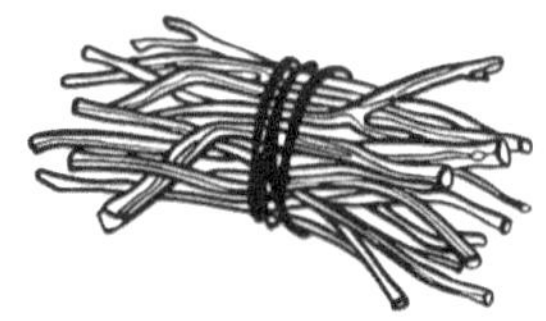

EyeSilimela (Month of the Pleiades) June 1974

I worried we'd pack up and move immediately. Yet two months later, as if we were stuck in time, we were still at Ilanga. I didn't ask, didn't speak of it. I carried a dark foreboding that if I did, the clock of change would begin to tick, and it would be my fault we had to leave.

We fell back into our routine, yet nothing was the same. Umama's eyes no longer sparkled when her daughters entered the room. Eternal tears filled her eyes.

Onele, at ten years old, proud to be called big girl instead of baby sister, started sucking her thumb again. When she saw me watching, the shame on her face hurt me so much I turned away.

Asanda quit assisting Dr. Vorster. Maybe she couldn't face him. Did she resent that he lived when Ubaba died? Or perhaps it was he who couldn't meet her eye. Did he feel guilty for putting our father in harm's way? She had been excited about transcribing his notes, thought the experience might increase her chances of getting into a university. Now, rather than calling out, "I'll be back for dinner after I do my work," she sneaked out to meet Leo. That suited me just fine. I lacked the energy and patience to deal with her snapping at me each time I nagged her to stop.

Acting normal at school was harder to carry off each day. I struggled to pay attention. My pencil weighed a ton. I focused on lifting it, then pressed it against the paper, unable to remember the important point Miss Yeboah said to write in our study notes. When another student spoke to me, I tensed like a string pulled too tight, ready to snap. Only Kalisha seemed to understand, making her voice softer, wrapping each word in cotton so it would do no harm.

Even Anthony changed. When I left my sweater draped over my chair, he ran after me and delivered it with the greatest care. Had to give him credit. He bowed like a gentleman. Once again, I felt a warmth similar to when Onele says she loves me.

I had no heart for writing articles for either the school or underground newspaper. And while I considered documenting my feelings and observations in my journal, instead I quit writing altogether. Rehashing the sadness overwhelmed me night after night. Besides, I wasn't the only one who was sad. My family talked less. Our tradition of playing cards or games before we went to bed seemed to be forgotten by all.

Yet, in a strange way, the silence comforted me, pulling my thoughts away from my family's grief, into the past, to a memory that helped me understand the turmoil my older sister was experiencing.

Last year, a mangy cat with matted fur and an infected leg climbed onto the big kitchen porch. We valued our feral cats' skills at keeping rodents off the premises, but this one, Rosie nursed to health and kept as her own. She said this cat was special, that its almond-shaped eyes, silky fur, and tufts between its toes meant it had descended from the Somali breed. That's how Miss Anna Belle became the only cat in Ilanga's history to sleep inside the women's dormitory.

Then, on a chilly June morning, the first month of winter, I found two kittens, so new to the world their eyes hadn't opened. Huddled tightly in a mass of motley fur, I assumed they were one until I scooped them out from under the bush beside the employee's laundry shack. When I carried them to Rosie, she explained their mother, a wiry gray cat with white paws, must have strayed too far. This was not a rare occurrence at the lodge.

Miss Anna Belle, once as wild as the other feral cats, now seemed to know she had a good home, and to secure her place, accommodated Rosie's every request. When Rosie placed the pair of gray feral babies in the woven basket that used to hold Rosie's shoes, next to Miss Anna Belle's litter of four, she snuggled them to her teats and licked their heads as if they were her own.

Auntie Grace claimed lessons hid in everyday life. I thought there might be one in this. Perhaps a warning of potential danger if, like those kittens' mother, my family strayed outside of Ilanga's borders? Or was it possible that an unseen force lurked in the dark? Watching, waiting to lure Asanda away from us—something with the power to separate us forever? Did my older sister experience a premonition, a message warning of danger that could be avoided only if she remained behind?

Or maybe Asanda wanted what Miss Anna Belle found at Ilanga; a place where she felt safe and the possibility of a home among people who were like her. Rosie said that whatever had happened to Miss Anna Belle left her with no home, no family. But Asanda had a family. Wherever our mother settled, that would become our home. Yet, if Umama chose Soweto, I couldn't see how my older sister would find people who cared for her like the Vorsters did, almost as if they were another set of relatives.

It was a lot to think about.

The following Saturday, Umama and I stood side by side, trying to duplicate Auntie Grace's *potjiekos*. Success depended on me. I had helped her every weekend in Soweto, so I was the keeper of the recipe. A voice inside me nagged, *You've forgotten something.*

Auntie Grace cooked on an open fire. We cooked on our indoor stove because Ilanga's owner didn't allow outdoor cooking near the rondavels' thatched roofs. We could have walked to the men's and women's dormitories where employees roasted meat and heated potjie pots over open firepits, but dragging our supplies and ingredients required too much effort. Then there was the difference I couldn't fix. Auntie Grace used chicken or pig instead of warthog.

The cooks had leftover warthog meat after feeding the lodge's guests, so it was up to the employees not to let it go to waste. On safari, guests watched warthogs on their calloused knees, rooting for tender shoots of grass. Many, repulsed by the horns that curl from these animals' mouths, refused to taste this ugly creature. Equally unappealing were the four hairy bumps on their faces, like more horns in the making. They snorted and squealed to warn the jeeps to keep their distance, so tourists feared warthogs rather than the animal they should—the hippo.

Ubaba had cautioned that the hippo was a killing machine, killed more people than any other mammal in Africa. Still, tourists cooed as if hippos were life-sized stuffed toys. The information my father held back was that while these enormous creatures appeared to be ignoring the entire safari, if the jeep's closeness offended them, the hippos would likely run full speed, up to thirty kilometers per hour, and ram the jeeps.

Deep in my thoughts, I realized neither Umama nor I had spoken since we selected the ingredients for this potjiekos. I pounded the meat with a saucer edge to tenderize it, sliced it into hunks, and spread them across the bottom of our pan. Atop the warthog, I layered carrots, cabbage, and cauliflower, then smacked my forehead. "Pumpkin. We don't have pumpkin. This potjiekos won't be as sweet as Auntie Grace's."

Umama chuckled. Focused on the forgotten ingredient, I realized she had spoken before I did and was waiting to hear my answer. "What did you say?"

"You are far away. I asked, where is your sister?"

It was unnecessary for her to identify which sister. We knew which one was always gone. Still, a shred of loyalty lurked in my nature, so I shrugged.

"We must have a family talk. And I want her home to eat with us."

Asanda would be at her usual place for this time of day. Onele and I used to sneak up to watch her kiss Leo. The first time we stumbled upon them, Onele was so repulsed, I thought Asanda might hear her gag. But since neither she nor Leo looked up, we used them as our entertainment for weeks.

After we lost interest, we walked heavy-footed, our best attempt to sound like adults approaching. When I tried imitating Baas John's voice, that also failed. Asanda simply shouted, "That's enough. You don't want me coming over there."

I wasn't afraid. I could pulverize her skinny butt, but Onele squealed and ran.

The next morning, after visiting the watering hole, my sister and I were restless and bored, so we dreamed up new mischief. I snuck the honey jar and rubbed the sticky goo into the large rock on which Asanda and Leo sat during their rendezvous. Before they got far into their first mushy kiss, Asanda sprung up and slapped her legs. The itty-bitty nibbles of sugar ants hardly hurt, yet the attack caused the panic we envisioned.

I clamped my palm over Onele's mouth when she snorted. Leo and Asanda, swiping their arms and legs furiously, moved to another rock, then got back at it. Just watching their antics made my legs itch. Then, we barely contained our laughter when, mid-kiss, they slapped themselves repeatedly. But the moment Leo slid his hand under Asanda's blouse, I led Onele from the scene of things she didn't need to see at only ten years of age.

The heat of Umama's glare pulled me from my thoughts. She stood with her hand on her hip, waiting for me to respond. I dreaded chasing after my sister, so I mumbled, "I'll find her in a minute."

Bubbles rose and danced at the edges of the cast iron potjie pot. To compensate for the missing pumpkin, I added a heaping teaspoon of *dukkah*, the nutty spice mix that was a gift from Ilanga's Egyptian cook. As it dissolved, the popping bubbles released the spice's smoky, earthy scents blended with a hint of something that smelled similar to the black licorice ole George kept in a tall glass jar at his store.

Umama, struck by a severe headache for the second time since my father's death, leaned against the doorjamb. I wanted to help her but did not know what to offer. I watched helplessly as she staggered to her room. Sweat beaded on my upper lip. I opened the kitchen window to let the heat escape, then stretched my neck, peeking out to see Onele shake the bushes.

"Come, lovely butterflies. I brought sweets for you." My little sister skipped away as I stepped out onto the pathway.

"Onele, come with me. Umama wants big sister home for dinner."

Onele scowled. I smirked as she wound up for a protest because I knew how to stop that. "Your favorite butterflies, the ones with blue patches on their wings, are flying toward the honey rock."

"No, they're not. You can't trick me. They like flowers, not honey. Anyway, I'm sick of watching Asanda and Leo slobber each other up. I want to go where the purple flowers grow." Onele threw herself into a full-force Eeyore imitation. While less effective than when she was five, her droopy eyes and frowny lips still pulled at my heart.

"Tomorrow. I promise. For now, it's important to Umama that Asanda comes home."

Onele's bottom lip swelled to the size of a gigantic cheese puff. I considered saying, *Stop pouting. You're not a baby anymore.* But she'd throw herself on the ground and make me drag her. So, I applied a logic even a ten-year-old should buy.

"Imagine how you'd suffer if a little girl who wasn't aware of how much you love your family trapped you in a canning jar."

Onele's expression changed from pouty to pure shame. I felt so bad,

I changed my approach. "Wouldn't you rather have marula jam in that jar?" Since she didn't respond, I assumed thoughts of our mother's sweet homemade jam did not sway her, so I replicated Umama's evil eye. "The Lord said, thou shall not kill."

Onele's eyes grew as wide as a green tree frog's and her voice became defiant. "The butterflies will die? I want them to live. See, I put leaves and flowers in the jar."

Worried about Umama waking from her nap before I brought Asanda home, I implemented our Bible school teacher's favored method of scaring students into compliance. "Remember the book of Deuteronomy? Curses fall upon those who disobey."

Onele's chin quivered. "I'll have marula jam."

"Excellent choice. First, let's go see if we can pry your sister's lips off that poor boy."

This time, we made no attempt to sneak up. As we stepped through the opening, Onele's giggles made me feel less mean, but startled the young lovers.

Asanda scowled. "What do you want, you stinking spies?"

Disturbing her kiss-fest tickled me so much I could hardly keep the gloating out of my voice. "Umama wants you home. Important family meeting."

Leo stretched out his arm, not releasing her hand until the last possible moment, then watched until Asanda stormed past the large crane flower bush and down the path. Onele and I followed, snickering and imitating the angry way she walked.

Inside our rondavel, the air hung heavy, as if nobody was there. I put my finger to my lips, "Shh. Umama must still be asleep," and motioned for us to go into the kitchen.

Without being told, Asanda opened the cupboard and removed four plates. My jaw nearly dropped to my chest. I started to crack a voodoo magic joke, then checked on the potjiekos instead of being mean. When I raised the lid, steam rose, giving the appearance that the pot of warthog had been full of rain clouds. My sisters sniffed, then grinned. They wouldn't miss the pumpkin.

Onele loved pretending she was the mother. She folded the paper napkins in perfect triangles and placed forks and spoons on top and a drinking glass on the opposite side. Then she repositioned Asanda's plates to the exact center of her arrangement. "Should I wake Umama?"

Our drowsy mother braced herself against the doorjamb. "I'm awake and feeling better. What thoughtful girls you are to cook for me."

I filled four bowls and set them on the table. After each bite, I snuck sideways glances at our mother. We lived in a house with real walls and running water—a stove, refrigerator, toilet of our own. What was Umama thinking? We couldn't leave Illana.

I was the only one aware of why she wanted to talk to us. If only I had warned my sisters, explained what was at risk, we could have worked as a united front. By presenting a calm, rational argument, the three of us might persuade Umama to remain in Ilanga. Stupid me. I should have prepared my sisters to work with me on this.

We sat so quietly waiting for our mother to speak that I heard the leaves rustle and roaches scamper on the path outside our door until phantom gunshots and blaring radios pushed to the forefront of my mind, reminding me of our Soweto neighborhood.

More reasons to stay in Ilanga.

Then there was Kalisha. I couldn't leave my new best friend. But a wave of guilt surprised me. Bini and I had blood-pledged we'd be best friends for life, regardless of how far away I ended up. I tried to convince myself that surely, she had a new best friend. After all, two years had passed. No matter how I set my mind on that, my heart knew it wasn't true. If I were gone a hundred years, Bini's loyalty wouldn't change. Mine shouldn't either.

I gulped a gristly bite of warthog. It roiled back up. I jumped and knocked my chair backward. In the bathroom, I splashed cold water on my face, then plastered a damp washcloth against my forehead. When I returned, Umama placed her hand on my neck. "No fever. Are you ill?"

"No, Umama. Mr. Warthog caught in my throat." Onele chuckled at my use of her nickname for our dinner meat. The mood lightened—until Umama brought it down again.

"Girls, I need to tell you something serious. Eshile already knows what your father told me in a dream, but we must discuss it as a family."

Asanda shot me her *you've-been-sucking-up-again* look. Onele smashed a gravy-covered potato with her fork as if oblivious to the tension in the air.

"Your father believes it best that we live in Soweto. He's strong about it. He assures me we must make our family whole, as whole as we can, now that he is gone."

I cringed when Asanda replied, "I am *not* going. Leo and I love each other."

Rosie had told me that the heart is like a goat that has to be tied up. I assumed that meant an untethered heart runs away. I chuckled imagining Umama tying Asanda to a tree. Probably wouldn't work. Leo seemed as in love with my sister as she was with him. He'd just find her and cut her loose. At that point, I was thinking I could use these words to write an American country western song when my mother's killer-eyebrow rose to an extraordinary height.

"*Uziembela emoyeni.* Asanda, you light a fire in the wind. Be careful, daughter. The ancestors frown on those who favor strangers over family."

Onele and I knew better than to defy Umama. Not that we were perfect angels. But if we disobeyed, we snuck about until caught, then spewed forth a litany of pre-prepared excuses and requests for forgiveness, followed by promises to never let it happen again. While we politely expressed our differences on important items, we were smart enough not to flat-out say *no* to our mother.

Onele clanked her fork against the table. "Please, Umama. I can't leave the butterflies. They need me. The Lord doesn't want them to die."

My father's unearthly presence bore down on me, making clear it was my responsibility to ascend to the role he and Great-Grandmother Haile expected of me. I patted Onele's shoulder. "Everything your butterflies need grows wild. They'll be fine."

"But Eshile, Kuhle hasn't had her new calf yet. We can't leave her when she might need our help."

"Kuhle birthed plenty of babies before we moved here. Dr. Vorster will care for her if she has problems."

"But our house is so pretty," whined Onele.

"Girls, rondavels are for men with families. Now that your father is gone, the owner requires that I move into the women's dormitory."

This new information from my mother caused me to backslide in my resolve. "I wouldn't mind living with Rosie."

Asanda's face brightened. "I'm fine living in the dorms."

My mother shook her head. "No children allowed, so that's out of the question."

Onele twisted her face into an expression of extreme pain, then stomped her foot. "Not fair, Umama. You work as hard as a man, harder than Mr. Okoro—grinning and scratching—when he's supposed to be cleaning the jeeps and vans."

"Yes, but his wife cleans guestrooms. They both work. Baas John requested an exception for us. The owner graciously granted permission to stay until the end of the year, but only until then."

"Is the owner aware I have a job? Tell him I'll feed the vultures for free if he lets us stay."

"Eshile, I admire how you smooth my path and stand by me at every turn. I appreciate that you make my life easier by doing more than your share. However, moving is out of our control. I thought you agreed?"

"Sorry, Umama. It's just that Soweto smells of *kak*. Rubbish every-where. Hauling water from the hydrant. We struggled so. Here we have real walls, not slats of wood and plastic. Remember when Baas John first showed us this wonderful home? Remember how grateful we were to sleep in beds?"

Onele stood and stomped her foot repeatedly. "I'm bringing my bed."

Umama chuckled. "Sorry, baby girl. This furniture belongs to the lodge. But I promise, never again will you sleep on a dirt floor. We'll buy beds."

"How, Umama? We barely had enough to eat in Soweto. You and Ubaba did your best. Still, we might have starved if not for the food Hulu snuck out of her kitchen and the chicken feet from the women who employed you."

"Eshile, you knew that? Oh, my, you were so young, I didn't realize. Our lives will be different this time."

"How?"

"Dr. Vorster recognized the danger he put your father in when he requested his promotion to driver, True, he had thought harm might come from the animals he treated, unpredictable in the wild, doubly dangerous when afraid and ill. So, he bought insurance for your father. Who could have predicted that a poacher would kill your father?"

Onele used her finger to wipe up the last bit of warthog gravy. "What's insurance?"

"Money, Onele. Money to help us survive without your father. Five thousand rand."

"Is that enough to buy a bed?"

"And a house to put it in."

"Our own house?"

"Small, but yes, a home of our own. You girls will share a bedroom, same as here."

Onele beamed, and my lips turned up despite my efforts to keep them turned down.

Asanda snarled, "I'm still *not* going."

∿

The next morning, I dangled my feet over the edge of my bunk, mentally saying goodbye to the curtains that hung over the window and the only closet I'd ever had to hold my things.

Umama shouted, "Girls, have you seen my pass?"

I leaned over the side. When Onele shrugged, I answered, "No, ma'am, we have not." Umama didn't seem to notice she received no response from Asanda, who had slipped out half an hour earlier.

The first few times Umama traveled off the Ilanga compound, she carried her pass. Since nobody demanded to see it, she stored it in her underwear drawer. But now her voice was frantic. "Help me, girls!"

I dashed into her room. Onele scurried past and crashed into the foot of the bed, knocking off the stack of Ubaba's belongings waiting for Baas John to collect and distribute to other employees. As I picked them up, I reached into a small pile of shirts, half expecting to feel my father's warmth, but the cloth was cool to my touch. Empty dresser drawers hung open. Umama's dresses, pagnes, and blouses looked like they had flown out of the closet and landed haphazardly on the bed. Her shoes had been tossed across the room. When she slumped to the floor, covering her eyes by cradling her face with her hands, I signaled Onele to start cleaning up the mess.

My sister wrinkled her cute pug nose and screwed her lips into a snarl. She was wound up, ready to protest. I shot her my *don't-you-dare* glare, and fortunately, she decided against throwing a fit. Frowning and mumbling under her breath, Onele picked up a red long-sleeved blouse made of silky fabric. No matter how she folded it, the rows of ruffled fabric slid this way, then that. When she placed it in Umama's top drawer, it looked as if she had wadded it in her fists.

Umama appeared dazed and seemed to have forgotten my sister and I were in the room. One by one, I lifted her pagnes hoping the pass would fall out. The yellow, black, and orange geometric print was her favorite. She wore it more than the other two, but nothing hid in its folds. After a thorough check, I hung each over a metal hanger, careful not to make wrinkles, all the while keeping an eye on Umama.

She startled when I spoke. "It's not here. Did you take it with you to Sunday services?"

"No. It has to be here. Where else could it be? What can happen next?" Umama scanned the bedroom. "Where's Asanda?"

Onele and I flapped the bedclothes, vigorously as if we thought the pass book might fly out.

"Don't know, Umama."

"Yes, you do, Eshile. She's with Leo, isn't she? Why you cover for her is a mystery."

"I'll look in the kitchen."

"No need. Neither your sister nor my pass book are there."

"Did anyone check the sofa cushions?" I headed to the living room, bent on dodging more questions, lifted the cushions and tunneled past the springs as if searching for buried treasure hidden in the inner workings of the sofa. Asanda walked in, tucking her rumpled blouse into her waistband. I was almost fourteen, and from watching Leo and my sister on the honey rock, I had an idea of how saying goodbye could be messy business.

I waited for Umama to ask what happened to Asanda's blouse. Instead, she said, "Stay here, girls. I must tell Baas John my pass is missing. It may be necessary to postpone our return to Soweto."

"I know where it is." My grinning elder sister headed to our bedroom.

I was speechless. Had Asanda not heard Umama? The pass book's disappearance would delay moving back to Soweto. Why didn't Asanda leave it be?

She returned holding a wrinkled paper sack and tossed it at our younger sister. Instead of catching it, Onele lowered her head, let the sack hit her body, and slid to the floor. Then she nudged it away with her toes. "That's not mine."

Umama's left eyebrow rose like a cobra preparing to strike.

After sneaking a sideways look at our mother's reddening face, Onele bent down, picked up the bag, and removed our mother's polished bone comb, a birthday gift from her brother, our Uncle Sammy. The second item she brought out was a small gold-colored metal tube.

Umama seized her worn-to-the-rim Berry Bon Bon lipstick from Onele. "What else have you got in there?"

Once again, Onele reached inside the bag and pulled out a pink brassiere.

Umama whipped it from her hands and dangled the threadbare bra by one strap. "What are you doing with these things?"

"Becoming a woman."

"What else did you take?"

Onele shrugged as though she had no idea what might be left in the sack, then dug to the bottom. Fumbling and twitching nervously, she revealed the yellowed pass book.

Umama snatched her pass from Onele. "Young lady, I have a few things to say to you."

CHAPTER ELEVEN

Monkey Trouble

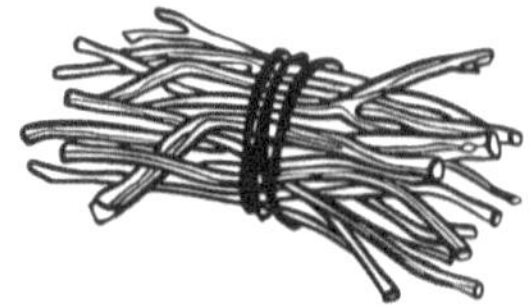

EyoMnga (Month of the Acacia Thorn Tree) December 1974

Our stay at Ilanga was coming to an end, and so was our mother's patience. Neither Onele nor I wished to tell Umama we'd been unsuccessful at doing what she told us to do. *Find Asanda.* This wouldn't go well for us.

We peered between trees and down every path, then made a second loop around the pool as a swim-suited tourist guzzled a can of beer, "I've seen hippos, wild dogs, giraffes, even lions, but no monkeys. Thought this place was famous for 'em."

Onele and I kept on walking until we reached our favorite perch above the watering hole. A guest had fallen ill that morning, and Umama had slipped me the unused sack lunch provided to those who go on daylong safaris. We devoured every bit of food except the banana (now too bruised and mushy) and a plastic-wrapped sausage we knew from experience tasted like a peppered licorice stick dipped in motor oil.

I stared at the banana's brown spots. Two short years ago, I would have relished any piece of fruit, no matter what its condition. Since our move to Ilanga, we never went to bed hungry and strutted around, proud of our firm, round tummies. Except for Asanda. She said White men preferred their women thin.

We returned the mushy banana and oily sausage to the sack, then resumed our search for our older sister. I stopped to consider one of the many posted signs. *Please don't feed the monkeys.*

We were leaving. How much trouble could we get in for breaking one measly rule? Our guest hadn't said he wanted to *feed* the monkeys. He only asked to see them. This I could fix. I justified the action I was about to take by replaying Baas John's instructions in my head. *"Our jobs are to ensure that our guests' every request is provided with a smile."*

"Onele, let's make his wish come true."

"Whose wish?"

"You heard the man by the pool. He wants to see monkeys." I held up the sack holding the banana and sausages.

"We'll get in trouble."

"Not if we're gone before anybody finds out."

Onele grinned. "Let's do it."

We strolled the path as though we were innocents, not a devious thought between us. Past the kitchen and the possibility of Umama's hawk-eyes, past the turnoff where Ubaba had gassed up the jeeps for safaris, then past Arno and Jabu still engaged in the beetle wars. We turned down a broad trail lined with raffia palms, then crept up the wooden steps to the more costly guestrooms.

These second-floor rooms opened onto a spacious balcony overlooking the swimming pool. Below us, the man who wished for monkeys stood in the pool's shallow end and chugged another beer. A light rain sprinkled the guests, but the day was warm. Nobody left. They lounged on thickly padded chairs or gathered in the shade of thatched grass umbrellas. Rain-covered leaves glistened as if coated with silver.

To our right, were six wood-framed glass doors. I expected the guests to be out of their rooms by now. In Baas John's orientation, he asked visitors to close their doors when they left to avoid invasions of tsetse flies, mosquitos, or wild monkeys. Surprisingly, several doors remained wide open.

Onele's expression told me she wondered if the risk was too great. I had the same thought, yet nudged my sister forward as my mouth overruled my brain. "Keep going."

We paused at the first open door. I stretched around the corner like a long-necked giraffe. The room appeared empty. We felt emboldened until we heard a drawer slam shut inside. I jerked back. We waited seconds, then peeked in again. The lights were off, nobody in sight.

I pointed to the far end of the balcony. "Let's hide behind those chairs." Onele ran so fast her feet were a blur. The paper sack rustled as I retrieved the banana, broke it in half, and spread its two parts on the rail. We scrambled behind a large bamboo guest chair. Then I dug into the sack again and handed her the sausage. "Rip the plastic."

A monkey walked the length of a tree branch. With each bouncy step, the limb sank from his weight until it touched the porch rail.

Onele grimaced when the plastic ripped between her teeth and the oily sausage seeped onto her lips. "A velvet monkey."

"Not velvet, baby sister. Vervet." I understood why she made this mistake. His long silver-gray hair appeared as soft as velvet, an invitation to reach out and touch, but he'd never allow that. He stretched his neck and sniffed. When the monkey caught a glimpse of us, he backed up the branch. But when we didn't shout or wave our arms, he jumped onto the rail.

Rocked back on his haunches, this vervet displayed his bright red penis and his blue *ibhola* sack. Glaring out from under a single, long white eyebrow shaped like a caterpillar hanging on for dear life, he kept his eyes on Onele and me while lifting the banana closest to him as if it had great value.

Caterpillar Brow produced the sharp crack of breaking twigs, the sound these monkeys used to warn off others. He raised the fruit in his spindly fingers and took his first bite. A younger male flew in and hit him in the side. Caterpillar Brow stayed true to the reputation of Vervet Monkeys expressing spite by baring his teeth, then swiftly threw the youngster over the rail.

The smaller vervet shrieked. Pool guests looked up as he crashed, bounced, then dashed away.

"Look! There they are!" The guest who had made the wish clambered out of the pool and punched his friend's biceps. "I just said I wanted to see monkeys."

Two females cozied up beside the remaining banana half. With dainty fingers, the larger female peeled it. The yellow flaps hid her bony hand when she held out the banana. Her friend broke off a piece. Instead of gobbling the way the males did, she nibbled as if having tea and scones.

"Did you see that, Onele?"

"They're sisters." Her sweet answer warmed my heart, turned it into the mush of milk-saturated oatmeal, but before I could hug her, the whisk of a monkey bolting past and into one of the guestrooms and a woman's scream captured my attention.

"I brought those M&M's from home! Come back here right now!"

A wide-eyed vervet, holding a dark brown baggie, peeked out the door. All monkeys are nimble, but this furball deserved a prize. He scampered out clutching the M&M's bag in one hand and stuffing multicolored sweets into his mouth with the other. Close on his tail, the woman's bare feet pounded the wooden balcony. He bounded away from the bath towel she swirled above her head like a helicopter blade. He escaped by leaping up to a branch, ripping off leaves as he climbed. His screech pierced my ears when three monkeys scurried from above him and tried to grab the bag. Then another, larger monkey, dropped from an overhead branch onto the M&M's thief. They scratched and snorted as they thudded only inches from where we hid. The candy bag ripped. Fur flew. A mob of monkeys bombarded the scattered sweets.

The woman dropped her towel and backed into her room.

"I have *soetkoekies* in my pocket," whispered Onele.

"Toss one."

A monkey from high in the rafters dropped like a paratrooper onto Onele's cinnamon sugar biscuit. Three more swung in from the sides. Bits of dry hard biscuit popped into the air and sailed across the balcony floor. As quickly as they appeared, the monkeys jumped onto tree branches, plunged to the ground, or leaped from one railing to another, positioning themselves to snatch the best biscuit crumbs.

Onele stepped out from behind the chair at the same instant a bobbing mass of golden blonde hair emerged from the second room. The woman, her long locks whipping from one side to the other, tracked the monkeys' movements as if watching a tennis match. I grabbed Onele's tee-shirt and yanked her back behind the chair. I thought the blonde saw me and expected her to scold us. Instead, she scurried inside and slammed her door, making the glass rattle as though rammed by a rhino.

The beer-drinking male guest beamed. "Wasn't that great? What a show!"

"Can we go now? Before Baas John catches us?" murmured Onele.

"Not yet. The other door's still open." I pointed to a vervet with a tiny furry bundle clinging to its back. She poked her face over the viewing platform's edge and squeezed her sleek body through the slats. She chattered softly until her moist pink tongue flicked at biscuit crumbs.

A miniature head arose. The fuzzy lump was her infant. It must have been born later than the rest. Its eyes, teensy black marbles, peered curiously from a face the color of a ripe peach.

When Mama Vervet rolled her shoulder, her baby released his grip and slid off. She placed him on the remaining trail of biscuit crumbs, put her thin lips close, and flicked her tongue without touching the tasty morsels. The frail replica batted his tiny eyelashes as if to signal his understanding of his mother's message. Teats swollen and raw, Mama hovered protectively to watch Baby Vervet eat. After licking up every last crumb, he climbed aboard Mama's back, and they sprang to the rafter above our heads. Onele stretched on tiptoes and offered the sausage. Mama wrapped her fingers around the greasy tube and sniffed. But after a quick taste, she handed it back to my sister.

"She doesn't like it either."

"Give her your last biscuit," I suggested.

Mama Vervet took the treat from Onele's fingers, then dove to the porch floor with Baby still clinging to her back. She broke the biscuit, then laid the pieces in a row. Her baby walked the line, much like hungry tourists at the lunch buffet. We sat silently until the last crumb was in his elfin mouth, and he climbed on Mama Vervet's back.

Onele whispered, "She let him have every bite. She's the best mother in the entire monkey world."

I nodded. "Not often a person gets to see something as marvelous as that."

After Mama and Baby bounded onto the branch of an acacia tree, Onele and I scurried down the steps. On the way home, we laughed and congratulated ourselves for not getting caught.

Our front door creaked when I opened it. Someone in the kitchen blew their nose. We walked in on Umama wiping her eyes with her apron corner.

"What's wrong, Umama?" I asked gently, afraid of what she might answer.

"Rosie's throwing us a party."

Saying Goodbye

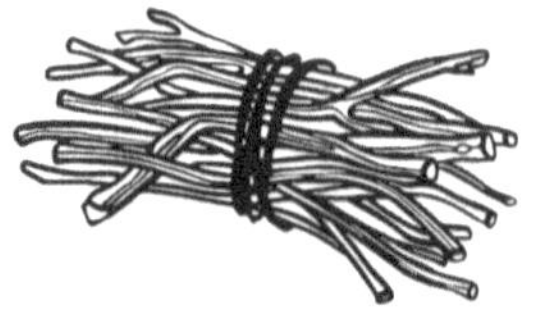

Two weeks later in *EyoMnga* (Month of the
Acacia Thorn Tree) December 1974

Through the open window drifted a distant roar, not loud and enraged, but muted and satisfied as though the lion's belly was full. I loved that peaceful time while everyone slept. I enjoyed the sense that I was the lone human hearing the midnight buzz of cicadas and trill of pointy-eared caracals in harmony with other midnight creatures. But that night, I found no peace. I conjured the gleam of long canine teeth as if the lion posed a threat to me—or my family. I pinched my eyes closed, but they wouldn't stay shut. My muscles twitched and my skin itched like I was under attack by fire ants.

The events responsible for our leaving Ilanga played in my brain. I struggled to recall every detail, from the moment I saw Baas John's van at school, Asanda and Onele in the rear seat, then Umama begging my father, "*Hayi, Hayi.* No, no, don't go."

I remembered holding my father's cold, limp hand and picking dried blood from where the IV needle pierced his skin. My mother's cries, "Help! We need help!" sent chills down my spine.

Metal wheels had clanged as the doctor and nurses ran into the room, their lab coats flapping madly against their legs. Someone shoved me outside the white curtain that encircled the hospital bed. As if it was happening again, I felt a hand on my upper arm, ushering me from my father's bedside, into the hall. My sisters and I cowered as a deathly quiet settled in.

I massaged my temples, thinking that might still my thoughts. Instead, every funeral detail came alive. The rope slipping from the men's hands and the coffin crashing to the bottom of the dark hole. The tap-pa, tap-pa of dirt hitting the golden wooden box echoed in my ears. Again, I saw Onele crawling to the rim of the grave and peering in. "*Climb out, Ubaba. Please climb out.*" Fear overcame me just as it had back then.

I staggered down my bunk bed ladder. Rosie had left a tin of golden flowers and dried leaves from the *imphepho* plant on our kitchen counter. I dropped a match into the container, blew gently on the flame, then drew the sedating smoke deep into my lungs. Each breath calmed my mind. The voices receded. How had Rosie known exactly what I needed? Once back in my bunk, I fell into a dreamless sleep.

When I awakened, my sisters' beds were empty. The position of the sun told me it was afternoon, explaining why our room was hot and stuffy. Voices drifted from the kitchen. To avoid being noticed, I slunk along the wall, crept into the bathroom, and remained in the shower until the water ran cold.

When I opened the bathroom door, my mother and sisters gazed expectantly at me. In one hand, I held the towel to keep it wrapped around me; with the other, I waved limply. Relieved when nobody spoke, I kept walking toward our bedroom.

I sat on the edge of Onele's bunk until I lost track of time. Then I rose, stood before the closet, and wondered what to wear to an event I'd rather die myself than attend. But by evening, I realized it was only polite for me to act happy that our friend Rosie was throwing a party in our honor. Sadness and a sense of loss are expected at farewell parties, yet shouldn't one also feel excitement about the future? I couldn't muster any of that. But during our walk to the gathering area between the men's and women's dormitories, I was grateful to be among people who cared for me and my family.

Women hovered, flitting like the butterflies Onele caught in Umama's jam jars. The men stayed a few steps aside, watching as though to catch me in case I collapsed. But I wasn't the only person at risk.

Onele, eyes swollen and as glassy as marbles, cowered and tucked Monkey tighter in her armpit when workers tried to hug or offer comfort in their own way. Asanda stood near the *braai* and stared into the flames. Rosie cleaved to Umama's side, leaving my mother only when Baas John shooed her away to tend to those who were preparing food.

Ubaba had many friends in Ilanga, more than I had known. These friends broke from the small clusters they had formed and approached us one by one. They smiled, but sadness darkened their eyes. My heart begged me to cling to these people who had become family. If I could absorb the warmth of the men's kind words and the women's loving hugs, it might have released my pain. Yet my body stiffened, and I pushed away.

Rows of folding tables and chairs circled the *braai*. Rosie cleared a spot on the food table. There she set a large bowl of lily pads. "Breathe in their sweetness, Eshile. Lilies are symbols of separation and rebirth."

I inhaled, slow and deep.

"Good girl. Now exhale. Expel it all. Release your grief to ride the breeze."

Of all the adults in Ilanga, I was closest to Rosie. Her heart was as soft as her plentiful body. For her, caring for others was more important than anything. So, this farewell party was the kind of tribute one could expect of her.

But I sensed Ubaba watching from the sky. What if he saw me laughing, chatting, and thought I had finished mourning him, thought I no longer cared?

Wilson, who always stood by to ensure my safety while I fed the vultures, now lit torches and jabbed their pointed ends into the dirt along the path and in between the tables. Wilson was a serious fellow with a gentle smile, but now, skin reddened by the closeness of the flames, his face brought to mind the horned *usathana*, the devil pictured in my Bible School workbook.

Realizing my mind was running wild, I vigorously shook my head to rid myself of these crazy thoughts.

The men muttered among themselves, then crowded around Umama and nudged Wilson forward. He presented my mother with a gold and black cloth pouch the size of a man's hand, which she sniffed, making me think she expected to find fragrant herbs or remedies. Umama looked at Wilson and cocked her head, waiting for him to reveal what was inside.

He shimmied like a puppy that had brought its owner their favorite slippers. "Open it. *Shesha*. Please hurry."

"*Shesha*. Be quick," echoed Jabu as he and Ubaba's other former beetle-sweeping partner grinned. Arno hopped from one foot to the other.

When Umama shook the cloth bag, its contents clinked and tinkled, the same sound Ubaba made when jingling the coins in his pocket. "What in the world?" Umama loosened the drawstring and peeked in. "*Hayi*, no. I cannot accept this."

The men whooped and danced in place. "*Yebo*, yes, yes. You must. To help with your trip. Your husband did much for us."

Umama dipped into the bag and brought out a handful of nickel-plated coins and two gold rands—one I assumed was from Baas John and the other from his boss.

I wondered if anyone else noticed the moisture collecting in the corner of my mother's eye. Onele tugged on my sleeve and put on her Eeyore face. "Eshile, there're no kids here. Please, let's go home."

"This isn't our home anymore, baby sister."

"Will our new home be as nice as we have here?"

I swayed. My vision darkened. Spots of color popped and fizzled. Our dirty rented shanty floated before me, bringing the stench of rubbish with it. My mind conjured Soweto street children holding up cupped hands; the youngest hung on to my skirt, but I had nothing to give.

Onele tugged again. "Can we go now?"

I rubbed my forehead to clear the dark memories, then pointed at Rosie's nieces, their braids tied with matching ribbons.

Onele jutted her chin. "They made fun of me when I asked them to play."

"Sorry. I should have helped you deal with them a while ago." Neither Onele nor I had the strength to say one more goodbye without bursting into tears, so we stole away from the party.

Except for the streak of moonlight glimmering through the windowpane, our rondavel was dark. We took off our shoes, padded to our room, and slipped into our pajamas. Onele begged me to sleep with her, as I had every night since our father died.

But I was zombie tired, drained from the emotions and kind intentions of the partygoers. I wanted to sleep alone. "I'll be right above you."

Her voice quivered. "Eshile, I'm afraid you'll leave me too."

I sighed, snuggled up to her, and mumbled, "I won't leave you."

Onele still had a stranglehold on my neck when Asanda's shouts blasted in from the living room. "Unfair! I hate you!"

Umama's voice was stern, but calm. "Sit, young lady."

Asanda threw herself down on the sofa with such anger that the cushions made a farting sound we could hear from our bunk. "I'm staying here."

"*No.* You are *not.*"

I peeled Onele's grip from around my neck, amazed she didn't awaken, and crept to our half-open door. Asanda had locked her arms across her chest.

Umama towered over her. "A family is a tree whose branches bend but do not break. Daughter, you shall not break us apart. Especially now, at this most trying time, we will remain whole and strong."

Asanda rose and glared eye to eye with Umama. "Leo will come to Soweto for me. You'll never see me again." My sister stormed out, slamming the door, leaving the wall quaking in her wake.

Umama turned her fiery snarl on me. "Bring me your sister."

I showed Umama my *do-I-have-to* face. The look she shot back told me I'd better get going or pay the consequences.

As I walked the gravel path, barefooted and in my pajamas, I thought about how I'd miss my sister if she married Leo. It wouldn't be the same as losing Ubaba because Asanda could come to Soweto for holidays. Besides that, I liked the idea of returning to Ilanga to visit her.

But was I failing Ubaba by not stopping her? He knew his girls would marry, talked of the many grandsons we would give him, compensation for the son Umama never had. Maybe he expected me to convince Asanda to marry a Soweto boy, so she'd remain near our mother. Surely, he remembered I had rarely, if ever, convinced Asanda to do anything. My chances of becoming Africa's prime minister and having thousands of adoring followers at my feet were greater than getting my sister to take orders from me.

But that didn't lessen my thoughts of rising to the rank of eldest daughter and enjoying the privileges of that position as I followed the lighted path, past the turnoff to the employee laundry. I was ready to have Umama treat me like an adult and rely on me for advice and support. Then it dawned on me—I was walking too slow. Much time had passed since she sent me to find Asanda. If I failed, I'd be the target of my mother's next yelling bout.

I hurried to the rock where Leo and Asanda hung out to neck. Clouds blocked the moonlight, but when she flipped her apricot hair, I noticed her. "Good, you're alone. Umama wants you. *Immediately.*"

"Beat it. I'm waiting for Leo."

"You're insane. I'm not taking the blame for you sitting there on your bony *impundu*." I plunked myself on a fallen tree branch. "Umama will rip your head off if she has to come after you herself."

"Mama's girl." The heat of Asanda's scowl baked my bare neck.

I ignored her by studying the flowers and shrubs as if they were more interesting until a rosy-faced lovebird poked out of a crevasse between two thick tree limbs. "Hello, little bird. Did you know the Lord commands children to obey their parents?"

The lovebird fluttered his chartreuse wings and responded with a high-pitched chirp.

"You are a smart bird, my friend. And you're quite right. Our Lord says this pleases Him."

"*Teef!*"

That was not the first time my sister called me bitch. I wore the title as a badge of honor. Having kept tally since she started sneaking off with Leo, the current total was twenty-two. I leapt off the fallen branch and followed her, smirking the entire way because I planned to bask in the praise I'd get for bringing her home.

Once inside our front door, Umama grabbed Asanda and shoved her into a chair. "Leave us, Eshile."

I had a good idea of what might happen next, so I headed to our bedroom. Onele didn't even stir when my foot slipped and rattled the ladder.

Asanda's voice rose to a pitch. She begged, pleaded, threatened. In many ways, I was naïve, but I prided myself on understanding the emotions a woman experiences when separated from the man she loves. Miss Yeboah's brother had sent her a novel from America titled, *A Girl of the Limberlost.* The pages were graying and frayed. That didn't matter to me. I loved the book.

Miss Yeboah loaned it to me for an English book report. As I read, the author's words transported me to Elnora's life on a farm in a state called Indiana, a place I held no hope of ever seeing in real life.

In my book report, I described how Elnora's heart broke when Philip left to care for his sick father. Then it turned out his father wasn't sick at all. Philip had returned to another girl. But that wasn't the important point. In my conclusion, I wrote, "It doesn't matter if it's the boy or girl who leaves, the pain is just as great."

My mother and sister continued arguing, yet even over their heated voices, I fell asleep. By morning, all was settled. Whether Asanda liked it, or not, she was returning to Soweto.

Asanda sulked, and I must say she was an expert in that field. For days, she spoke to our mother only after Umama shot her the squinty-eyed killer-eyebrow. She didn't speak to me or Onele at all. She wouldn't even look at us unless we infringed upon her space. I was okay with her rotten attitude until she smacked my bottom because I stepped over the pile of possessions she was packing in her woven bag.

"Don't touch my things with your stinking feet." Asanda's lip curled in disgust.

I made a fist and wound up to let her have it. Despite my anger, my arm froze. The blow might bruise her pale skin. I remembered Hulu saying that police don't look fondly on Blacks, even children, who beat Whites, thus we had grown up under the fear of arrest. In one swift and solid move, I grabbed the pillow off her bunk and threw it at her face, expecting her to return the favor by slamming it into my head.

She let the pillow tumble to the floor.

I took this as a sign I had the upper hand. A self-satisfying gloat spread from my chest and stretched my lips into a smirky grin—until I realized my sister was broken—her heart, her spirit, all because of who she was forced to leave behind.

Having not yet experienced love, I relied on the books I'd read to understand her sense of tragedy and the pain she must feel from losing the boy (she called him a man) who was the love of her life. The thing I did feel personally and deeply was the potential loss of the protection Ilanga provided from the dangers that had ruled her life under apartheid. Soweto was not a safe place for a White girl to live, especially not with a mixed Black and Coloured family.

Overwhelmed by shame, I picked up the pillow, smoothed its wrinkles, and set it back on her bed. A lump clogged my throat. I couldn't speak without crying, so rather than apologizing like I should, I returned to searching for my new shoes.

In Soweto, I had owned one pair of scuffed brown leather lace-ups. Here at Ilanga, Ubaba's wages were ample to purchase us each three pairs—sturdy new lace-ups for school, white *takkies* for play, and patent leather flats for Sunday. Solid proof we were better off in Ilanga. My *takkies* would be most comfortable for traveling. The other two pairs, I wrapped in tissue to prevent them from rubbing and getting scratched. With the changes we faced, who knew when Umama could afford to buy me more?

Nonchalantly, I slipped into the closet and stretched on tiptoe to where I hid my journal in the darkest corner, out of sight, and beyond the reach of prying hands and big noses. I hooked my finger into the binding. As I glanced over my shoulder to be sure my sisters had not looked up, my journal slid. I fumbled, and it crashed on the floor, opening to the exact page I feared someone might see.

Since my father's death, I hadn't written for the underground newspaper Rosie had connected me with. But now, as our lives calmed, I renewed my efforts to organize my notes into an article to submit to *Inyaniso Yethu*, Xhosa for *Our Truth*. This was the perfect place to publish my observations. I'd spent weeks shaping my thoughts about how, through reinvigorated implementation of the Group Areas Act, apartheid made it illegal for my grandfather to own the International

Imports Emporium, the business he had built from the ground up. But even more than stripping him of his livelihood, the loss of his standing in the community was responsible for a decline in his stamina and health, possibly even causing his stroke. I was confident this had happened to others, but nobody was talking about it, much less writing about it.

As I emerged from the closet, my foot accidentally touched the belongings Onele had piled on the quilt Rosie made.

She snarled, "Get off. Everything on this quilt is mine."

"Sorry, Your Majesty."

That was when I noticed Monkey—his left button eye missing, the right hanging from a loose string, and yellowed stuffing balls escaping from this ratty creature's belly seam. He stank of rancid milk mixed among other unidentifiable odors of the food or drink Onele had dribbled on his patchy fur. Umama had charged me with the disposal of worn-out belongings. Once again, my anger over having to return to Soweto, like an evil spirit inside me, overtook my common sense. Onele, intent on folding her tee-shirts, didn't see me coming.

I grabbed Monkey.

Packing had been a simple chore when we moved from Soweto to Ilanga. Our clothes and the single special thing Umama allowed us each to bring gave my sisters and me little to fight about, even though we disobeyed and sneaked additional items into our bags. I surveyed the clothes, books, toiletries, games, dolls, and souvenirs we had laid out. We owned much more now. On this return trip, Umama allowed us to bring it all, unless it was rubbish, which, to my way of thinking, Monkey was.

The power our mother bestowed on me surged—until Onele slapped Monkey from my hand.

"My property."

"He's dirty and ripped. Umama said we're not taking rubbish."

"Monkey's not rubbish. He's my friend."

Baas John had secured the lodge owner's permission to drive my family to Soweto in the eight-seater van. The area behind the seats was large enough to carry all our belongings. I don't know why I was dead set on getting rid of Monkey, except his skinny arms and legs and stomach pooch reminded me of when we were hungry and poor. Still, that was no excuse to hurt my sister. I had no right to strike out. Plus, it did nothing to release my rage.

Fortunately, I came to my senses, let Onele keep her disgusting monkey, then hid my shame for being such a bully by checking under the bunk beds for forgotten items. Both my sisters returned to their packing. A somber bunch, we needed to get this done.

The previous day, my last at school, had been a different matter. Miss Yeboah brought my classmates and me individual servings of *malvapoeding*, a sweet rich cake, wrapped in pink tissue. Further, as if that weren't amazing enough, she packed a tub of homemade guava ice cream in ice as if we were celebrating my birthday instead of saying farewell. We ate from bright blue paper plates printed with *Bon Voyage*. The most kindhearted thing a teacher ever did for me. And I mean ever.

After Miss Yeboah dismissed us, students gathered to say a last goodbye. When most had wandered out, Abigail, who wrote poetry for the school newspaper, leaned close. "Your words need to be heard. You must keep writing, no matter where you live."

I gulped to gain my composure, yet my voice crackled. "Thank you, Abigail. I believe writing is my purpose in life."

At the fork in the path, before Kalisha and I parted ways, we clung to each other, promising to write every day. I released my friend and watched her walk away. Her shoulders drooped and trembled. She was crying too.

An older girl from the higher standard, who never talked to us younger kids, called out, "I'll miss you, Eshile." I was contemplating what it was about me she'd miss when Anthony ran up, grabbed my shoulders, and yanked me to him so fast it jarred my brain.

I walked slowly, purposefully not catching up with my sisters, so I could ponder Anthony's violent hug. Could Umama be correct? That he showed his affection by tormenting me? I was baffled. While hidden among the bushes, I'd watched Leo hug Asanda many times. His embrace had no resemblance to such a rugged clutch.

Boys were a mystery, and I'd run out of time to settle this issue between me and Anthony. Onele hung back and took my hand. Asanda walked only steps in front of us, yet I didn't dare ask her what she thought about the meaning hidden in Anthony's goodbye hug. As angry as she was with me and with the world as a whole, the best I'd have gotten from her was a resounding, "Bug off."

Going Home

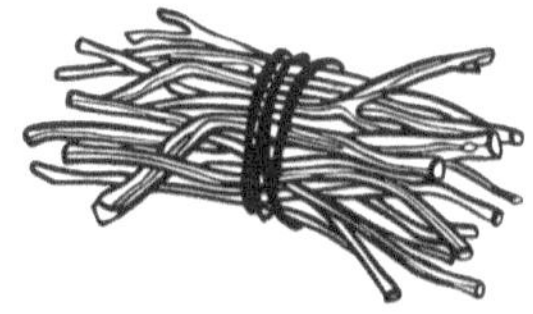

The following day, *EyoMnga* (Month of the Acacia Thorn Tree) December 1974

My gaze moved from the back of Baas John's head, down his neck. His massive shoulders carried our load as if it was the most natural thing for him to do. The van didn't seem so spacious once we loaded our boxes, bags, and the old jute rug that came from Soweto only to return with us.

"Asanda touched me," whined Onele.

Our big sister shoved her away. "Your fault. You're too close."

Umama must have been exhausted because she ignored my squabbling sisters and grabbed the door handle, grunting as she hauled herself into the passenger seat.

The jeeps used to haul tourists from one event to another lined the road at the entrance to the Ilanga Safari Lodge. A delivery truck blocked the circular driveway, so Baas John backed the van. Instead of moving toward the sausage trees, we moved away. A sensation of living my life in reverse washed over me.

Baas John yanked the steering wheel. I swayed and came to rest against the door. As we headed down the road, the engine drone soothed me, reminding me of falling asleep in the safari jeep the day my sisters and I had taken the places of ill guests. A warmth, like freshly baked bread, swelled my chest with pride as I recalled Ubaba teaching the lodge's guests about the magnificent animals of South Africa. Then I chuckled under my breath remembering Onele straggling as we got out of the jeep, chattering as if she were a *hadeda* bird. "Wait for me, wait for me."

I went through my mental list of bird sounds I loved, trying to lock them in my brain—the unique calls and colors such as the squeaky peeps of rosy-faced, chartreuse-feathered lovebirds and the high-pitched chirps of fiery-necked nightjars. Once returned to the city, I would miss the shrieking screams and sneezy barks of vultures fighting over bloody bones. Even more, I'd miss the coins I earned supervising these diving birds' wild and crazy, dive-bombing shows.

Surely, there were birds in Soweto, but as hard as I tried, I couldn't remember any flying gracefully above my head or making a single chirp. The loud music, gunshots, fireworks, and swearing men must have scared them away.

The crunch of gravel beneath the tires lured me into the present. Everything was changing, except for Asanda sulking in the rear seat. That was as constant as our drippy bathroom faucet.

Asanda had protested when we moved to Ilanga. Now she protested our move away. It seemed that, like Rosie's cat Miss Anna Belle, once my sister settled in, she wanted to stay. Perhaps I worried needlessly about my sister traveling with Leo to an American university. But if she had no intention of leaving me behind in South Africa, why did she study so hard to keep her grades high? Last night when I tried to comfort her by saying I was glad she was coming with us, she muttered, "Won't be for long."

Did this young man who loved her, and she loved back, drive her quest? Did she search for the acceptance of belonging? In both Soweto and Johannesburg, Asanda lived with uncertainty. But then, we all did. Apartheid put my family at risk of arrest, or even worse.

A flit of tension skimmed my spine just remembering our fear each time my family took the bus, especially when we gathered beneath the *Nie-blankes* sign marking where Blacks, Coloureds, and Indians were required to wait. Our mother's fear was so great that it spread to the rest of us. Asanda, even when too young to be out of our mother's reach, couldn't stand with us, her family. Even though it broke Umama's heart, she trained her to step away and take her place under the *Net-blankes* sign alongside other Whites. It felt wrong to return to that, but what else could we do?

Like the quilts I helped Hulu sew, my family was a patchwork of unique shades and colors. Yet, in Ilanga, nobody treated us differently because of it. Maybe it would have been kinder to leave my sister there. I gritted my teeth at each blast of gravel against the van's underside. No matter how much I massaged my forehead, the tinny patter sent stronger and stronger bolts of pain slicing from one ear to the other.

The baobab loomed ahead, as impressive as when my family and I first walked this road. Since this magnificent tree hadn't disintegrated into ash, she must have reconciled her differences with the gods. I wondered if she remembered how I longed to touch her beautiful trunk as I stood in awe of her dried, upended roots, sprouting like a hairdo gone bad.

I never disturbed the baobab or her white flowers, so evil spirits had no reason to send a lion to eat me. Now that we were leaving, I regretted not testing Umama's warning. Even if the baobab cursed me, it was unlikely a lion would find me in Soweto. Baas John would stop beside the baobab if I asked, but my regret was not strong enough to make it worth suffering Umama's wrath for delaying our departure. I should have returned to test the tree's powers for myself, learned the truth, when I had the chance—one more thing I waited too long to do.

I shook off my foolish thoughts. Only a crazy person would believe that stupid curse.

Still, a lion caused Ubaba's death. It didn't maul him, didn't pull the trigger. Yet if the lion hadn't been there, my father wouldn't be dead. Anger burned in my gut. But he never touched that cursed tree, so that wasn't the reason the ancestors took him while we still needed him here on Earth. Through the window, I watched the place I loved go by and, once again, worried that we were making a huge mistake.

The previous night's rainstorm had washed Africa clean. The bushes lining our route blurred into a moist wall of green. I knew my heart would long for Ilanga's rains—some gentle, others thunderous storms— and how afterward, the clean leaves sparkled, and flowering bushes released their scents. In Soweto, the rain had leaked through our shanty roof to soak us where we slept on the ground, on our thin woven grass mats, and caused the *kakhuis* to overflow and run its contents down our alleyway.

I scowled over my shoulder. "Asanda, stop kicking my seat." I had more to say, but the words caught in my throat. The rearview window filled with the enormous sign that had greeted us when we arrived two years ago.

Welcome!

Ilanga Safari Lodge

After Baas John turned onto the highway, he pressed down on the gas pedal and the van lurched forward. The journey from Soweto to the lodge took two full days, from early morning until late at night: our return by van—ten hours. Had I been such a baby that I made the trip into more than it was? But when I remembered the creepy old man who slipped his grimy hand up my skirt and the strange market where we bedded down outside, I realized time passes slower and events loom larger when saturated with uncertainty and fear.

On this trip, I was safe from such dangers. And the noises. No snickering boys clambered up into the truck bed to sit by my sisters and me. No gunshots in the dark.

I rested my face against the windowpane. The glass warmed my cheek. The flow from the air-cooler vents tickled my nose. Two years ago, I never expected to experience such luxury. I'd never heard of cooling yourself any other way than folding up a newspaper, then flapping it as fast as you could.

Baas John settled into a steady pace, around seventy-two kilometers, maybe forty-five miles per hour. Onele abandoned Asanda and joined me. She stretched and rested her head in my lap, hugging Monkey so tight another ball of stuffing, the color of oatmeal left too long, popped out. I should have told Onele to climb back over the seat and snuggle with Asanda. This move was harder on her than either Onele or me. But when my baby sister patted my knee, the gesture comforted me so much that I couldn't part with her affection.

I glanced over my shoulder to send Asanda a message of sympathy, a meager effort to show support. Her body had slumped. The circles beneath her red eyes were as dark as her loneliness and despair. For the first time, it fully sunk in that when our White father abandoned Umama to return to his home in the Netherlands, he deserted my sister and me as well.

According to family stories, within months of his leaving, my mother bounced back and into Ubaba's arms. Everyone, except for family who knew the truth, assumed he was my father. But our Dutch father's disappearance left Asanda alone in a crowd of people, none of whom looked like her. She rarely shared how out of place she felt or the guilt she suffered from knowing her difference put our loved ones in danger. But now that I was older, I recognized the signs—the quick darting of her eyes, the shrinking into the shadows.

Our relationship was complicated by my jealousy of the special treatment her whiteness brought and her resentment of me because I fit in. But never did I doubt our devotion to our family and our affection for each other. I signaled a look of reassurance, but Asanda had turned away, her gaze frozen on something outside the window. I leaned my head back, let the van's rolling motion slow my thoughts and dull my brain.

The change in tire noise awakened me when Baas John drove off the road, then stopped.

A fellow perched on an upside-down bucket patted the lid of a dented metal cooler and called out, "Cold drinks. Very cheap, my friends."

Umama opened the van's rear doors and pulled out a wicker basket made from roots and bark. Onele and I hopped out. Asanda slid out slowly. I kicked aside several green marulas the tree had shed too soon, then spread our blanket in the shade.

My mother handed us each one of Rosie's palm-sized pies. The aroma of ground beef and onions seeped through the wax paper. Rosie expressed her love through food, and now the familiar scent carried memories of its magical ability to soothe the sadness in my heart. Golden flakes of crust fell onto my jeans. I licked a finger, tapped up the fallen crumbs, and let them melt on my tongue.

The young fellow rose from his overturned bucket and raised the lid on his cooler. After purchasing five bottles of Coca-Cola, dripping from the melted ice, Baas John offered him one of Rosie's Nigerian meat pies.

"*Hayi enkosi*. No thank you, Baas. Cannot accept."

I stopped stuffing my mouth. This lad was proud. A striking gold design, encircling the neckline of his collarless cotton shirt, extended down his chest. Even though the pocket and hem were frayed, his *dashiki* shirt was spotless and pressed. How different he looked from the Soweto boys who harassed people on the streets until they bought their wares or gave them coins.

"Please. The meat pie will turn bad." After the boy shyly accepted, Baas John asked, "Do you live here?"

"*Ewe*, Baas. My *kraal*." The boy pointed to a cluster of circular thatched-roof huts. "I was born in this village."

Three women wearing multicolored skirts, hair tucked under a contrasting cloth *doek*, were sweeping loose dirt from the clearing. Their voices resonated across the distance like the music of the glass tube chimes that hung in the Ilanga Safari Lodge entryway.

I lay on the blanket and imagined living in this peaceful village rather than returning to Soweto. If I wrote about this, many *Staan Op!* readers would think I had imagined it. I resolved to write about this boy's village, anyway. I envisioned the bolder of my readership packing their meager belongings, then setting out to find such a home for themselves and their families.

Goats bleated and bumped inside a tree trunk enclosure as they vied for the best straw. While we ate, a black goat, with white spots and a white tuft at the end of his short tail, vigorously rubbed its horns and skull against the pen.

I sniffed. "Do you smell vinegar?"

The lad smiled bashfully. "Ah, that is Absko. He reminds the ladies how handsome and virile he is and that he is… ah… interested in love."

White and gray patches of altocumulus clouds clumped overhead. Set in a background of blue, the pattern reminded me of the flowered button-up shirt my father wore when he visited my dreams. Were the clouds a symbol of Ubaba sending me a universe full of good fortune?

But when the breeze blew the clouds apart, was that also a sign? An end to a season of prosperity? Acid burned up my throat, into my mouth. Hopefulness turned into dread. My insides knotted as I swallowed the last bite of Rosie's meat pie. The reminder of starvation's nagging pain felt like a splinter lodged too deep to pry out, bringing back an ache I had come to accept as a child.

We gathered our belongings and said goodbye to the young man. Around 5 p.m., we stopped again to stretch our legs. Umama was eager to keep going, so we didn't eat dinner. I couldn't have eaten, anyway.

My stomach cramped and rolled—whether from excitement or dread, I wasn't sure. The brown terrain transformed into grassy fields. Villages arose from the banks of the Olifants River. Further along, we passed housing areas built of plywood, plastic sheets, and corrugated iron. At the end of each row, piles of rubbish loomed as tall as the shanties. The drizzle of rain held down the dust but heightened the stink.

For miles, the van bounced out of one muddy rut into another. When the road smoothed, we approached a sign.

Welcome to Johannesburg

Umama touched Baas John's elbow, then pointed to a row of homes set back from the street by lush green yards. "My parents lived near here before the government forced them to close their international imports store."

Onele reached over the seat and tapped Umama's shoulder. "May we stop at Hulu's old house?"

"No point in that."

Onele put on her combination Eeyore and *can't-you-help* look. I pretended not to notice. Some other family probably lived in our grandparents' house, most likely a White family. I had no desire to see that. Yet recollections of the enormous kitchen where we cooked food to celebrate Sunday dinners, birthdays, holidays, and ceremonies that marked the passage of our lives rolled over me like a rain-filled cloud. But Hulu no longer lived in the lemon meringue house, so neither did the love. It was just a wooden structure, one more symbol of how apartheid rips a person's life apart.

Baas John jerked the steering wheel, swerving to avoid a red fender that looked like other cars had hit it many times. The sudden motion jolted me from my thoughts. For the next thirty minutes, the houses changed style and shape, to smaller, older, less well kept. Lawns turned browner and overgrown with weeds. Stacks of threadbare and peeling tires overtook several lots.

A man stepped into the street to wave us down. "Good tires for sale."

Baas John waved in a friendly manner without slowing. I stared, thinking about the treasures my father used to drag home from the rubbish dump and try to sell to our neighbors.

The front area of another house featured a collection of old toilets and cracked bathroom sinks. Within a few more blocks, the yards were little more than dirt. Boxes, rags, and bottles littered the clay streets. A kid with a bloated stomach and blistering sores around her lips lifted a squished milk carton from a plastic bin and sniffed. At the border of the roadway, a youngster bent over a pile of rubbish, possibly searching for the mate of the shabby shoe he had tied by its laces to his belt loop. He waded knee-deep in the rubble and watched us round the corner.

The only green in this neighborhood was fresh weeds at the edges of a straggling stream made by a leaky water hydrant. When I rolled down the window, the thing I had dreaded most, the reek of *kak*, blew in. The stench of shit burned my nose. Children sorted debris, searching for something of value, or to eat. Flies swarmed on the rubbish. Women sitting on overturned buckets glanced up as we passed. Baas John nodded to three boys clustered at the side of the road. They dishonored him by making a V with their fingers and showing him the backs of their hands.

Soweto. We are back.

CHAPTER FOURTEEN

Arrived

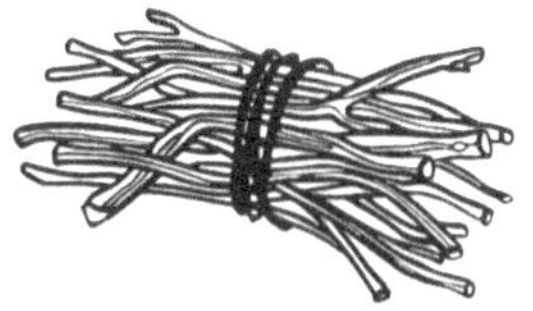

Minutes Later, *EyoMnga* (Month of the
Acacia Thorn Tree) December 1974

As we emerged on the far side of shantytown, Umama called out the streets on which Baas John should turn. We passed a church, white paint peeling from its walls, and Johnson's Sandwich Shop, his rickety rocker still perched at the edge of the porch. I searched for ole George as we drove past his market, watched until it shrank in the distance, but it didn't appear anyone was inside.

Baas John drove on. We entered a neighborhood in which most houses had grass, many enhanced by the flowerbeds beneath the front windows. A knee-high rock fence surrounded one yard. I sensed we must be close, but I wasn't sure until Umama pointed, and Baas John pulled into a gravel driveway.

"Lookie, look!" squealed Onele.

The color wasn't as intense, but there could be no mistake. They had it painted yellow while we were gone. Now, at the driveway's end sat my grandparents' tiny, single-story version of the lemon meringue house, Hulu's attempt to recreate herself back into the Johannesburg home she loved so much. The sun was low, but an hour remained until it would sink below the horizon and two hours until the nine o'clock blast of the curfew horn.

Hulu ran out, wringing her hands on her apron. The van rolled to a stop. My grandmother ripped open the door, and Umama slid into her mother's outstretched arms. Laughing and hugging, tears streamed down their faces. Auntie Grace wrapped her arms around them both.

I turned toward a scraping sound. Uncle Abel steadied Umkhulu as he leaned hard on hand-carved canes. My grandfather's arms trembled, and his left foot dragged. The right half of his face smiled at me; the other side was paralyzed into a frown. When Umama had explained that her father couldn't come to Ubaba's funeral because he had a stroke, I shrugged it off. Umkhulu had been quick to call Ubaba *inja youmoya*, dog of the wind, a man having no plan. He repeated it so often I thought his lack of respect for my father was why he didn't make the trip to Ilanga.

Facing my unforgiving attitude made me hot and clammy, as if shame oozed from my pores.

Still, I drew away when my grandfather raised one cane off the ground and awkwardly placed his hand across my back. Hunched over his canes, we were the same height. He stank like an old wet blanket. Saliva pooled in the corner of his frozen mouth, and his head twitched as he angled for me to kiss his cheek. His skin, as fragile as tracing paper, clung to my lips, cold, the same as Ubaba's when I leaned into his coffin to kiss him goodbye.

Hulu released my mother and gathered my sisters and me in her arms. She hugged and kissed us until even Onele tried to wriggle free.

"Spent days preparing this meal." Hulu motioned toward her front door. "Come eat. You too, Baas John. The ancestors answered my prayers through you. I owe you a splendid meal."

It wasn't necessary for Hulu to tell us how long she'd been cooking for me to know a feast awaited. Herb-rubbed meat and curried vegetable scents rode the breeze. From where we stood in the yard, I caught the sweet aroma of a familiar dessert and wished I'd been there to line the cake pans with *kusmalva* leaves. I hurried to the kitchen to see what I could do to help.

In our excitement to carry the serving dishes to the table, my sisters and I bumped into each other. Twelve chairs surrounded Hulu's table in Johannesburg. When in full force, one chair was available for a guest, our most frequent being ole George because he used to sneak away from home when his wife Oba's four sisters visited.

This table was smaller, only eight chairs, but I was glad. Empty chairs would remind me of my loved ones who used to sit in them. My lips turned up at the thought of Uncle Sammy with his enormous laugh and his tales of traveling to cities outside Soweto, enticing me to want to do the same. I had sensed his pride as he presented us with gifts from faraway places, even though we pretended not to know he sanitized these adventures by leaving out the drug dealing and other gang activities that enabled him to purchase such extravagant gifts. And Auntie Nofoto, the shyest, sweetest of us all. So protective of her birth family that she hid from them the abuse her husband heaped upon her in their own home until there was no hiding it.

If we still had twelve dining chairs, their spirits would hover over these vacant seats, making me miss them even more. I only wished Hulu had a chair for Ubaba.

That night, including Baas John, we were nine, so Abel carried in a metal folding chair from the shed where Umkhulu had sold his wares before it became too much for him. After we sat, Hulu put her hands out to Umama on her right and Auntie Grace on her left. We bowed our heads. My grandmother began by thanking God for the roasted hen. Then she asked our ancestors to please send rain. "My vegetable garden dried up."

Umkhulu slurred his words, but we nodded because we understood when he stuttered, "Sa-Amen."

Hulu ignored her husband. She had more for which she planned to express her thanks. "Almighty Lord, we join our hands in praise of You for bringing my girls home. They were as thin as twigs when You shaped their lives, so they had to go away. But I accept Your plan. Never have I seen my granddaughters so healthy and strong, my daughter so brave. We are grateful for Your comfort and guidance. Your wisdom rises above all else."

"Sa-s-Amen. B-beat this chicken now."

"Beat the chicken," giggled Onele.

"Eat, ninny," I whispered. "He's saying eat the chicken."

Uncle Abel chuckled until Auntie Grace poked her fork tines into his hand.

Hulu, head still bowed, pulled in a deep breath. "Evil spirits, *bose geeste,* worked to break my family apart. They took loved ones, two of my beloved children, Nofoto and Sammy. But they reside, protected from all harm, in Your house now."

"Sa-s-Amen. B-bood prayer, wife."

"With You also is our Ubaba. While some of us lost patience with the man," Hulu shot her husband a glare of condemnation, "Umama loved her husband as You love Your lambs, fully and without condition. I feared she might not endure his loss. But You made her strong and brought her home. We pledge to bundle her in our protective embrace forever more."

"Sa-s-Amen."

I kept my head bowed and my eyes open. Hulu shot her husband *the-look.* It was clear, no matter how many times my grandfather tried to say amen, Hulu wouldn't stop until she'd said what she needed to say.

"And bless Baas John, a generous and compassionate man. I praise you, Lord, for sending him to watch after my girls. Now, we beg of You, please watch over him as he returns to Ilanga. Praises be to You, our God."

Auntie Grace interjected, "Thank you, Lord." When Abel snatched up his fork and licked his lips, I heard a thunk that sounded like she kicked him beneath the table.

Abel stared morosely at the roasted chicken.

Hulu continued. "We are grateful for the nourishment You place before us and the home in which we gather today. In the name of the Father, Son, and Holy Ghost, we exalt You eternally for every blessing You have seen fit to bestow on our family. Husband, you may say amen."

"Sa-s-Amen!"

"Finally, we can eat!" Onele applauded merrily.

In a flash, Asanda captured our younger sister's hands and shoved them down onto her lap.

As we passed the serving platters, Onele and I told Hulu and Umkhulu how we watched Kuhle's baby grow, leaving out the part about how sad we were to leave before her next baby elephant was born. I shared the way Rosie nursed Usana, the infant kudu, to health after poachers killed its parents. Onele cut me off and dived into a full-fledged description of how we enticed the monkeys with biscuits and a banana. Now it was my turn to kick someone under the table. I also shot Onele my *shut-up* glare. I couldn't believe she forgot that neither Umama nor Baas John knew we caused the monkey invasion.

"Eshile kicked m—" Onele's eyes widened as she realized my kick saved her from our mother's wrath. She mouthed, "Thank you," and changed the topic. "Hulu, did I tell you we had our own bedroom?"

Hulu gave my little sister one of those smiles that lets you know you are loved. "Did you praise the ancestors?"

"We had to share the closet, but I had a bed and my own big white fluffy pillow." Onele seemed oblivious to the rising of Umama's killer-eyebrow and the impending threat of the *it's-a-sin-to-brag* lecture. "Yes, Hulu. We thanked the ancestors for our beds and all the other blessings the Lord gave us in Ilanga."

Umama smiled softly and her eyebrow sank to its normal position.

Hulu gestured to Asanda. "Did you like your new school?"

"Better than here. The head teacher said they'd award me a scholarship. No chance of that now that we've left."

The lull in the conversation left me worried Umama might return to Onele's verge on a confession and dig for more information about the monkey incident. I stood and gathered up as many dinner plates as I could carry. There was no need to scrape the dishes before putting them in the sink. Hulu's cooking was so delicious that everybody wiped any remaining sauce or meat juice with their last bite of bread. I slipped the plates beneath the soapy water, careful not to clank them. I needed to hear what people were saying.

Hulu cut the *kusmalva* cake. Forks clicked. Compliments flowed. My family chattered like vervet monkeys swinging from tree to tree. Would I ever hear that sound again? Baas John's deep voice rose above the others. "Best meal I ever ate. Hulu, please marry me and teach my kitchen workers your recipes."

After our laughter quieted, chair legs scraped the floor when everyone pushed back from the table. Abel always slapped his friends on the back when parting. He whacked Baas John several times.

One by one, family members straggled into the kitchen, depositing their dessert plates on the counter. Baas John entered last.

"I'm going, Eshile. Just came to tell you goodbye."

I hadn't thought this through. Baas John leaving? I might never see him again. All that he had done for us. Provided our amazing home. Given Umama her job in the kitchen. Made sure we had all the food we wanted. Promoted my father to a position that let him respect himself, feel like a man. And he had given me a job of responsibility.

Baas John patted my shoulder. "I'll miss you, Eshile. But I'm glad you're with your people."

"But you're my people too!" I fell against Baas John, wrapped my arms around his waist, and buried my face in the folds of his tunic. A sob caught in my throat. I needed to thank him, go on for hours about how grateful I had only then realized I was. But I just clung to him, my tears leaving a jagged wet spot on his tunic, right where his heart would be.

Baas John broke my embrace, then returned to the living room. When I turned back to the sink, the rising steam added to the moisture filling my eyes.

Feet shuffled toward the front door. Umama's voice quavered. "I will never forget, Baas John. I swear, I'll repay your generosity."

"Nothing to repay. May life go well for you and your daughters."

Gears ground. The van backed onto the road. I should have gone outside along with everybody else, but I had collapsed into a kitchen chair, unable to stand. Then Abel's truck motor roared. I dropped the washcloth on the floor and bolted outside. I was too late to even wave.

My family trudged toward me. Their laughter had faded. No one spoke, but that was okay with me. I didn't want to talk to anyone either, so I silently followed them inside.

Umkhulu's plate was the only dish remaining on the table. He might have scooped up a bit of cake icing, but nothing else. I could see why he had become so thin. My childhood image of him as a big burly bear evaporated before my eyes.

I carried his plate to the kitchen, placed a second plate upside down on top to keep his cake from drying out, and yanked on the metal handle to open the tiny refrigerator door. I sniffed, hoping to catch a whiff of the fresh scents I loved inside Hulu's refrigerator in Johannesburg, in the lemon meringue house she loved so much. A little over two years ago, before we ever knew such a place as Ilanga existed, Hulu's Harvest Gold refrigerator seemed enormous. I remembered looking up to the top shelf that held a carton of milk and three glass containers—freshly squeezed mango juice, homemade Amarula, and sweet tea. I had been barely tall enough to lift the heavy pitcher of rooibos tea, mint leaves floating on top, and pour myself a glass.

The middle shelf would have held spinach, jute mallow, and Hulu's wooden bowl of *tatashe*. She loved to cook this red pepper stew, the recipe passed down from Great-Grandmother Haile's mother. The third shelf usually held a row of tender golden mangos lined up as if they were children waiting for the school bus. The bottom bin always held a bowl of ground beef and onions wrapped in wax paper, Hulu's technique to contain the eye-watering odor. It never worked. Onion bite mingled with the delicious mango scents from the higher shelves.

Sadness burned at the edges of my heart as I stared into this tiny refrigerator that sat in a miniature version of Hulu's lemon meringue house. I slid Umkhulu's plate onto the empty rack, then shut the refrigerator door.

CHAPTER FIFTEEN

Too Close, Too Much

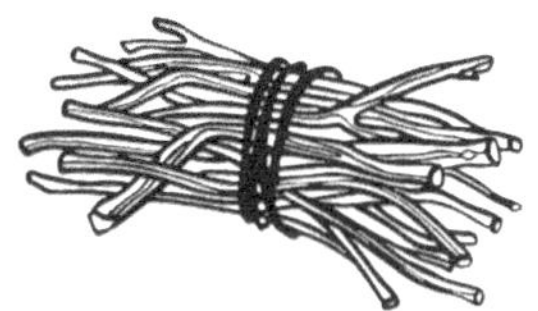

EyeNkanga (Month of Small Yellow Daisies) November 1975

Umama hadn't said how long we might live in her parents' small house. I closed my eyes and imagined our bodies pressed against the walls and our arms and legs sticking out open windows because we were stuffed in so tight. I decided to give it a week, then move in with Auntie Grace until Umama found us our own place.

To make dinner, we used every pot, pan, and plate Hulu still owned. I had washed them all and now they sat stacked on the counter, dripping water. Either Onele or Asanda should dry. But I guessed I was on my own. A bit huffy, I flung open the cupboard door beneath the sink, then snatched a towel off the hook. Even though stained and frayed, I recognized it. Umkhulu ordered these, imprinted with giraffe faces, from a mail-order catalog from Japan and sold them in his International Imports Emporium. He told customers they were native art from a local village, then bragged to friends and family about how great his profit was.

I tipped the rinse water out of Hulu's roasting pan and dried it with the imposter towel. Finding no place to set the clean pan on the counter, I remembered she kept it in the oven. Unlike the large oven in Johannesburg, this one only held this single roasting pan.

Soft voices and scuffling sounds floated my way. My head felt stuffed with straw. I was ready to go to bed, wherever that might end up, in this one-bedroom house. My arms were tired, my legs ached. I'd had enough. I dropped the towel atop the pile of plates and marched into the living room to tell my sisters wet dishes awaited them.

A bed sheet unfurled as if hit by a sudden gust. I jerked back when it snapped me in the face, then rolled my eyeballs, and prepared to shoot the sheet flapper my infamous *you're-disgusting* look, until I noticed the offender was Umama.

My little sister stuck out her pouty lip. "I'm sleeping in Umkhulu's recliner."

Umama grabbed Onele's elbow, nearly ripping her off her feet. "No, you're not. And I'm too tired to tolerate your prissing about. You'll sleep with your sisters."

"Can't. Floor's too hard."

Umama spread the sheet atop two blankets. "You've bedded down on harder than this."

Onele plunked into Umkhulu's chair and tucked his lap blanket under her armpits, locking it to her body. "I'm sleeping here."

"One more word and you'll have to sleep face down after I smack your butt."

"Umama, b-blet her be." Spit sprayed out the corner of Umkhulu's mouth, the side not paralyzed from the stroke. "B-bedder dan listin to her kumpane, colplain. Bloody hell."

This required a moment to interpret. But when he shouted, "*Bathuke bonke,*" the words came out perfectly. Our grandfather had cursed in his native *isiZulu* tongue.

Hulu led Umkhulu away from pouting Onele and scowling Umama. He banged his canes against the furniture so hard he stumbled. I leapt up to help, but my grandmother slipped her arm around his waist before I got to him. He leaned heavily against Hulu's slight frame as she guided him to the bedroom.

We each took a turn in the only bathroom. Onele was first. Umama last, flipped off the light, then curled up on Hulu's sofa. Though too tall to stretch out, my mother must have been comfortable because her breathing slowed and deepened almost immediately. Onele stayed in Umkhulu's chair. I sensed her gloating from where Asanda and I lay on the blankets, careful not to touch each other.

I listened for the cicadas to sing. But outside, boys' taunting voices rose in the night, feet scuffled, then bottles crashed against a neighbor's wall. A car engine revved. I pretended it was a lion's roar. My eyes closed, but my mind raced. I flipped onto my stomach, then onto my side. Asanda hissed, "Hold still," and shoved a foot against my bottom.

I slapped her leg. There was no end to Hulu's generosity, and I loved her for it. But it was difficult to squeeze six people into that house.

I felt a waft of shame. My expectations had changed. Prior to Ilanga, I wouldn't have had a single negative thought about sleeping on soft, thick blankets. Probably would have considered it an extravagance since my family had slept on grass mats rolled out on our shanty's earthen floor.

Even though my grandmother closed their bedroom door, Umkhulu's coughs ripped through the air, deep and raw, like Anthony hawking out his record-breaking spit wads. My grandfather called out, "Hep me, Hulu. Hep me." Hulu soothed him the way she had baby Onele when she suffered from colic. I could almost feel her firm pats on his back as he cried.

Cooling air blasted through the open window. No longer a gentle breeze, it howled and spun Hulu's lampshade.

"Wife, doon lit me die."

In a flash, the room flared as if the street boys had shot off firecrackers. Before the eerie shadows faded and darkened again, thunder rocked the house. Onele leapt from the recliner and nosedived in between Asanda and me.

Asanda elbowed her. "How's anybody supposed to sleep?"

Our frightened little sister lifted my arm and wriggled in until snuggled tight. I wasn't sure who was most comforted, her or me. As the rain pattered down, my breathing slowed. Perhaps that was the end of the storm.

Then the sky lit up as if we were under cannon fire. The earth shook, making me think a lightning bolt had hit nearby. A boom of thunder rattled the windows.

"Get ud-udder the b-bed! Gangs shitting again!"

Onele giggled, "Umkhulu said shitting."

"Shooting," I snickered. Old enough to feel the shame of such an inappropriate laugh, I covered my mouth with one palm and Onele's with the other. She slapped my hand away.

Asanda yanked off the sheet and scrambled into Onele's place in Umkhulu's reclining chair. "I've had it with you two babies."

I glared. "We need that bed sheet."

Asanda wadded it into a ball and flung it into my face.

Of course, our squabbling awakened Umama. She rolled off the sofa and closed the window, then loomed over us. "Stop. Go to sleep. You don't want me settling this."

The room glowed as if every light switched on at once. Onele squealed.

"Girls, what did I tell you?"

A wave of rolling thunder finished in a resounding crack. Onele wrapped her pillow around her head, tight against her ears. Lightning sparks left behind the same burnt electric odor as fireworks from a New Year's celebration. Then suddenly, these bursts departed as quickly as they had filled the sky.

I startled at my grandfather's sharp snort, and then again when Hulu snapped, "You're snoring like a hairy baboon! Roll over, old man."

But within minutes, the only sounds were the soothing thrum of pouring rain and the slow resonance of my family sleeping. My brain conjured the image of Soweto washed clean. This I wanted to see, so

I carefully untangled my younger sister's arms from around my neck, slipped off the bed, and sneaked to the door. It creaked when I pulled it open, but no one stirred.

I heard the swoosh a second before sinking ankle-deep into the muck. The dirt road, transformed into a river of mud and slop from the *kakhuis,* had widened into Hulu's and the neighbors' yards. The stench was horrible—a vile combination of rain-soaked dirt and human waste.

My bare feet made a sucking sound as I stepped backward. I swished each foot at the surface of the fast-moving stream, where it almost looked like clear water, then stepped inside and tiptoed to the kitchen. After dampening the giraffe-face towel, I retraced my steps and wiped the puddles as best I could in the dark.

It was hopeless. In the morning, my smeared footprints would alert Umama to what I'd done.

CHAPTER SIXTEEN

Settling

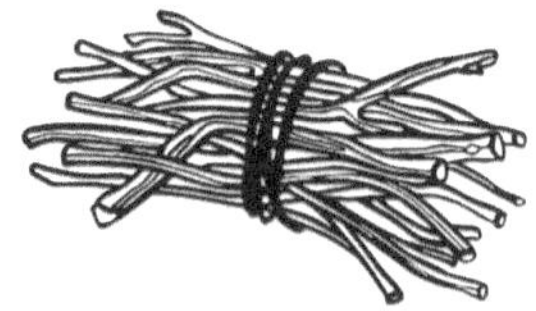

EyoMnga (Month of the Acacia Thorn Tree) December 1975

We loved our grandparents. Still, settling in did not go as smoothly as I expected. We had a thorny start. You can't just come back. Things aren't the same.

The size of my grandparents' house was perfect for two but had insufficient space for six plus all our belongings. Umkhulu's night pills, day pills, heart medications, not to mention herbs and potions, and stalks of incense covered half the kitchen counters. His oxygen tanks, canes, metal walker, and a battered wheelchair were everywhere.

But it was more than squeezing in with our grandparents in their little home. There was also the issue of privacy. I'm sure my grandfather never thought he'd find five females sharing his one small bathroom. In all fairness, it was rough for all of us. As quickly as we'd each taken a turn, we started over again.

Yet it was our emotions that kept us on edge. The tangible shifts from struggling to cope with the loss of our father, conflicting feelings about returning to Soweto, and anticipation singed by fear of what our future held seemed like a minefield lying in wait for one of us to misstep.

While Hulu used her calming nature, negotiating skills, and loving understanding to prevent many a blowup, my strategy was to hide out in Umkhulu's old shed. I'd open the door wide enough to let in the sun but angled it so no one inside the house could see me, sit in an old plastic chair, and document my woes in my journal.

But not everything that happened was bad. I experienced a shift inside my head, possibly in my soul. Instead of saying the first thought that came into my brain and doing whatever I wished, I considered my words before letting them escape my mouth. While my desire to be the favorite still lurked, it no longer drove my actions. Still, at fourteen, the same age as Umama when she gave birth to Asanda, I should have done better.

Regret hardened in my heart, weighing me down like stones. I'm sure my sisters hurt as badly as I, and my mother even more. How could a child compare their loss to that of a wife, a partner in life? Was it different for a sibling who is almost an adult, on the verge of independence like Asanda? Perhaps the healing process is less acute than for a young girl like Onele, only eleven, and needing her father's daily guidance and love. Was there a difference? I couldn't know for sure.

I understood that nothing I did should add to their grief. Yet with all my thought, I didn't always get it right. That caused me a considerable amount of shame. Such as the unforgivable words I uttered two weeks later.

We'd been house hunting every day. Fortunately, Umkhulu's stroke left his financial wisdom untouched. He calculated the amount of insurance money Umama could spend to purchase a place of our own and what she should save for expenses until she secured a job. While maths came easy to him, he struggled to say, "Man-to-man is bedder to bargain the b-b-brice of a house." And since our mother put up no argument, he called upon a friendship from his Johannesburg days.

Turned out Umkhulu was correct. Once the owner interpreted what our grandfather was asking, he reduced the price.

My sisters and I danced across our grandparents' tiny living room. Our mother thanked our grandfather profusely, causing his chest to swell as it did in the past when he was a successful businessman.

After signing the papers and completing the financial transaction, we stood out front, in awe of the first home we ever owned, admiring its blue-painted exterior, the hue of the December summer sky, and its windowsills painted white like sugar frosting. Then my rawest thoughts slipped out of my mouth, ruining how good the afternoon was going. "I'd rather have Ubaba than this house." Even I was shocked to hear myself be so cruel as to imply they didn't feel the same.

Umama gasped as if hit in the stomach. I wanted to express sorrow for my unkind comment. Instead, I bit my lower lip so I wouldn't cry.

We were standing there, each absorbed in our own thoughts, nobody knowing what to say when ole George pulled up in his flatbed truck. He had bought his wife the dining table she'd begged for. Oba offered us her old set. Her new one, all the latest rage, had metal legs and a top much the same as the linoleum on her floor. I preferred the old table of solid wood, even with its wobbly legs, because it gave us opportunities to carve messages on its underside, the way we had done to the small table in our shanty.

After unloading the table and chairs, George drove us to town to buy beds. We chose bunk beds similar to the ones we had in Ilanga. As quickly as the beds were unloaded and placed in our room, we ripped the bedclothes from their transparent wrappers. Onele fluffed her pillow and propped Monkey against it, placing his hands behind his head so that one would swear he was saying, "It's good to be home."

After ole George left, I scrubbed and polished the end tables Umama bought from a street market vendor. It took me hours to buff out the scratches and polish them up to her standards. But it was worth the work, and who knew she had such fine bargaining skills? She topped the table off with a lamp from Howard's Second Hand Store. Someone had painted a leopard skin design over the original green glass, and the black shade had no rips or tears—barely faded at all. Umama was thrilled with this lamp that cost her two fifty-cent coins plus four beef meat pies until she plugged it in. Then she changed the bulb and inspected the cord. It still didn't light.

Umama surveyed the room and sighed. "I imagine George can fix the lamp next time he comes by. Girls, we've worked hard. Tomorrow we'll visit our former neighbors."

Her statement surprised me. "Why? You swore you never wanted to go back."

"It would be hard to return to the way we lived. I wasn't ready to face it again, but now I am. I long to see my friends."

Asanda jutted out her chin. "I'm not going."

Umama's eyebrow rose, but not to the danger zone. "Yes, daughter, you are."

Umama claimed the walk to our old neighborhood was thirty minutes, but it seemed longer. So much was hard to look at. Had living conditions gotten worse? Or hadn't I comprehended how poor we were? Stinking *kak* floated in the runoff from the community water hydrant. A naked toddler jumped to cross the stream. His legs were too short. Filth splashed. He wiped his face with his damp, dirty hand.

After we turned the corner, Umama stopped in the middle of the block. "Oh, Lord. The rubble. Why would anybody collect plastic chairs with most of their legs broken off? You can't repair them. No earthly reason to save them."

As we continued walking, I couldn't believe what I was seeing. The yard where Umama stopped was especially shocking. I asked, "Are you sure this is the row we used to live on? I don't remember all this old bathroom stuff. Who keeps cracked toilet seats?"

Onele giggled, "They'd pinch your bottom."

I squinted at the next shanty. It looked familiar, then I realized it had been ours. "Umama, there's a hundred pots and pans thrown about. Why keep this in our yard?"

"Not ours any more. Looks like these folks eke out their existence by hauling other people's discards from the dump, then selling the stuff to folks who have even less."

"But, Umama, the fence Ubaba built is gone. Anybody can walk in and take all this junk."

"Who would want it?" Umama let out her first full-fledged laugh since her husband died. "Besides, that fence didn't even keep the neighbor's toddler out. Remember when he fell against it, and they both toppled over? It certainly wouldn't have kept a thief out."

Before I could nod, a massive snarling head, eyes aglow, glared out from behind a crooked stack of used tires. Slobber hung like globs of gelatin from his gleaming canine teeth. When he hit the end of his chain, his enormous feet flew out from under him. Onele shrieked and wrapped the flare of Umama's skirt around her as if it might protect her from the monster dog.

Asanda let go of the scarf covering her face, grabbed my arm, and pulled me back. "Thank you," I gasped.

Umama didn't flinch. She held her ground. "At least they replaced those plastic walls with wood."

Ife, our former neighbor, stepped out of her shanty to our right. "Don't go near that brute. He killed the old cat that kept the rats from getting inside my place." Then she recognized us. "Praise the gods, you are home. I told everybody you couldn't stay away. Come on over. Let's have tea."

Umama hugged Ife as if she loved her as much as Auntie Grace. Another mystifying adult behavior. As Soweto's most accomplished gossip, our busybody neighbor used to take every opportunity to tell Umama that her daughters ran wild, her crazy witch doctor sister killed people who didn't deserve to die, and Dinga dug up her meager garden again. Before we moved to Ilanga, complaints about Ife rolled off Umama's tongue. Yet that day she gave our elderly neighbor a second squeeze. "I missed you plenty."

And the biggest surprise, Dinga trotted out of her shanty, wagging his long skinny tail. Ife had kept our dog. Her threats to shoot him the next time he lifted his leg on her shanty walls had turned out to be only that—threats. Besides, she didn't own a gun. In fact, she didn't have much of anything.

Dinga perked his floppy ears toward Onele's voice, then ran as if to plow her down and launched himself into her arms. They crashed to the ground. Onele squealed and laughed as they rolled on a patch of weeds.

It had hurt when Umama said, "You know Dinga likes Onele best," but now I loved how crazy the two of them were acting. Dinga pinned my sister down, covered her face with drool and sloppy licks, and whipped his tail against her legs.

"I took care of your mutt for you."

"Ife, he wasn't ours," says Umama. "Just a neighborhood stray. No need for you to keep that old dog for us."

"He thought he was yours. Poor mutt pined and whined, watching for you. He wouldn't even chase the rubbish truck." Ife motioned toward our former yard. "As soon as that monster dog took a nap, Dinga sneaked past to see if you were all inside. I kept telling him he just needed to be patient, that you'd return."

Onele squeezed Dinga so tight his eyes bugged. Even Asanda took a brief break from fuming and pouting and rubbed his favorite spot behind his ears. Who knew? That mangy old dog had believed his family would return. He could teach people a thing or two about loyalty and love.

Onele poked out her lower lip. "I told you we should keep Dinga's leash."

I scruffed her hair, then scratched Dinga between his shoulder blades. "You don't need it, baby girl. That dog's not leaving your side."

After drinking the tea Ife brewed over her hot plate, we hugged goodbye. Ife's eyes glistened, damp with tears, when we promised to return soon. We left the rows of shanties and stepped out onto Ngobse Street.

Dinga crashed into Umama's legs when she paused to gaze back toward Ife's falling-down shanty. "We'll bring food once a week."

Dinga yapped happily as if he agreed with Umama's proposal.

"Umama, that's not enough. Ife can hardly walk. Her place stinks. Blowflies everywhere. Rubbish piled up."

"Fine, Eshile. I guess that means you will gather all that up and carry it to the dump again?"

"Yes, and we must do more. You saw how bony she is, couldn't weigh over forty kilograms. She gave Dinga food she should have eaten herself. Now she's weak. Her skin looks weird, too pale, like she's sick."

I shot Asanda a look of surprised amazement when she said, "Eshile's right. Ife's awfully thin."

"So, what are you girls saying?"

Asanda nods for me to explain. "Ife denied herself to feed Dinga. Can't you see? Not because she loves that dog. Because she loves us. Please, Umama. We must bring her to live with us."

"Your heart is tender, Eshile. Yet you are my strongest daughter. I offer an extra prayer for you every night. Great-Grandmother Haile warned me that you have many sticks to gather and the load ahead is heavy."

My mother's words settled solidly in my body. I did my best to replicate Onele's saddest Eeyore expression as I offered my last attempt to persuade her. "Besides, we have an empty bunk bed."

"I suppose you're right. So, don't be sad, my sweet daughter. As soon as we settle a bit more, we'll bring her home with us. But now, I have a surprise for you. We're taking a different route home."

"Why, Umama?"

"We're going to stop at Rufaro and Matilde's. Hulu says they moved into a tiny home nearby. Just a couple of blocks away."

The weight lifted. The warmth and security of loved ones returning to their proper place filled my heart.

Onele patted her empty pockets. "Do you think Matilde still carries Bonomo's Turkish Taffy?"

Dinga smacked his lips. We burst out laughing and picked up our pace.

CHAPTER SEVENTEEN

Differences

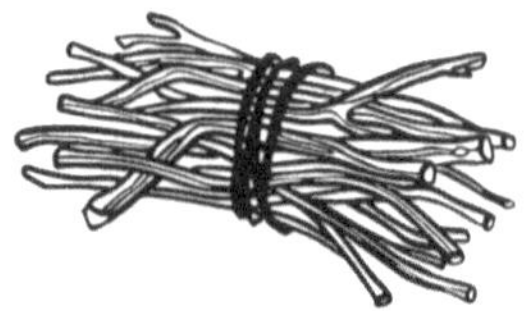

EyoMqungtu (Month of the Tambuki Grass) January 1976

Bini claimed most of the students I knew remained in our class because they had progressed through the standards from middle school to high school, the same as she and I. Because of her assurances that I'd feel right at home, I expected to be greeted by happy faces and welcome-backs and slide easily into the way things were before.

But that's not how it went. First, the school secretary met me at the doorway and squeezed the breath out of me. "We love you, Eshile. I am so sorry for your loss."

I sniffled my way down the hall. Students whispered. When I approached, they fell silent and stepped away as if I were Moses parting the waters. I couldn't help thinking it would be better if they didn't know of my father's murder.

My chair at the table Bini and I had shared sat empty as if waiting all this time for me to return. My friend signaled for me to sit down. "I didn't let anybody take your place."

Before Ilanga, I had begged, pleaded, and wheedled to attend a better school, one the quality of the Catholic school Asanda attended. But when I slid into my old chair, it felt like a piece of home.

Most of my classmates were girls. In the week that followed, each came to me, but not alone. Perhaps they anticipated my reaction, that I might burst into tears. To fortify themselves, they developed the strategy of coming in clusters of three or four. They offered comfort, but in their uncertainty of how to act or what to say, I felt worse.

With their every nervous sentence, memories of biting disinfectant odors filled my nose. I heard a ghostly version of Umama crying out, "Help! We need help!" Once again, I felt the cold puff of air from when the nurse yanked the curtain along the metal pole, separating me from my father's bed.

Then feelings I experienced last month, just two days before New Year's Eve, swooped in atop my own sense of loss. Oba, ole George's wife, died suddenly and unexpectedly. I couldn't imagine the pain of going to bed beside the person you had loved for most of your life, then awakening to find her gone. George had explained, "The doctor said her heart just stopped." Then he asked a question for which I had no answer. "Why didn't the Lord take me too? No reason for me to be here anymore."

My family comforted our dear friend by inviting him to dinner, taking him leftovers, and doing his laundry, but nothing seemed to make a difference. I wondered if my friends now felt the same about their efforts to comfort me. These girls were kind. Yet, as tender as they tried to be, none recognized how overwhelmed I was by the heavy, empty feeling of loneliness. I wanted to tell them that I cherished them for their bravery and their desire to ease my discomfort. But while phrases of gratitude rolled through my brain as easily as writing in my journal, all I managed was to mumble, "Thank you."

I also suffered pangs of shame because I considered myself too old to act this way. Besides, I was not the only girl whose father passed. While I lived in Ilanga, a rival gang, the Black Jacks, killed Zola's father.

And another girl's father died from a rockslide in a diamond mine, the same as my Uncle Sammy.

Only two of the boys originally in our class still attended. The others dropped out to find work. Many fled to the mines; some for the maize, bean, or cocoa fields. A new boy, skin as light as mine, blocked my path. "My father says yours was a hero. He stood up for what Africa means. I wish I'd known him, but we moved to Soweto after you left."

These types of unexpected acts of kindness hit me hard. I found it impossible to look him in the eyes.

He shuffled his feet, reached out to touch my arm, then let his hand drop limply to his side. "Sorry, didn't mean to make you cry."

I didn't have the strength to hold back my silent tears of pride. His powerful arms encircled me. I leaned my head against his shoulder, sinking deeper into our awkward hug.

Even the teachers appeared uncomfortable. When my maths teacher, Mr. Nnadi, asked if I completed the homework, I sucked my bottom lip and lowered my eyes. He patted my arm as if I was fragile. "No need."

Words came to me easily. Numbers, not so much. Mr. Nnadi's reprieve made me so happy that I suffered a bit of guilt.

Later in the afternoon, our science teacher directed us to open our books to where the class last left off. In Ilanga, Miss Yeboah focused lessons on the environment and the animal world. The study of genetics was unfamiliar. I felt overwhelmed, yet knew I needed to pay attention so I could catch up.

That day, I learned an important bit of science. Half of a human's genes come from their mother, the other half from their father. While easy to comprehend, that bit of science raised questions in my head, questions such as since Asanda and I had the same genetic makeup, why was she remarkably lighter than I? I wanted to ask but decided that wasn't a conversation best held in public. Plus, more than our color difference, how did this genetic code explain why she was so different from me in every irritating way?

The following day, our science teacher explained the concept of cloning to create a genetic duplicate. I loved my older sister. And while my new understanding left me appreciating her unique personality, the thought of another her—I wasn't certain the world needed that.

These questions returned to me throughout the day. As I mulled over what I'd learned, I concluded my fascination with why Asanda and I were different colors was more of a thorn in my side than a fascination. If I was the same color as Asanda, I could have attended the Catholic school and gotten the superior education I so craved. While there was nothing anyone could do about this, it was the unfairness that drove my jealousy, and all that jealousy did was drive a wedge between my older sister and me.

It was time for a change. Gazing heavenward, I prayed to Great-Grandmother Haile, asking for her help with becoming more tolerant.

I waited weeks for my Great-Grandmother's response, a sign she'd heard me. Every day felt like a sea of sadness, leaving me abandoned and unable to pull myself out. I moped around, doing and saying as little as possible. It would have suited me to quit school, pull the covers over my head, and stay in bed. But Bini wasn't about to let that happen. Still, I took no particular notice of what other students did until Gabisile—her friends called her Gabby with good reason—stood in the schoolyard and shouted, "We reject Afrikaans."

Our teachers did their best to instruct using these foreign words, words whose meanings they scrambled to learn themselves. It wasn't going well. Mr. Nnadi was our only teacher who spoke fluent Afrikaans. But when it came to maths, that made it worse for me. A subject I didn't get in a language I couldn't understand. How was that a proper learning experience? But when I raised my hand and asked, Mr. Nnadi's face flushed red. "I do as directed. That is all I can say."

Others said plenty. Gabby's brother was a member of the student group, Black Consciousness. Every time he came home from his university, he boasted that more teenagers had joined the movement, and they were creating a united student voice. And he said that just like them, we had the power to be a driving force in the defeat of apartheid.

I hung on his every word. Was he right? I had doubts. We were just kids. What could we do?

But Gabby believed in her brother. She created flyers—some in English, others in Xhosa—none in Afrikaans, using lined notebook paper and taped them on the school walls, up and down the halls.

REFUSE TO SPEAK

THE LANGUAGE

OF OUR OPPRESSORS!

Someone ripped off the homemade flyers before most pupils saw them. Undeterred, Gabby created more. Then a three-day suspension convinced her to abandon making flyers. Instead, she turned to giving speeches just outside the schoolyard perimeter, explaining she was duty bound to spread the word. The principal informed Gabby's mother that he had suspended her daughter for another five days. Strategic, yet undeterred, upon her return, Gabby scaled her efforts to smaller crowds. She gathered five or six classmates at a time and rallied them to the cause.

Bini said she overheard the school secretary say the teachers met with the principal and discussed the mounting dissent. They explained tension was at a breaking point among the students and teachers, and that was why our White principal now kept his door closed.

Support grew when the White South African government dismissed our local school board for resisting their demand to teach in Afrikaans. Bini's mother maintained that government officials did this to scare others into abiding by the law, but it had the opposite effect. During the subsequent months, teachers and parents met in private places. Black organizers rallied through underground communication networks. Pupils from other schools spoke out, often more forcefully than our own Gabby. Across our township, student leaders stepped forth and planned a peaceful demonstration.

I understood the rising opposition to Afrikaans but still felt steeped in sadness. Like a robot, I trudged to school and finished most of my assignments. After class and on weekends, Bini swirled around me, working harder than anyone to make me think my life had returned to normal. Through all this, my best friend and I existed like a unit of one on the fringes of the growing hostility.

Monday morning, I set my books on the table Bini and I shared as a desk. "*Bah.* I have Asanda's English book." I waved it at my teacher as I rushed out. "Be right back."

I tapped on my sister's closed classroom door, then pressed the textbook against the small, cracked window. The teacher waved me in. The older students watched as if an alien had invaded their territory, but what I saw kept me from approaching Asanda. My sister sat hunched over her desk in the last row, closest to the wall, bringing to my mind the image of the only white daisy a wildfire had missed while using its flames to darken the rest of the savanna.

"Yes?" Asanda's teacher peered at me. "What can I do for you?"

"I have my sister's English book. May I give it to her?"

The teacher nodded and turned to face the chalkboard.

I sensed Asanda's discomfort. Our teachers, the people Umama taught us to emulate, looked nothing like her. And not a single student was light skinned like her. I was reminded of a novel about a young girl who didn't realize she was Coloured until seeing a photograph in which she recognized everyone except herself. Until then, she had thought she looked like everybody else. I wondered how that realization had happened for my sister. Sudden and hard like it had for Janie, the character in the book? Could Asanda pinpoint when she knew? Or did awareness come about gradually as my sister grew older? Perhaps recognition of one's place among others occurred as a natural progression along with each measure our family took to keep us all safe.

This novel, *Their Eyes Were Watching God*, had been difficult to read. For me, the Black Southern dialect was a foreign version of English. It also brought difficult thoughts to mind, thoughts of my family made up of different shades, all the way up to our grandparents. Hulu's lightness, a result of her mother's rape by a missionary, was not unlike Janie's story. Would color ever not matter? It was difficult to imagine such a day.

I handed Asanda the textbook. "I am so sorry." She cocked her head, giving me half a nod, as if understanding I was saying more than, 'I am sorry I took your book.'

Her exclusion from the bonds these people shared struck me like an arrow between the shoulder blades. Conscious of the aloneness she endured, I stared at my feet, methodically taking one step after another down the hall, into my classroom, until I slid back into my chair beside my friend Bini. Outwardly, I'm sure I looked calm, but my thoughts didn't settle.

Upon our return to Soweto, Umama informed Asanda that she would attend school in Soweto. My sister threw a week of fits. But I didn't try to calm her, didn't call her a spoiled brat. I rooted for her success. If she went to the Catholic school, perhaps I could too. As Umama showed Asanda her new uniform, the one required to attend Soweto schools, I egged my sister on until she calmly and firmly replied, "I don't fit in. Not going. That's final."

"You are bigger than this pettiness," said Umama. "You will go. My daughters will be educated."

Umama and Asanda faced each other. I expected them to growl like lionesses, daring the other to move forward. But when Asanda broke her stare, Umama's shoulders softened. My sister leaned in and cried against our mother's breast.

"You are my eldest daughter. Your life is not easy, and I bear the responsibility for that. The ancestors tell me you face difficulties ahead, in some ways more trials than your sisters. You must strengthen your resolve and prepare for what is ahead. But you won't go alone. Great-Grandmother Haile, Auntie Nofoto, and even my brother Sammy assure me they will guide you to a good life."

I wasn't about to put my doubts up against Umama's convictions. I fit in. I always had. Still, the possibility of my sister never feeling secure in who she is or with whom she belongs, perhaps living in isolation for the rest of her life, weighed heavy in my thoughts.

The Rand Daily Mail, May 1976.

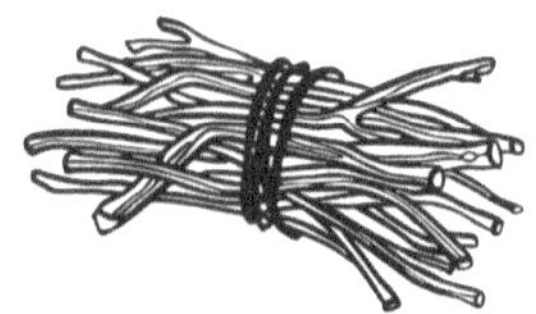

"The broad masses of Soweto are perfectly content, perfectly happy. Black-White relationships at present are as healthy as can be. There is no danger whatever of a blow-up in Soweto." —Mr. Manie Mulder, Chairman, West Rand Administrative Board.

CHAPTER NINETEEN

The Protest

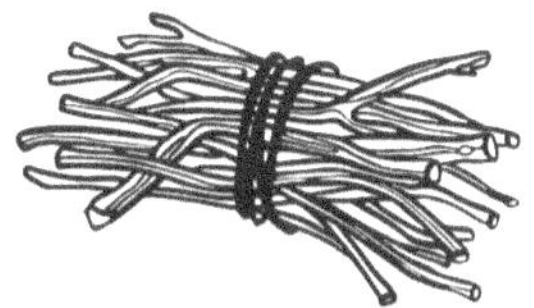

EyeSilimela (Month of the Pleiades) June 1976

It was a winter evening, Tuesday, June 15, 1976. Umama habitually waited until Sunday night to ask if we finished our homework. I hoped she wouldn't realize, even though the week was not yet half over, I was behind. I struggled to concentrate. My brain hardly functioned inside the soft fog that enveloped me at the moment of Ubaba's death and still clouded my thoughts, not yet letting the sun break through. Every assignment, especially the maths, took longer than previously. That night, everyone was asleep before I felt satisfied with my work.

When I finally rested my head on my pillow, the barrage of rumors concerning the students' plan for the next day bounced in my brain, keeping me awake all night. Tingles of excitement ran along my arms. Maybe excitement—might well have been fear.

Bini and I always made the trek to school together. Before we left her house, her mother slipped us each a fat slice of *biltong*. Of all the dried beef in Soweto, hers was my favorite. Most cooks used coriander and cloves, but Bini's mother sprinkled sugar and nutmeg on hers. Saliva pooled while I decided whether to devour my slice or wait until recess.

The day before, I had allowed myself to eat the biltong after language class, a reward for not fussing about being forced to recite baby words over and again in Afrikaans. We all knew how to spell dog in *isiZulu* and *isiXhosa*. *I-n-j-a*. But Afrikaans? Who needed a third way? *H-o-n-d*? Besides, I learned hound in English. Wasn't it enough to speak three languages? Did I need a fourth?

I couldn't understand how the Department of Bantu Education became powerful enough to decree Afrikaans instead of English as the instructional language in Black schools. Most importantly, I wasn't alone in thinking English and our native languages served us better.

At Umama's invitation, the former collection of gossiping women resumed their Friday night gatherings, now held in our new house's yard. The woman whose husband worked at a liquor store brought a six-pack of beer imported from a place called Amsterdam. These women could find something to say about everything. And being free was not an attribute that saved this beer from the same fate.

"No wonder Dutch people are sickly pale. This beer is weak." Yet for all her complaining, Auntie Grace emptied her glass.

I chuckled because, while a jug of her husband's homemade *tembo* beer sat in our refrigerator, no one seemed interested in it until they'd finished the last drop of Heineken. Then, as the women switched beers, they shifted their disdain away from the pale alcohol to the laws requiring they speak Afrikaans to their White employers.

"Riles me like a bull elephant with his foot caught in the mud." Beer sprayed from Auntie Buhle's mouth. "Our ancestors lived in Africa before the Dutch."

"And now there's a hundred times more Blacks than White Africans," added Zola's mother.

"Why aren't they learning our languages instead of forcing theirs on us?" I was free to ask because now that I had turned fifteen, the women no longer banished me to the shadows, out of earshot of the conversation.

"Eshile, that's the best question you could ask. How would you answer it for yourself?"

"Honestly, Auntie Grace, I think they're afraid."

As my auntie nodded in agreement and I mulled over other possible reasons, Bini's mom broke up my thoughts. "You girls heard what happened to Miss Cisse, didn't you? The teacher stabbed last week, on her way home from a clandestine teachers' meeting at Queen Alice's Shebeen… Well, she died."

A million questions sat on my tongue, but the lump in my throat kept me from speaking. As I struggled to choke down what felt like a giant wad of mushy bread, the women moved on to the increasing number of gangs moving into Soweto. It wasn't until the following Monday morning, as Bini and I strolled to school that I asked my friend the questions occupying my mind.

"Bini, did you know Miss Cisse?"

"No, but I heard she taught Standard Three. And one night, my mom saw her cover her face with a scarf, then slip in the back door where Shaka's group meets."

"I knew her."

"No, you didn't."

"Honest, Bini. I did."

"Why are you saying that? Are you planning an article about her political views? Are you going to say her support of student protests led to her death?"

"No, I wouldn't do that. Uncle Sammy was crazy about her. He had his hair blown out at Mabel's Beauty Parlor because he thought Miss Cisse would take notice of him looking so good in his new 'do. When she didn't, he used me as cover. He made me take him to the library. Bini, you knew my uncle. Probably the only time Sammy ever stepped foot inside. But she went every Thursday after school. My job was to ask her advice on which book to read next while Sammy charmed her with his flirty smile. Before he departed for the diamond mines, he gave her a bronze bracelet and promised he'd look her up when he got back."

"Did they kiss?"

"Kiss? Bini, what are you talking about? Teachers don't kiss boys who drop out of school."

"Too bad for your uncle. They say she is—was really pretty. Now they're both… I'm sooo sorry, Eshile. My big mouth…." Bini hung her head.

I felt sorry for my friend. To relieve her embarrassment, I said, "Gabby thinks our English and Social Studies teachers will walk with the students today. I'm not so sure. I haven't heard a word about teachers being involved."

"You know what I think, Eshile? I think they'll call off the protest. Too dangerous for children."

I thought for a moment before answering my friend. "I think the kids who had Miss Cisse as a teacher will march as a gesture of respect. She stood up for them, so they won't want to let her down."

When we entered the schoolyard, human electricity buzzed in the air. Students stood in clusters, leaning close to keep others from hearing what they said. Some students hung at the perimeter of the schoolyard while others milled around as if unsure of what to do. The principal's secretary, assisted by several teachers, herded us through the front door. When I overheard someone say the organizers canceled the protest, I released the breath I'd been holding inside.

Bini and I entered our classroom. Our first lesson was science; the second, Afrikaans. A steady stream of students walked past our open door. Shuffling footsteps in the hallway blended with their hushed voices. I felt the strength of it in my bones. Distractedly, I fingered the strip of homemade biltong in my pocket.

I glanced at Bini. Her eyes darted, then settled back on me. When the students in the front row rose, we followed suit. As we passed our teacher, I noticed four wide-eyed children stayed at their tables, and our teacher remained at her desk. If she was staying, perhaps we might too. I hesitated, but my best friend headed out the door and joined the line. I hurried to catch up, just in time to see Bini hesitate, then take the poster on a stick held out by Gabby.

We do not want Afrikaans

More pupils than not carried signs printed with thick black ink. Students, their spirits high, streamed past our principal. He spoke in his deep, quiet voice. "We wish you good luck. Your teachers and I support your efforts."

As we left, a girl from my science class shoved a homemade sign in my face. Needing a moment to make a choice, I ducked away. Yet, when she pressed the wooden stick into my hand, I gripped it tight.

To hell with Afrikaans

As we exited the schoolyard and formed long lines, taking up the width of the road, all I thought of was what would happen if Umama saw me carrying a sign with the word hell on it. She did not abide her girls using foul language. Saying she'd be unhappy didn't come close to what I could expect. She'd make me pay dearly. I searched for a spot to ditch the sign but found myself locked in, shoulder to shoulder with my classmates. To avoid being called a traitor, I raised my sign to my chin.

More protesters joined at each street. Without any noticeable prompt, hundreds sang *Nkosi Sikelel' iAfrika*. They lifted their voices for the second verse. *O fedise dintwa le matshwenyeho*. In *isiZulu*, the students offered words of prayer to end war, poverty, and the troubles faced each day.

A young Black man standing atop a tractor called out, "Brothers and sisters, I appeal to you. Keep calm. Remain cool. Police are coming. Do not taunt. We are not here to fight."

At the corner, roughly twenty female students joined those singing. Two girls in the lead carried a cloth banner on which they'd painted their message.

Don't shoot

We are not fighting

"Shoot? Bini, do you think they'll be shooting?" Fear climbed my neck.

"Don't be silly. We're just walking."

Bini and I fell in behind a pack of teenagers. Dust coated my throat, making it impossible for me to continue singing the prayerful song. We approached lines of students parading off the Phefeni Junior High School grounds. Policemen blocked our way. The marchers, unaware of the blockade, pushed forward from behind, their hot, heavy mass of bodies filling the intersection.

Gray smoke seeped from under the bonnet of a stalled police car. A White officer leapt behind the car's boot for protection, then lobbed a tear gas canister between a cluster of five fellas. They seemed stunned for a moment, then cried out and covered their weeping eyes with handkerchiefs, rags, or shirttails. Gasping and choking from the tear gas, they circled the vehicle. As flames billowed from the engine, the teenage boys threw rocks that pelted the officer and shattered the car's windows.

"Hurry," screamed Bini. "That car's gonna blow."

I wheezed from the dirt kicked up by fleeing students. When I stopped to catch my breath, a second stream of smokey fumes shot out of a tear gas canister as it rolled toward us. Bini and I scrambled in the opposite direction. My lungs burned. My heart pounded. I watched my feet so I wouldn't stumble on the rubbish in the street. Students stopped singing *Nkosi Sikelel' iAfrika* and raised their voices in screams of warning and fear.

Out of nowhere, Bini leapt in front of me, threw out her arm, and hit me in the chest, stopping me three steps from two policemen using the open doors of their Land Rover as shields. They lifted their rifles, and then as if it were the most natural action, fired into a cluster of shrieking kids. I dug my fingernails into Bini's arm and yanked her away from the crowd.

A huge policeman, his pasty skin streaked with grime, rolled a second tear gas canister in our direction. We bolted. Others were not so lucky. The gas enveloped them. Students darted in every direction, smoke dazed and coughing as if their insides were coming up. I stooped and gagged up yellow slime.

A group of female students emerged from a side street, waving their signs. Police, protected by riot shields, encircled them. The shortest officer, no taller than the sixth-grade girls, commanded his dog to attack. Two teenage boys jumped between the younger girls and the German Shepherd. The dog sank his teeth into the leg of the fella still wearing his school uniform. The other young man pelted the snarling animal with rocks. When a large stone hit the police dog's eye, he whimpered but didn't let go. Slobber flew as he shook his head and ripped the boy's pants. The officer swung his *truncheon*, hitting the teenager's shoulder so hard the wooden billy club flew from his hand.

Two women, one still holding a blue spiral notepad, rushed from a red brick building to help these young people. When a policeman pulled his handgun from its holster, she waved the notepad, flapping its pages violently. "Run, kids! He's going to shoot you!"

A bullet whined. Bini spun. A boy crumpled at her feet. Police opened fire. Panicked students rammed into each other, then bounced off in confusion. Other children jumped over sprawled bodies. A boy screamed, "They shot Hector!"

A tall young man kneeled on the ground, slid his arms beneath the wounded boy, then lifted his limp body. The terrified girl at his side frantically waved her arms. "Help us! My brother's shot!"

Bini pointed. "That's Antoinette."

Five or six kids rushed up from behind and pushed us into the crowd. We followed like a flock of lambs. Sweaty bodies bumped me. I tried to knock them off, but their hands were everywhere, grabbing my blouse, pulling my arm, hitting my hips as if trying to propel themselves in front of me.

I caught a glimpse of Gabby on the corner of the block, but a tall man, maybe her brother, whisked her up as if she were a child and bounded in the opposite direction when an armored troop carrier entered from the side street. One policeman stood tall and stiff, raised his machine gun, and peered down the barrel. A second officer rose through the opening just enough to rest his elbows on the *hippo's* metal roof and aim his machine gun toward a cluster of children. Standing tall in the turret, these police officers fired over the heads of protesters. Bini and I sprinted into an alley. Other students followed. A small girl clung to my shirttail as if I could pull her to safety. I seized her blouse collar to keep us from being separated.

Shots rang in the air. A sharp metallic taste coated my mouth. I watched, horrified, as Bini tumbled and tucked into a ball. Sweaty palms hit me hard, slid down my back, and then grasped at the hem of my uniform skirt. Bloody fingers left hot streaks on my legs. I lost my grip on the child, and the crowd pulled her away from me. As the small girl disappeared between running legs.

I cried out, "I'm sorry," and swerved past two girls hunched on the ground. The one holding the other's head in her lap sobbed uncontrollably. I hesitated, but it was too late to help.

Then I saw my friend—lying motionless in the dirt. As I came even with Bini, she rose and gasped for air. I steadied her and helped her stand. Then we ran. Bini's shorter legs churned at twice the rate of mine. Her chest heaved in its fight for air. I worried she'd pass out, so I veered onto Vincent Street and slowed our pace. A row of *hippos* blocked the road. Bullets cut through a mist of tear gas and whizzed past our skulls. We screamed, bolted into an alley, then cowered in the shadows.

Bini latched onto my arm, bent over, and heaved. Violent and wet, a gritty slime, remnants of her breakfast, splattered my bare legs. I held her shoulders, coaxed her upright, and nudged her toward the intersection.

We approached the corner, then pulled up short. Two heavyset guys ripped open the door of a black sedan and hauled out a White man wearing a suit and tie. The car continued to roll as the boys wrestled the man to the ground. A wiry young fella trotted alongside, unscrewed the gas cap, and stuffed a rag in the opening. I held my breath until the flame of his cigarette lighter caught, then Bini and I took off, fast.

Only a few meters ahead, a policeman shoved a boy who looked to be approximately thirteen against a storefront window. The glass shattered, and the boy tumbled inside, blood shooting from his head and the bend of his elbow. Another young man wearing a sweaty dirt-stained tee-shirt tackled an older officer. A protester wearing a black do-rag kicked the officer in the gut. When the policeman tried to rise, a girl, the hem of her school uniform hanging loose, bombarded him with rocks. The sweaty tee-shirted man pulled a steel *billhook* from his waistband. His knuckles paled from gripping the wooden handle so tight. Raising the flat, curved steel blade above his head, he thrust his *billhook* with tremendous force until blood spurted from the officer's stomach. Do-rag and Sweaty tee-shirt both turned to run, but police-men in camouflage garb pinned the fellas against the blast-proof hull of a *hippo*, while another pulled the groaning White officer to the side of the street.

My friend's face was stricken with horror. "Eshile, this demonstration was supposed to be peaceful."

I shoved Bini more roughly than I meant to. "Go! Let's get out of here."

We raced past the post office. Armed guards stood outside. At the bank, three young girls gaped helplessly as officers threw a limp Black body into a van.

My chest heaved. Bini panted like a dog. I glanced around for a place to hide. Not a single open store. We left the road to evade the *hippos* and pulsing crowds. I became confused, unsure where we were, until we came to the rows of brick hostels that housed men who left their tribal villages to work in the city.

Bini and I walked as rapidly as our unsteady legs could manage. We crossed the train tracks, then hurried through an empty lot. I didn't see a single person, yet fear quivered along my spine.

"Eshile, which way should we go?"

Dazed and confused, I shrugged, then hesitantly headed left, past a laundromat, a petrol station, and Mable's Beauty Parlor. I pointed up the next street we approached.

"Look, Bini! Ole George's market."

Bini pumped her fist into the air as a sign of victory. Then we jogged to the market. Bini stumbled and fell on the wooden step. Blood seeped from her knee.

Newspaper covered the windows. I peeked through where the pages didn't meet. The market was dark inside. My hand trembled on the doorknob. It didn't spin, so I yanked, but the door lock held. I bit my lip and banged on the glass. Bini didn't need to see me cry.

When the newspaper moved, ole George's nose, still crooked from a childhood scrap, poked through. I'd have recognized it anywhere.

"Get up, Bini!"

The door flew open. Two powerful hands yanked me inside, then dropped me on the pine floor. Next ole George picked up Bini. She had passed out. He bent her at the waist and draped her body over his arm. Her arms and legs dangled like a kitten hanging from its mother's mouth.

George slammed the door and locked the deadbolt. "Quick, Eshile! Hide in the stockroom."

Bini stirred as he laid her on the metal cot where he slept when the store might be at risk. He motioned for me to sit beside her. When I wiped sweat from her face, her eyelids fluttered. The pressure against my chest kept me from filling my lungs, but I couldn't hold in my fear any longer. Tears stung my eyes.

"Eshile, what were you girls doing out there? Teachers should do the protesting if they don't like teaching in Afrikaans. You're children. It's not right."

"The march was to be peaceful."

"Peaceful," snorted ole George. "Too much anger, too much hatred. Peace just can't be."

"Nobody thought the police would shoot students."

"Surely your mother knew what would happen. Can't believe she let you go."

"Not sure she let me. I begged, and she didn't say no. I took that as an okay, but she was asleep when I left. George, I'm in big trouble."

"Are your sisters out there?"

"No, no. Asanda ditched school to work for Mr. Wepener. Onele's at home. Umama said she was too small, so she wouldn't allow Onele out today. But she didn't forbid me."

"She thought you were old enough?"

"We were supposed to be just a bunch of students walking through town trying to make officials understand we want to learn the way we always have, in English and our native languages—what's the harm in that?"

"And you thought the Whites in charge would sit still for this rebellion? Thousands marching out of their schools and through the streets?" He rubbed his forehead. "You kids must be smarter than that. Surely, your mothers are. What were they thinking?"

Bini opened her eyes and pushed up to lean against the wall. "I promised my mother today would be nonviolent. How am I going to tell her what happened?"

"Bad news travels on the wings of the wagtail. I'm sure both your mothers have already heard. They're probably pulling out their hair. Or running in the streets, looking for you girls."

"Those men are destroying our culture. Teacher said they're holding Black people down, making us learn Afrikaans, so we'll do what White bosses want. George, there's more of us than them. Why can't they learn our languages?"

"It's still not right that you kids are out there like that."

"So many, George. When our school reached the corner of Moema and Vilakazi streets, hundreds were waiting to join the march. Bini and I followed them into the Orlando football stadium. Tsietsi Mashinini, do you know of him, George?" When he shook his head, I continued. "He's a Methodist preacher. He climbed atop a tractor so everyone could see him, then urged us to be peaceful. Reminded us that we were not to fight."

"We didn't fight, but we sure did run," said Bini. "We were among the last to leave the stadium and as we did, we heard gunshots."

"We didn't see it, but word came back through the crowd an officer had shot Hastings Ndlovu. Then the police at the front of our line of students opened fire. We, everybody panicked, George, and I slipped on the gravel. Then when we were running down the street, I'm so sorry—the fellow who works for you on the weekends—"

"Hector?"

"Police shot him. We saw him fall. I don't think he made a sound. Maybe he did, I don't know. Kids were shrieking, crying—police shouting for us to halt."

"They shot Hector Pieterson? He's a child. Only thirteen, been working at my market since he was ten."

"A bigger boy scooped him up. It was horrible, George, blood pouring from Hector's head and dribbling out his mouth. His sister screamed for help."

"Shot… Oh, my God… Hector's like a son to me. I pray he'll be okay."

"Don't know, George. Lots of blood. People ran right past them. Nobody stopped. Nobody helped. I couldn't move, even though I wanted to." I rubbed my elbow where it burned from sliding on the gravel as if that excused my inaction.

"I'm too scared to go home," whispered Bini.

"Me too. Umama's gonna kill me."

Ole George grimaced. "If I know your mother, she surely will."

"We should stay the night. Umama will have her fit, then be okay by the time we make it home."

"*Hayi, hayi.* No, no, Eshile. I fear what your mother might do to me. Got to take you home. Your mothers will be so happy you're okay, they'll smother you with kisses. Oh, you'll still get punished. I guarantee you, whatever Umama does, you're gonna remember it for a very long time."

Bini giggled nervously. I shot her my *that's-not-funny* face.

"I'll take a peek out. Girls, you stay here."

We did as George said—for seconds—then tiptoed up behind him.

"*UThixo uyadala.*"

I never knew ole George to swear. It stopped me in my tracks. Bini covered her mouth, but wet laughter sprayed through her fingers, noisy as a sloppy fart.

"Do you girls ever mind?"

"Sorry, George. We tried, but we need to know if the police are coming after us."

"I doubt they're interested in you two."

"But George, what if Eshile's be right? Somebody might tell them you took us in."

George kept a wooden bin of red apples by the window to draw in customers. The apples quivered in place. Several tumbled off the pile and rolled across the floor. We let them go.

Ole George lifted the tape, allowing us to peek around the newspaper. Two *hippos* rumbled past Johnson's Sandwich Shop, sending a vibration through the earth that rocked the late Mr. Johnson's old wooden chair as if his spirit was sitting there watching the danger roll by. Hair rose on my arms, prickling my skin.

The grinding motor sounds retreated as the *hippos* pulled away from ole George's. The rotten-egg stink of their exhaust hung behind and seeped through the cracks between the market's slatted wooden walls. Gray clouds of smoke billowed beyond Missy Meaby's Midtown Fruit Mart.

Another *hippo* rumbled up the street. I held my breath when it clanked to a halt. Two soldiers stood and pointed their rifles at the glass window of Dottie's Dress Shop, then the *hippo* rolled up even with the market.

George let the corner of the newspaper slide from his fingers. "Down! Guns aimed at our heads."

We dropped to our bellies. Ole George rolled to a protected position behind the wood wall and motioned for us to join him. But Bini headed for the storage room, butt-scooting like Dinga dragging his bottom in the dirt. If I hadn't been about to pee my pants from fear, I would have laughed. Instead, I hunched on my hands and knees and crawled after my friend. But when Bini slammed the storage door, blocking my entry, sweat oozed from my pores. I stank like a dead fish.

Ole George hunched over and hurried to the storeroom door. "Bini, open up. It's just us."

I curled up in a ball on the floor, pinched my eyelids closed, and prayed like crazy to Great-Grandmother Haile and uThixo as ole George coaxed Bini to let us in. Just when I moved on to baby Jesus, the *hippo* groaned.

George turned back toward the window. I grabbed his ankle. "No! They'll see you."

"They're leaving. I think that's the last of the armored cars. Eshile, let go of my leg."

"No, George. They might be tricking you. Waiting for us to come out."

He shook his leg with enough force to break my grip. I knew he was afraid because his hand trembled when he peeled back a corner of the newspaper. I crawled on all fours after him.

"All clear, Eshile. Stand up and look."

I snagged George's khaki slacks, climbed up his leg, and pressed my face against the glass. Across the street, three doors down, small black clouds exploded and spread their smoke over the top of Ethel's Laundromat. I thought the windows would shatter right out of their frames. "Was that a bomb?"

"Smell that? Fire. Maybe another store, or somebody's home. Can't see flames. Got to look out back."

I clung to George.

"Might be Mrs. Andile's house, nothing but splintery dried wood. Let go, Eshile. Her husband asked me to watch out for her. Been doing it since he passed."

I sucked in smoke-filled air and clenched ole George's belt at the hollow of his spine to keep him from leaving.

He dragged me toward the storage room while digging in his pocket for his silver key ring. "Go on in with Bini. Lock the door. Mrs. Andile should be okay, but I got to be sure, got to get eyes on her house."

George pried me loose, then unlocked the stockroom. My knees buckled. Bini was nowhere in sight. "Bini, are you okay? Come on out. Ole George won't let anything happen to us."

The blanket atop the cot trembled. Bini had pressed herself so flat against the mattress that I hadn't noticed her. When she peeped out, her face was as red and swollen as a ripe *ackee* fruit ready to pop.

Bini took the hand George offered, but when he tugged, she yanked the blanket back over her head. "Come out, girl. Let me get to that box of Bonomo's Turkish Taffy bars on the top shelf."

Bini popped up. We no longer heard armored cars or gunshots, so I joined Bini on the cot, leaned back, and relaxed against the wall. Ole George reached over our heads, then held out a palmful of strawberry taffy bars.

She ripped the wrapper. "Please, George, we need to stay here tonight."

"Your mothers will kill me if I don't bring you home. You know they're worried sick."

I asked, "Will we go when it's dark?"

"None of my ancestors are strong enough to protect us after the sun sets. Neither are yours, or you wouldn't be here." Ole George slapped his thigh and snickered at his own joke. "Finish your sweets. We'll go when I'm sure it's safe."

My eyes slid closed but flapped wide open when the wall trembled, and jars slid off the upper shelf. "Earthquake."

"Earthquake? Never heard of an earthquake in Soweto. Never had anything rattle my Oba's Ginger Jams off the shelf."

That was the first time I'd heard ole George say his wife's name since we buried her three months prior. The look of loss that crossed his face hurt me so deeply I couldn't say a word.

Wide-eyed, Bini asked, "What is it then?"

"More *hippos*. That's the only thing that makes sense. Not safe to check on Mrs. Andile now."

Bini gripped my hand. "They could crash through the store—shoot us dead."

"Not gonna happen," said ole George. "They're rounding up protesters. Doubt they're interested in an old man taking two young girls home."

I glanced at Bini and then back to George. "But we're protesters."

"Not now. Now you're my little girls. So, stop fretting. I'm keeping you safe."

Bini's shallow choppy breath was as quick as her mama cat's when she pushed out her last litter of kittens. My hands were sweaty; my mouth so dry the taffy still sat in my mouth as hard as a rock. I loved ole George but was far from confident he could protect us against armed *hippos*.

"We'll go soon. I don't want your mothers hurrying me along to join the ancestors." George pulled the chain to turn off the overhead light.

"I'll keep watch. Don't move until I say all's clear."

Bini and I hugged our legs to our chests. We must have dozed because when the metal-framed bed shimmied, we shrieked and sprang to our feet.

"Sorry, girls. It's just me. I bumped the cot."

"You scared us, George. We thought the *hippos* were after us again."

"*Hayi*, no, but officers are patrolling the streets. Not safe to walk about, yet I need to get you girls home, and I must drive by Mrs. Andile's to take a closer look." George held open the rear door. "Come on. My truck's parked behind the store."

I craned my neck around the doorjamb. Over rooftops, a drone of activity hung in the heavy air. Ole George nudged Bini outside, then moved past her, motioning us to follow. Bini pressed her body against the rough, sun-bleached wall and slithered toward the truck. Her skirt snagged on the splintered wood. I held on to her shirttail but cranked my head to make sure no one snuck up behind.

The flatbed's rusty door creaked when George opened it. I knew it was my fear that made it sound so loud. Still, I glanced around again, just in case. Bini placed one foot on the running board, then lunged. I scrambled in behind her.

We slid down in the seat until our heads sank lower than the passenger-side window frame. When the motor backfired, Bini hurled herself to the floor. George wiped glistening sweat from his forehead, then gripped the steering wheel. I peeked out.

Relief flooded George's face as we passed Mrs. Andile's tiny house. "Looks like she's fine."

A thick, foul-smelling smoke hovered on the next street. We choked and coughed until George drove out the other side. Three dilapidated *bakkie* pickup trucks raced past us, blaring their horns. I cast an eye toward a whistling noise, but a boom startled me back down in the seat.

"It-it's okay, girls. Th-that's aways off." I knew George was more frightened than he looked because he never stuttered. Bini, quivering violently, tucked her head between her knees. The screams and shouts in the distance, feet pounding the streets, and the rattle and clang of the armored troop carriers melded into an eerie hum that encased us and absorbed the truck's engine sounds. I stayed low, seeing only roofs and treetops until ole George said, "Eshile, we're on your street. Umama's out front, watching for you."

When George halted the truck and climbed out, Umama, crying like a winter storm, swooped me up as if I were a baby, even though I was almost as tall as her, then barreled into the house. Ife slammed the door behind her.

"Wait, Umama! Get Bini!" I wriggled from her grip and turned to run back out, but Umkhulu blocked my way with his walker.

"I-I worried 'bout my favorite gi-gi-girl."

Favorite? I was stunned. But before I had a chance to think that over, Bini blasted through the door and rammed into me. George rushed in behind her, poked his head back out, took a swift look up and down the street, then pulled the door shut.

Umama wrapped her arms around me and Bini and sobbed, "Thank you, my friend. You are a gift from God. May the ancestors bless you for keeping these children safe."

Ife, leaning hard on her cane, patted George firmly on the back when he bent, clenched his knees, and gasped for air.

Umama cocked her head. "George, what did you say?"

"I love these girls."

I loved him too, but a slimy wad clogged my throat and blocked me from speaking. Surely, he knew, I told myself.

George straightened to his full height before my grandfather. "How'd you get here, old man?"

"Ba-ba-balked."

"With your walker, you're as slow as a three-toed sloth. Too dangerous. I'll drive you and Bini. Then I got to get home to the wife…." George's face reddened, and his voice faded when he realized he had just spoken of Oba as if she were still alive.

The same thing happened to Umama just a few days prior. When Onele rattled on for way too long about how she wanted to visit a friend at school, our mother had said, "Ask your father when he gets home."

To break the embarrassed silence, I asked, "Umama, can't Bini stay? Please."

"Not tonight, Eshile. Bini's mom was here at least ten times. She's in a frenzy." But when Bini and I stuck out our lower lips, she sighed. "Friday night she can stay."

I hadn't noticed Onele until she leaned her hot sticky body against me. "I waited and waited for you. We heard guns. I was afraid they shot you."

Umama brushed a stray curl from Onele's swollen eyes. "She cried herself to sleep."

Leaning on his walker, Umkhulu clanked and rattled as we walked George and Bini out to the truck. "Got to tell Bu-Bulu you're safe, or she'll be next one b-bunning through the streets."

"Umkhulu, I won't be able to sleep." I placed my hand on his forearm. "What if the police come to arrest me?"

"Do not bo-burry, sweet Eshile." My grandfather sucked down a deep breath, then forced his words to come out right. "However long the night, the day will break."

The Day After

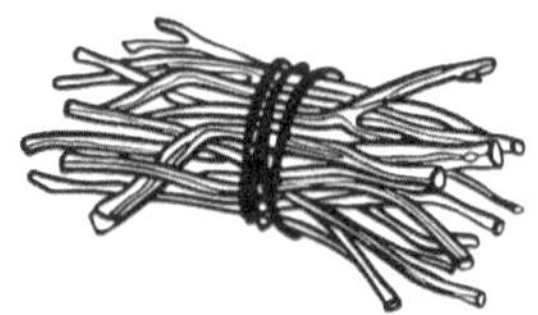

EyeSilimela (Month of the Pleiades) June 1976

Except for Saturdays, Umama shook us awake while the light was dingy gray. But now the sun shone bright. Sweat pooled in my armpits and the creases underneath my chin. I flipped toward the bunk ladder, only to be hit with hot, moist doggy breath. Steadying himself by digging his sharp toenails into my shoulder, Dinga bestowed me with a juicy dog kiss, then joyfully ran his tongue up Onele's cheek while beating her back with his happiness tail.

"Hi, baby sister. How long have you and Dinga been perched on my ladder, staring at me?"

"Hours. Ife kicked me out of the kitchen because Umama's talking with our aunties about some dumb newspaper."

"They didn't go to work?"

Dinga leapt from the ladder, yelping when he crumpled on the floor. Onele scampered down and rushed to the bedroom door. "Umama, Eshile's awake." Dinga bit into her hem and jerked her backward. She crammed her fingers between Dinga's lips, trying to unclamp his teeth. "Umama, Dinga's eating my skirt."

I sent a quick prayer to Great-Grandmother Haile. *"Please don't let the police come for me and Bini today."*

I yawned and stretched my neck toward the women's voices. Their hushed undertones told me they were gossiping. I didn't like missing out, so I rolled out of bed and scooted closer in my bare feet.

Ife stood on tiptoes, straining over Auntie Buhle's arm to read a large sheet of paper, the cheapest grade, the kind used mostly for Black publications. "He was just a child."

"A year younger than Eshile." I cat-walked up behind Umama. Printed in bold letters, *The World* newspaper's headline read:

4 DEAD, 11 HURT AS KIDS RIOT.

I shouted, "That's not true! I saw many more! They're lying!"

In one of the rare moments of weakness I'd ever witnessed in my mother, her chin quivered and her voice quaked. "It could have been you...."

Auntie Grace clicked her tongue. "Hector Pieterson, such a shame. Never had the chance to become a man."

"Nice, polite boy. He packed my groceries at George's market." Auntie Buhle wrung her hands. "Always put my bread and eggs at the top of the bags."

Auntie Grace pointed to the front-page photo. "Look at that poor girl's face. Caption says she's Hector's older sister."

Umama ran her fingers over the photograph. "Antoinette Sithole. A student herself, seventeen years old. How will she ever get over this?"

I had no memory of seeing my mother reading a newspaper before this morning. She always said she had too much work to waste the day sticking her nose into other people's business, which always made me laugh given the *skindering* that went on each Friday night in our front yard. But I didn't force the point because as long as she wasn't reading newspapers, she wouldn't see my articles published in Mr. Walker's underground newspaper, *Staan Op!*

But now she was reading every word.

Auntie Buhle braced herself against our table. The wooden legs creaked. I held still, listening.

"Who took that picture?" asked Ife.

"The caption says a Black man named Sam Nzima," said Buhle. "He's not a student."

Three teenagers, faces distorted by fear, filled the middle of the page. I pinched my eyes tight and once again saw them running straight at Bini and me. Eyes closed, blood pooled around his mouth and temple, Hector lay limp in the arms of an older boy. His sister had waved frantically. Many students followed, but no longer in the neat line of a parade. They weaved and crashed into each other, bringing some to their knees. A few peeled off into the side street. A woman wearing a plaid dress, the solitary adult who might have offered aid, stood mute and motionless. Nobody broke from the crowd to take Hector from the bigger boy.

I trembled at the sound of Hector's sister's screams inside my head, just as I did then. There must have been other noises—shouting, crying, people falling. But the background absorbed all that. I heard only Antoinette's scream for help.

The rattling of a newspaper page brought me back to reality. I opened my eyes and leaned around Auntie Grace's backside as she tapped the caption below the photo with her index finger. "This article says the older boy is unidentified. But Abel said he heard it was Mbuysia Makhubo who carried Hector to the Phefeni Clinic. Only it was too late. He died from his wounds."

A tremor vibrated along my spine. If Umama had allowed Onele to come yesterday, I might have been that sister, running, crying out for help.

Umama straightened and folded the newspaper. "That's enough, Eshile."

"Umama, I need to read it."

"Not now."

The front door slammed. Umama glanced out the window, then

bolted toward the door. Fear seized me.

"Police?"

Umama called over her shoulder. "*Hayi*, no. Your idiot sister and that damn dog are running in the street." The door slammed behind her.

Auntie Grace motioned at the clock. "Lordy, it's noon. What do you want, Eshile? Breakfast or lunch?"

"Lunch, please."

"Good. We'll all eat." Auntie Buhle opened the refrigerator door. "What have we got?"

Auntie Grace glanced toward our bedroom. "Is your big sister still sleeping?"

"I don't know where she is. She must have snuck out before I woke."

"What's wrong with that girl? Your mother doesn't need this right now."

Ife opened the drawer holding spatulas, knives, and cooking spoons. "Get dressed, Eshile. And wash your pretty face. You'll feel better."

When I came out of the bathroom, our small kitchen hummed like a huge electric fan. Ife, wearing her purple flowered dressing gown, tapped two spoons together, then repeated the rhythm. Umama had explained that Ife relived her youth in Namibia through her native music, *Marabi*.

Earlier that month, two Saturday nights in a row, Bini and I had sneaked out late to listen to a jazz band that always drew large crowds when it came to Soweto. Since we were too young to go inside Queen Alice's Shebeen, we sat beneath the open windows. We giggled at the inebriated men and their goofy attempts to persuade women to dance. The more of Alice's illegal brew the men drank, the more desperate and foolish they became. The approaches they took and the words they plied the women with became funnier, dumber, totally ridiculous, until it was clear to Bini and me these poor guys should give up all hope. Yet as entertaining as these fellas were, it was the music that captivated me. And now the beat of Ife's music brought to mind the sounds that jazz band made.

Ife must have read my thoughts, or perhaps my sad expression. "Just so happy you girls are safe that I can't stop myself from dancing with joy."

Auntie Buhle, cast-iron frypan in her hand, attempted to move up beside Auntie Grace and claim a burner. That maneuver became harder each year. Auntie Grace's hips were now as wide as the stove. Except for her husband Abel, nobody appreciated her cooking more than she did herself. I chuckled when, in a single graceful maneuver, Auntie Grace nudged Buhle with enough force to knock her aside like a sliding bowling pin and slip the leftover mielie bread into the oven.

When we last lived in Soweto, hunger never quite went away. But Mom's job supplemented the insurance money, so we now ate well. I sent a quick thank you to the ancestors.

Auntie Grace glared. That was sufficient to keep Buhle out of her way until she filled the frypan with *boerewors*. They sizzled and released beef and lamb scents into the warm air. Grease bubbled and popped. My stomach growled.

Umama took ripe mangos from the refrigerator, then handed me a knife. I peeled and sliced the fruit while Onele opened the silverware drawer and set the table without being told.

The mood was jovial when Asanda returned. Instead of snapping, "Where the *usathana* have you been?" Umama greeted her with, "Good, you're in time. Pour the juice." Then she lifted the lid of her largest pot and sniffed the rising steam. "Yum. Love the smell of warm corn." Using the ladle, she filled seven bowls with last week's rewarmed *isophi* soup.

Dinga thumped his long thin tail against the floor, keeping the same beat as Ife replicating *Marabi* style music with her two spoons.

As I pulled my chair to sit with my sisters and these four women I loved, I realized we were all pretending nothing had happened yesterday. No protest, no armored vehicles or guns, no children dead.

❧

The following day, I heard a timid knock. Still worried about the police, I crept toward the sound. But officers didn't tap, they banged their wooden batons, so I opened the door.

My best friend's mother slipped inside. "Bini wanted to walk with me today. I told her no. Sorry, Eshile, but I'm not ready to let her out. If you write a quick note, I'll give it to her when I get home from work."

I retrieved my notebook, pulled out a chair, and sharpened my yellow #2 pencil. While I wrote, Umama and Bini's mother bent over that day's newspaper, spread out on the table. A photo shows the government's West Rand Administrative Building on fire.

Auntie Grace followed the caption with her finger. "Says here many stores were burned and looted."

Umama read aloud, "Dr. Klein at Baragwanath Hospital reported that the resuscitation room was filled with bloodied children all with red 'Urgent Direct' stickers stuck to their foreheads. One boy wearing a school uniform had a bullet wound to one side of his head and blood spilling out the exit wound on the other side. The gurgle of death was in his throat. That boy was Hastings Ndlovu."

Then on the second day after the protest, as I sat at the table writing in my journal, Umama opened the latest edition of the newspaper and pointed. "Imagine that. Yesterday four hundred White college students marched through Johannesburg's city center protesting the slaughter of our children."

"White?" asked Bini's mother.

"Can you believe it? From the University of the Witwatersrand."

Days later, Umama said, "Now look at this article. It says hundreds of Native African workers organized a strike."

As Umama turned the page, I imagined myself entering a factory, then asking the White owner how he felt watching his Black employees walk off the job. That was a story I wanted the world to read. I made a note in my journal to remind myself to write it.

Bini's mother glanced at me as if she had read my thoughts. "Still scary out there. I'm hearing of more riots in neighboring townships. Who'd have thought a bunch of kids could start all that?"

"Twenty thousand is more than a bunch." My mother stared at me. I sensed her mood, heavy with worry.

I imagined moving among my fellow students, recording their statements. Feeling the pride I'd experience watching people read the articles I wrote, I lifted my chin and pressed so hard my pencil etched my words into the next page of my journal.

Umama insisted on returning to work. I begged her not to—contending the headaches she was experiencing meant that she was not strong enough to be out when so much more could go wrong. When my pleas failed to persuade her, I argued that fear of being fired and sinking back into poverty should not override her good sense. She responded that the ongoing bursts of protest (the press called them riots) weren't a threat to her. Her face said more. The way her eyebrows pinched together told me she wasn't sure.

Umama planned to keep my sisters and me home for an entire week. Turned out, it wasn't her decision to make. Our schools closed for over a month.

Onele flicked on the radio. "Jabber, jabber, jabber. This is boring. Can we buy a television?"

I perked up. "Excellent idea, Onele. They've been available for six months now. We should know what's going on outside our little world."

Umama blew a heavy breath out of her mouth. "Eshile, we deal with enough without worrying about the world's problems."

"Which problems would be too much, Umama?"

Ife perked up. "Atomic bombs, wars, and disease—dangers to our people."

I piped in, "The big danger is not knowing! How can we prepare?"

Umama stared me down. "Prepare? Eshile, how do you suggest we prepare for any of those? Dig a bomb shelter and buy gas masks? Haven't seen many of them at the street market."

"Eddie has them in a cardboard box beneath his folding table."

The look Umama shot our way caused Onele and I to let go of our arguments. It was clear nothing we said would change our mother's mind about buying a television, so we busied ourselves playing Mancala. Ife watched and offered crazy advice. When we lived in Soweto before, Ife used to play. And while we'd only been gone two years, she now struggled to remember whether to move her stones to the right or left.

That Ife easily recited the recipes her mother cooked in her childhood village in Namibia, close to the border of South Africa, amazed me. I kept a sheet of notebook paper on the counter to record the ingredients and steps she took to prepare these traditional foods. Somebody needed to write a recipe book before these treasures faded from her memory. Maybe me. While a cookbook wouldn't help me fulfill my dream of becoming a journalist, I would find satisfaction in presenting her recipes as a tribute to her early life before the memories faded from existence.

Ife changed after coming to live with us. She was still nosy and told stories from long ago, tattling on people I didn't know and didn't care about, but she wasn't cranky or mean anymore. I enjoyed our time alone. And her little face was no longer drawn from hunger and worry. Ife's cheeks had the healthy roundness and rosy hue of ripe apples.

My family enjoyed the exotic Namibian dishes she taught me to cook for breakfast and lunch. Ife never cooked dinner herself. She claimed to be worn out by then. But when she thought nobody was watching, she'd change the channel to Springbok Radio, turn the volume a little higher, and shuffle through the latest dance steps Bini and I had taught her.

For our month at home, Ife napped after lunch, muttering in her sleep while Onele painted watercolor scenes from Ilanga. Onele proved to have quite an artist's touch. When the little girl next door visited, my sister taught her to paint elephants with an amazing resemblance to Kuhle and her baby Yama.

I spent my extra time drafting articles for publication in *Staan Op!* and reading interesting books. Shaka bragged about reading *Looking on Darkness* under the covers in his bed every night. "No African has ever before written about race relations in this way."

Not only was this André Brink's first novel, but it was the first Afrikaans book to be banned by our government. What an honor. I could only aspire to find my first novel in a trunk, padlocked with the largest lock anyone has ever seen, just to keep people from reading its controversial message. I asked to borrow the book when he finished.

Shaka shook his head violently, "No! Never!"

"Why not? I'm fifteen."

"Your mother will pound my head with her mallet until my brains shoot out like the innards of a squash."

"Shaka, you exaggerate."

"I do not. The book is full of sex, the wrong kind of sex, the kind you go to jail for. A Black man and White woman…"

I gave Shaka my look of *what-the-heck-are-you-talking-about*. "Are you the only person in Soweto that doesn't know my birth father is Dutch?"

"But Eshile, there's more." Shaka stepped closer and shielded his mouth from the view of others. "The author suggests that to transform the culture of South Africa, our people must prepare for a revolution. I fear you'd get caught with the book and end up imprisoned on Robben Island."

I wanted to read the book so badly that I offered him the ten-cent coin his father paid me for my latest article.

Brink's novel was two years old when Shaka loaned it to me, yet it looked as if it had traveled the world and been read by many. In my country, no one had written such a daring story before—a White African man using the drama of a Black man awaiting trial for the murder of his White lover to speak out boldly against apartheid. I had many uncomfortable moments as I read—mixed race relationships, murder, never-ending danger.

Several days later, I was sitting at the table reading another chapter of *Looking into the Darkness* while Asanda licked her envelope and slapped the seal shut on the letter she had written to Leo. Normally, she sneaked out to the post office, but that day she stuffed the letter inside her bra and squirmed in her chair. When she glanced sidewise at me, I wondered if she sensed how I was struggling with the passages I had just read. They seemed similar to what my sister might feel. I shivered to shake off the unease, closed my book, and opened today's newspaper.

Umama continued purchasing a newspaper after the Student Protest of June 16. She never talked to me about what she read, yet I knew it upset her. The pages quivered in her hands. Did she fear what might happen if I followed my dream to write such articles myself? I was fairly confident she hadn't found the article hidden in my drawer, beneath my underwear, safely waiting until I handed it off to Shaka for consideration in *Staan Op!*

Yet the more her hands shook, the more I worried. Was I wrong? So many times, I hadn't been honest about what I'd done, where I'd gone, or what I'd written. Yet even thoughts I kept private, somehow my mother found out. I never could explain how she did.

Yesterday's issue of *The World* printed the government report stating the police killed 23 student protesters. That morning's paper put the tally at 176 pupils slaughtered by police, noting that others estimated 700. Not a single newspaper report disputed the total of over 1,000 injured.

If I had written that article, the caption would have read:

`Children carry posters. Police shoot bullets.`

That day's lead article reported school attendance in most townships was close to normal. But in Soweto, 250,000 pupils stayed away. The few who showed up at our 256 schools were sent home.

Another reporter wrote of a student group that pelted others who tried to enter Soweto schoolyards. The boy down the street said Gabby led the group. I knew that wasn't possible. She spoke out but wasn't violent. My first morning at school after returning from Ilanga, Gabby had hugged me tighter than anyone and whispered in my ear. "Your father proved to be a fine man. Your pain must be unbearable. What can I do?"

I clung to her as thoughts sludged through my brain. What could I ask for that might release me from this sadness? Of course, nothing could, but her tenderness touched my heart. I couldn't picture her throwing a rock. There was no way she would harm another student.

Asanda, patting her chest as if to make sure her letter hadn't fallen out, pulled me out of my thoughts. I tried not to laugh. Since she still hadn't gotten the cleavage she'd hoped for, there was plenty of room for the envelope inside her bra and not much chance it would fall out. When Asanda first joined Umama in the living room, she spoke softly, but her voice rose.

"I'll go straight to the bus stop. I promise not to hang out. You can trust me."

My mouth dropped open. Was my sister joking? I knew she had gone to a street party with Robbie when she was supposedly at the library. And then, on another hot Saturday night, she and a bunch of Robbie's friends rode in his *kombi* van to swim in the Klip River. In fact, I could list the times she went where she was allowed and in the company of people Umama approved on the back of a single postcard from the Ilanga Safari Lodge Souvenir Shop. I left the eating table, sidled closer for a better view, waiting for Umama's eyebrow to shoot up.

What I saw confused me. What the heck was going on? Our mother was looking at Asanda with one of her rare sympathetic expressions.

And Asanda was doing a remarkable imitation of Onele's saddest Eeyore face. "Mr. Wepener said he must replace me if I don't return to work now."

"How do you know that?"

In a split second, Asanda devised a crazy lie. "Robbie spoke to him at the bus stop, then stopped by while you were at work because Mr. Wepener wanted to know if I was sick or hurt in the student protest."

I snickered. Surely our mother was too smart to forget the facts of that day. I doubted I was the only one who remembered Mr. Wepener offering her double her hourly wage to skip school and go to work. Then he and Asanda stayed inside his office until after the march ended. So, Mr. Wepener knew she wasn't at the protest, and surely Umama remembered that. Besides, there was no scenario in which I could imagine my sister's boss holding a conversation with Robbie at the side of any road. Mr. Wepener, of Luter, Koton, and Wepener, would never be at the stop where she waited for Robbie to appear in his kombi van. Like most White lawyers, he had a big shiny car.

When my mother's brow rose a half an inch, I thought she had lured Asanda into her lie-catching trap. "Why is it important you go in now?"

"Mr. Wepener's behind on cases because I'm not there to type."

"Three days a week," says Umama. "Don't even think of asking for more. Your studies are more important. Straight there and back."

I was stunned, yet I kept my sister's secret. What I knew was more valuable than a gold coin for bartering her silence the need arose.

Two days later, there was another knock on our door. I was pretty sure if the police were coming for me, they would have done it before then. Nevertheless, that knock, quick and loud, made the hair on my neck stand.

"Onele, take Ife to our room and shut the door." The front doorknob rattled, but we always locked our doors, even when at home. Cautiously, I asked, "Who is it?"

"It's me, Eshile." I pulled Bini inside.

Her mother stood staunchly in the doorway and shook her index finger. "If I get wind of you two going out, Bini won't be visiting you again for a very long while."

For once, Bini and I minded our mothers. I wrote an article for *Staan Op!* and one for the school bulletin. But mostly, Bini, Onele, and I staved off boredom by playing Monopoly and Mancala, trying new hairstyles on each other, and memorizing the lyrics to the songs we heard on Springbok Radio. We didn't sneak out even once. We joked about our mothers being afraid of their own shadows. Bini and I told Onele that we were only staying home because our mothers were so traumatized. But the truth was every car that backfired or sped by my house scared us enough that we were happy staying inside.

Then when Umama brought home the big surprise, neither Bini nor I even hinted at going out. We thought it strange when Umama borrowed the neighbor kid's wagon to go to the street market. But she brushed off our questions, saying she needed extra groceries because we kids were there all the time.

Bini and I were painting each other's toenails when we heard the wagon squeak and rattle up to our house. We spread our toes and walked awkwardly toward the door to help my mother with her purchases. The wagon was piled high with vegetables, fruit, meat, laundry soap, and a set of bath towels. In the center, sat a brown plastic box.

Umama, wearing a silly grin, said, "Just put all this inside the door. I want to get the wagon back to the boy next door."

I squealed, "A television! You bought a television?"

"Get it in, quick! Don't want to advertise that I bought this from Eddie. Not much of what he sells is legal. God only knows how he gets his hands on used televisions, but he had two today. We've been through so much, I couldn't resist. I told myself we needed some fun."

"Umama, you need not justify this to us! It's fabulous. I can't believe you bought it!" Bini and I each took one side and carried it in. Onele stared with her mouth wide open.

"Set it on the table. Eddie showed me how to hook it up," said Umama.

"This is amazing," murmured Bini.

I quite agreed. Prime Minister Verwoerd had blocked the bringing of television for years. He compared it to atomic bombs, poison gas, and other physical and spiritual dangers the government must shield its residents from. Broadcasting backed the Prime Minister's efforts by saying television promoted English and was a threat to Afrikaner culture and way of life.

Fortunately, not everyone agreed. But after a year of testing, the government allowed all of South Africa access to public television. I had expected years to pass before my frugal mother would even consider it for our house. As shocking as the personality change appeared, I didn't question it for fear she would borrow the neighbor kid's wagon again, pack the television up, and return it to Eddie.

The government only allowed the broadcast of one channel. While many shows promoted apartheid propaganda, we still found plenty to watch. For the rest of the month, our school remained closed, Bini, Onele, and I watched a dance show for teenagers, then practiced the disco moves over and over until we got the movements right. Another of our favorite programs was the American series, *Happy Days*. We tied pink scarves around our necks, emulated Joanie Cunningham's girlish laugh, and imagined ourselves living in Milwaukee, Wisconsin, though we were unsure where that was.

When weary of pretending we were kids we'd never be, living in a place we'd never see, we scoured the newspaper for reports of other protests. I'm not sure that was a good idea, because it always resulted in Bini recounting her nightmares of the soldiers in the *hippo* aiming their rifles at ole George's market. Her descriptions were so vivid, we both ended up quivering as she whispered her fears.

I missed my classmates and classes, except for maths. Thirty-five days of canceled school may sound like a kid's dream come true, but in truth, even with the marvelous addition of a television, it was a long time to entertain ourselves.

After Bini's mother came to collect her, I read every book in the house, not that we had very many. But once again, I brought out one of my favorites—*Their Eyes Were Watching God* by Zora Neale Hurston. That this novel, written by a woman in 1937, made its way from America, into my hands, struck me as a miracle. Set in Florida, the dialogue's deep southern dialect obscured much of the meaning, making it a difficult book to read. But on my second read, I felt the spirit of this light-skinned girl named Janie as she escaped relationships every bit as abusive as what my Auntie Nofoto had suffered from her husband.

If only Jackson had died like Janie's first husband did—before he had the chance to kill his wife. They had so much in common, Janie and Nofoto. Both were smart and beautiful women who strove unsuccessfully to please their prosperous older husbands. Yet Janie survived to become an independent woman who shaped her own destiny. I dwelled on how unfair it was, that unlike Janie's husband, Jackson was an evil man who trafficked children and lived to kill my Auntie Nofoto. Thinking he was probably still alive was almost more than I could bear.

Even though that novel offered much for me to ponder, I complained I was going backward instead of learning more. Thankfully, Umama veered six blocks off her route after work and stopped at Mr. Wallace's Used Bookstore and Print Shop. He selected materials to satisfy my desire to learn, including a manual on how to keep houseplants alive. We didn't have any indoor plants, but I studied the book from cover to cover just in case I came upon the opportunity at a later date.

The week before Soweto schools reopened, our mothers allowed us to go to the street market with them. Pockets of students gathered, then marched through the streets with their signs. I would have liked to brave the danger, join those whose presence said more than words ever could, and write my own stories, but Umama said she'd kill me herself. Bini tried to lighten my guilt over not joining the cause by telling me these kids were older. But that wasn't completely true.

Looking back on the time we spent at home, I realized I was learning more than I thought, and I was far from being the only person thinking about why some people were bold enough to create change. Shaka brought by a newspaper in which an American asked why the Pretoria Government required Black schools beyond Standard Five to teach in Afrikaans. And why would students do something so volatile as to march in the streets, given the sensitivity of the time and place?

Why, indeed? After all, the language mandate was only one of thousands of laws and regulations meant to hold Native Africans down.

CHAPTER TWENTY-ONE

I Must Choose

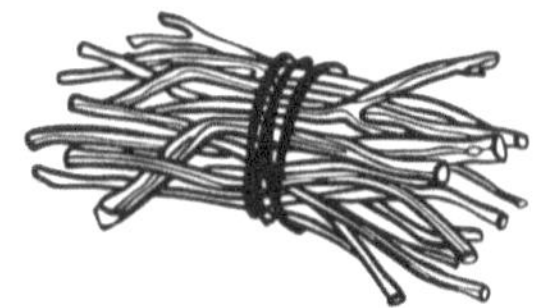

EyeKhala (Month of the Aloes) July 1976

Protests continued springing up throughout July. Some well planned, others appeared spontaneous; all intended to send the same message of our need to rule ourselves. Yet, I saw no evidence to support those who said this signaled the fall of apartheid. Still, I prayed they were right and wrote articles that might contribute to the cause.

Shaka kept me informed of the underground rumors about where and when a railroad or government building might be the scene of a bomb or fire. This inside information made it fairly safe for us to go out. Along with work and school, and all the other activities that make one's life normal, my mother got back to turning our new house into a home.

She selected coffee-brown fabric from the new Pick & Sew. Auntie Grace turned the cloth into living room draperies that slid on a bronze-colored bar to block the afternoon sun. With the leftovers, she made two matching throw pillows that I stuffed with cotton balls. We found bedroom curtains at Woolies Department Store—tiny bluebirds printed on soft fabric for the room my sisters, Ife, and I shared, and yellow roses for Umama's room. Over the weeks, we brought home a few more pots and pans, a full set of unbent silverware, and dishes the color of heavy cream.

The bathroom wall paint had cracked and peeled due to the lack of care by the previous owner. Umama and I sanded and scraped, then painted it pastel green. We even found a matching bathmat and a shower curtain printed with leaves of the same soft color.

Ole George fixed the lamp my mother purchased at Howard's Second Hand Store. It cast a soft glow that lit the room perfectly for evening television watching—a luxury I never dreamed we would experience. While I still missed Ilanga, still grieved my inability to visit my father's grave, the coziness of our new home softened my pain.

I often felt hopeful for our future there, yet on that last night, sleep did not come easy. My father visited me, floating in and out of my dreams. His face, shrouded in gray clouds, made me believe he was caught somewhere between earth and the afterlife. Though his image was distorted, I would have recognized him anywhere by what he wore. For the funeral, I helped Umama dress Ubaba in the borrowed—perhaps donated is a better word—blue suit. Then we wrapped him in an oxhide. He remained so encased when Baas John helped my mother close the coffin lid. That's why I couldn't imagine how he got his hands on his favorite shirt. While I never solved that mystery, I understood when he wore his old, flowered button-up, it meant he brought good luck.

Still, my father foresaw trials ahead. He warned of forces that would strive to break our family bonds and explained that responsibility for my sisters and mother fell to me. Ubaba cautioned my load would be heavy.

When he warned I might believe all is hopeless, my message to him was, "Some days, I already do."

"*Daughter, you may crave to give up, but you must not.*"

"My career, Ubaba. I plan to be a journalist. But even the articles I write now might get me arrested, possibly Umama too."

"*The ancestors chose you.*"

"What they ask is too much."

"*They only ask as those before us have—that you put community above your will.*"

"But Ubaba, isn't it my duty to report injustices committed against my people and my community?"

"*What an old man sees sitting down, a young man cannot see standing up.*"

"I don't understand."

"*Beloved daughter, I am saying, over time, as you mature, you will gain experiences that bring understanding of the ancestors' choice of you as the matriarch.*"

"I love my family. Nothing is more important."

"*Then, perhaps, your choice is clear.*"

"It's not that easy. Writing is my life. Given what is happening under apartheid rule, I can't be silent."

"*Remember, my daughter, sticks in a bundle are unbreakable.*"

"Doesn't the proverb mean that if I keep my family near, they will provide the strength I need for what I must do?"

"*And that is the choice, my daughter. What must you do?*"

I'd grown up well versed in this proverb, *sticks in a bundle are unbreakable.* Passed from Great-Grandmother Haile to Hulu, then from Hulu to Umama and my aunties. Now, my father spoke as if it were his own. I tossed and turned, reached out to pull him close. Emerging from this fitful sleep, I heard his voice, as soft as a feather against my ears.

"*You have sticks to gather. Some will break apart. But know this daughter, whenever faced with troubles, you will sense me at your side.*"

As Ubaba faded into the cottony grayness, my dream transported me to the watering hole's viewing platform, surrounded by lush greenery and morning mist. My sisters' and my legs dangled at three different lengths. Onele and Asanda leaned against me. I drew strength from their warmth. I understood, regardless of our differences, the touch of our shoulders created a bond with greater meaning than warding off the chill. This bond would bind us through all the future brought.

The image in my mind was so immediate, so clear and true, that when I filled my lungs, I smelled the sweet earth of Ilanga. In the deepest crevasses of my mind, a lion roared his threat from deep in the veld, warning me of the many dangers ahead and the strength I needed to overcome them all. Yet I didn't tremble with fear. I was unafraid; confident the covenant my people shared was strong, not unlike the one God had made with His.

Unbreakable.

Acknowledgements

Some say the proverb, "It takes a village to raise a child," is of African origin. Others claim it is a universal saying that can be attributed to several cultural regions. Without a doubt, the proverb explains my ability to write the trilogy of *Sticks in a Bundle*.

I thank my husband and editor-in-chief, Mike Spencer. I am grateful for his encouragement, love, technical skills, and hours of proofreading. Without his support, I'd still be writing instead of publishing this work.

The first page of *Sticks in a Bundle* was penned in the summer of 2018. From that date until publication, fellow authors and friends have contributed to its development. Through this process, they made *Sticks* a better book and me a better writer. I thank the members of the Writers' Bloc (Oceanside, CA) and the California Writers Circle (Orange County) for their friendship and support.

Thank you to Cherri Randall, author and editor, who guided me early on with the development of Eshile's story, and who is one of her greatest fans. I greatly appreciate my friends and fellow authors, Josephine Strand, Anita Downing, and Marlis Manley who served as alpha readers and offered a final round of suggestions. Your input was invaluable.

I am grateful to Simon Hough, at www.wordhook.com, for turning my mental images and illusive thoughts into gorgeous book covers for the Sticks in a Bundle trilogy. I also thank him for his patience and professional skills in formatting my books.

Finally, a million thanks go to my faithful fans and the many book clubs that have adopted Sticks in a Bundle. I appreciate your support!

Introducing Pat Spencer, Ph.D.

Dr. Pat Spencer has a lifetime of publishing fiction and nonfiction. She lived in three countries and seven states. Pat loves to travel and spent time in Europe, South Africa, Botswana, Zambia, Zimbabwe, Namibia, New Zealand, Australia, Italy, Greece, Mexico, the Galapagos, and the Bahamas, as well as Alaska and the Hawaiian Islands. She has road-tripped across the continental United States several times. Pat enjoys getting to know people and learning about their culture.

Dr. Spencer, a retired professor and community college president, lives in Southern California with her husband. She speaks to service and community organizations on human trafficking, writing processes, and her books. When not writing, Pat golfs, reads, walks the beach, hangs out with family and friends, or frequents book clubs and writing critique groups.

Please visit her online at:

Website: https://patspencer.net

Facebook: https://www.facebook.com/pat.spencer.9849/

Instagram: DrPatSpencer

Twitter: @DrPatSpencer

Golden Boxty in the Frypan

Pat Spencer

Available Online and through
Major Booksellers

In *Golden Boxty in the Frypan*, Pat Spencer captivates readers with a heart-rending and absorbing coming-of-age saga inspired by true life. Her poignant story captures the hearts of readers as they follow Katie's journey through poverty, illness, and discrimination in Philadelphia to a glorious train trip out west in search of the American dream. But just as she thinks the worst is behind her, a twist of fate reverses her good fortune. Katie must wrestle with her fears, face her insecurities, and assume the role of mother for her three youngest brothers.

Golden Boxty in the Frypan is an unforgettable novel that brings to life the hardships and joys of a multigenerational Irish family struggling to stay together during the Great Depression. Fans of books like *This Tender Land* and *Angela's Ashes* will appreciate the complex characters and themes of love, friendship, and family that make this book an emotional roller coaster. In the end, Katie must overcome the toughest of circumstances and orchestrate an escape from a sinister orphanage to secure a safe life for herself and her siblings. Don't miss this powerful story of resilience and hope.

Treat yourself to a copy of *Golden Boxty in the Frypan* today!

Story of a Stolen Girl

Pat Spencer

Available Online and through
Major Booksellers

Darby Richards, UCLA freshman, remembers attending a private gambling club at the invitation of her psychology professor, but not how she ended up in Ankara, Turkey. Her life is in danger. She tries to escape at each twist and turn.

Everyone searches for Darby. Authorities are baffled. Her mother, Nina, is desperate. Nothing in her career as an architect prepared her to enter the underbelly of society serving world leaders, corporate CEOs, and even the President's Cabinet. But when authorities fail to rescue Darby, this widowed mother attempts something no other mom has ever tried before. If she fails, her daughter will be lost forever.

Story of a Stolen Girl explores the unbreakable bond that forms between women in peril. This intense page-turner contains no graphic sex or violence. Fans of *The Story Keeper* and *Then She was Gone* are captivated by this thrilling story of female heroes.

Don't miss out. Treat yourself to a copy of *Story of a Stolen Girl* today.

A Baker's Dozen For Writers:
13 Tips for Great Storytelling

Pat Spencer

Available Online and through Major Booksellers

Unlock your potential with *A Baker's Dozen for Writers: 13 Tips for Great Storytelling* by award-winning author, Pat Spencer. If you seek to free your imagination from its past confines, this book is perfect for you. With wit and charm, Dr. Spencer shares her expertise on how to write bolder, clearer, and more engagingly.

As a published author of fiction and nonfiction, Pat Spencer's engaging approach to storytelling makes this book a must read for those who want to create stories that captivate readers. Spencer's thirteen tips will enable you to infuse passion, symbolism, body language, action beats, and sensory experiences into your prose.

If you liked Stephen King's *On Writing* or Anne Lamott's *Bird by Bird*, you'll *love* Pat Spencer's *A Baker's Dozen For Writers: 13 Tips for Great Storytelling*. Whether a seasoned writer or just starting out, this book is a valuable resource for you. So why wait? Unshackle your creativity.

Treat yourself to this essential guide and create captivating stories today.

Sticks in a Bundle: The Decision

Book III

Pat Spencer

Available Online and through Major Booksellers

Winter 2024

Sticks in a Bundle: The Decision is the final piece of Eshile Mthembu's powerful and poignant tale. Join Eshile on the bumpy road, leaving behind her teenage years and entering womanhood. On this journey, she struggles with the complications that accompany maturity—love, duty, and accountability. She's strong and resourceful yet battles self-doubt when called upon to resolve challenges greater than any she ever envisioned for her future.

The 1980s bring no relief from apartheid or the devastation it wreaks on Eshile's family, friends, and community. Publishing her words in a South African underground newspaper places everyone she loves in harm's way. Still, she risks everything by assuming leadership in the fight against prejudice and discrimination. Ultimately, Eshile must balance the safety and expectations of others against what her heart craves. Does she follow her dreams or accept the responsibilities asked of her? Which life will she choose to live?

Fans of historical and literary fiction are captivated by Eshile's inspiring tale of love, strength, and resilience in the face of adversity. Comparable to bestselling titles such as *The Color Purple and Homegoing*, this extraordinary coming-of-age saga, *Sticks in a Bundle: The Decision*, will have you sitting on the edge of your seat.

The Unfortunate Conversation
Pat Spencer
Coming in 2025

On a desperate winter night in 1938, Isabelle, an emotionally overwhelmed fifteen-year-old, abandons the moral code by which her parents raised her. When the swole of her belly reveals what she's done, her father, the Very Reverend Patrick Maguire of Galway's Collegiate Church of St. Nicholas, banishes her to the infamous Bon Secours Mother and Baby home in Tuam, Ireland.

In the wake of World War II, an American couple purchases Isabelle's infant from the nuns. Isabelle takes a grueling job on the Queen Mary's last voyage before its conversion to a troop transport ship. The decisions Isabelle makes determine the future she will face—continued tragedy or a grand adventure and reunion with her child.

The Unfortunate Conversation, a gripping historical novel, propels readers on a coming-of-age journey through the highs and lows of human experience. Fans of *The Light Between Oceans* and *'Tis* will gravitate to *The Unfortunate Conversation.*

Don't miss this powerful tale of love, desperation, betrayal, and determination to find happiness.